# The

# STAR of XERXES

THE
CATALONE
PRESS

Canadian Cataloguing in Publication Data

MacKinnon, Mary Stewart, 1937-
        The Star of Xerxes : historical novel of the 5th
century B.C.
ISBN 0-9698337-4-1

        I. Title.
PS8575.K48S73 1996  C813'.54  C96-900545-8
PR9199.3.M3296S73 1996




Printed by City Printers
Sydney, N.S. Canada


Published by
The Catalone Press
P.O. Box 1878
Sydney, NS
Canada

# The

# Star of Xerxes

Mary Stewart MacKinnon

THE
CATALONE
PRESS

For Angus, who always encouraged me.

## Author's Preface

The Star of Xerxes is a work of fiction based on the Biblical
Book of Esther. It is a fascinating story, but it always raised
questions in my mind. What was it about Esther that enabled
her to become queen of Persia? It could not have been just her
beauty, because there could have been no lack of beautiful
Persian women. How did it come about that she, with her
background as a Jewish exile, could assume a position of such
prominence in what was at that time the most sophisticated
court in the world?
It was to answer such questions that I began to write this book.
While I kept closely to the plot of the story, many of the
secondary characters are my own invention. For the sake of
simplicity I made Artaxerxes the eldest son, although of
course, he was the second son of Xerxes, Darius being the
eldest. I also used episodes from Josephus, and material from
the *Biblical Commentary of Jamieson, Fosset and Brown*. For
the descriptions of the Persian army, and some parts of
Xerxes' speeches I am indebted to the *Histories of Heroditus*.
For the descriptions of the palace of Darius I consulted *Darius,
les Perses et l'Empire* by Pierre Brian

Mary Stewart MacKinnon
Arnish, Cape Breton, July 1996

# CHAPTER 1

The Palace of Darius, now the winter residence of King Xerxes, stood on a cliff above the river Ulai, with the city of Shushan curving below it like a studded necklace. To the rear, the land sloped down to tree-fringed meadows, meeting the river again as it meandered its way to the sea nearly two hundred miles to the south. A solid stone bridge joined the city to the Processional Way which lead to the palace, and provided a docking area for the boats of the fishermen and merchants who used the river to ply their trades.

On a summer day in the fourth year of King Xerxes' reign, no one looking at the massive exterior walls of the palace could have guessed at the chaos within. In every corner, frenzied activity had displaced the languor that usually prevailed at this time of year. Chamberlains snapped at each other and yelled at the eunuchs. Eunuchs hurled orders at servants, and the servants took to beating the slaves. All because a few hours earlier, the king's advance guard had arrived unexpectedly at the palace gates, shouting entry to sleepy watchmen, whose peace had not been disturbed in such fashion since the departure of the king in the early spring.

The captain of the king's guard, not known for his patience, had demanded to see the chief chamberlain and immediately a eunuch was sent to rouse him. Hazael, whose ripe years should have precluded rude awakenings in the middle of the night, vented his wrath on the messenger for some minutes until he was sufficiently wide awake to realize that the matter concerned the king and must therefore be attended to without delay. Summoning the captain, he donned his bedrobe and waited with some impatience to hear what he had to say.

The king, it transpired, was on his way to Shushan.

"You rouse me to tell me that?" growled Hazael. "We know to expect the king at the onset of winter as usual."

"The king will be here by sunset," said the captain, and enjoyed the look of consternation on the face of the chief chamberlain. "He has decided to return to Shushan early this year."

"But why? What is afoot? Is there some emergency?" Hazael brushed the last vestiges of sleep from his eyes. "Why was I not informed sooner?"

The captain's mouth thinned. "I know nothing, my lord chamberlain. The king does not make me privy to his plans. I was told to advise you of his imminent arrival, and now with your leave, I will see to my horses and men."

The lord chamberlain dismissed him with a wave of the hand, his mind already focused on the almost superhuman task of preparing the huge palace to receive the king and his equally huge entourage at what was virtually a moment's notice.

There was no more sleep for anyone. The whole palace staff, who up till then had been had been enjoying the easing of duties afforded by the king's absence, were pressed into action. By daybreak the bakeries and kitchens hummed with activity. Armies of slaves were washing marble floors and beating priceless carpets, opening up and dusting unused rooms, and everyone scuttled about, getting in each other's way, all driven by the urgency of completing their tasks in the short time that was left. Throughout the commotion, in the midst of all the to-ing and fro-ing, the question uppermost in everyone's mind and asked a thousand times over was, Why is the king coming now?

\*

Across the river from the palace, the same question floated in the mind of a young woman as she sat on the terrace of her home. She stared at the dark, impregnable bulwarks, wishing with all her might that she could see what was going on behind them, just as she had done so many times before, but today it was especially frustrating because of the events of the previous night.

She had awakened around midnight hearing the pounding of hooves on the main thoroughfare of the city. Leaping quickly out of bed, she had raced up to the rooftop just in time to see the glint of moonlight on the helmets of the King's Guard and the flutter of penants as the troop of horsemen clattered across the bridge and proceeded along the Processional Way towards the palace. Her heart thudded with excitement. The King's Guard meant the presence of the king himself! At this time of year? It was unheard of for King Xerxes to retire to Shushan before the winter set in, busy as he usually was with campaigns and progresses around the empire. There must be something extraordinary afoot. Perhaps a war had started or a rebellion, and the king was coming to amass his troops. Whatever it was, it meant enough excitement and activity to rouse the city from its summer somnolence. Overnight there would be an influx of merchants, artisans, entertainers and every kind of follower of the king's court. She returned to bed full of happy anticipation.

At the market early in the morning, she listened to the conversations of the townspeople, hoping to pick up snippets of information. No one seemed to know anything definite about the king's return, although there was plenty of rumour and speculation. Even when the cavalcade of baggage vans that inevitably followed the king's court began to pass through on their way to the palace, the citizens could get no satisfactory answers to the questions they fired at the waggoners. Whatever the reason, it was not common knowledge. She went home frustrated and impatient, knowing she would have to wait all day long until her cousin Mordecai came home, to find out what was going on.

And now it was evening, and he was late. Rising up, she paced back and fore across the terrace, pausing at one end to look over the parapet to the street below, only to find it deserted. She sat down again and closed her eyes, assuming an air of serenity that was at odds with the turmoil inside her. It was no wonder that Mordecai was late today, she rationalized. As an officer of the court he was bound to be occupied with palace business.

The noisy daytime bustle of the city had muted to a distant murmur and she could hear noisy insects whirring among the roses which grew in profusion over the terrace and tumbled down into the courtyard below. A bird twittered occasionally in the trees lining the high walls of the garden, and every now and then a gentle breeze brought to her nostrils the scent of flowers mingled with the odours of a thousand cooking pots as the citizens of Shushan prepared their evening meal.

When she opened her eyes it was quite dark. Fetching a taper from inside, she lit the torches in the sconces on either side of the door. The thought occurred to her that Mordecai might have to stay the night at the palace, but she pushed it from her mind. That would be unbearable.

At last she heard it, the sound she had been waiting for. The gate clicked and in a flash she was clattering down the steps as Mordecai entered.

"What kept you so late, cousin? I thought you were never coming!"

"Ah, Esther." He smiled and laid a hand on her shoulder as they mounted the steps together. "I almost did stay the night at the palace, but I knew I would never get any rest if I did. What a turmoil. And I was afraid you would die of curiosity if I didn't get back to answer all your questions. And it's well that I did. It's not every day I get a welcome like this!"

She laughed obligingly at his jest and tucked her arm into his. "I sent Zorpah to bed. Her feet were swelling up again, so I told her I'd serve your dinner. It's all ready."

"And of course you thought you would get more information if Zorpah wasn't around!"

"Mordecai!"

"All right, I'm teasing. But I know your curiosity. No questions until I've eaten. I'm starving. There was no time to eat all day. I'll just wash and change."

He disappeared into his room, and she busied herself laying out the dishes on the table. She had just finished when Mordecai reappeared, adjusting the clasp on his fresh white shirt. It struck her how handsome he was still, even though his black hair curling damply at his neck had an occasional streak of grey. Any woman would be proud to have him for a husband, a thought that reminded her of the suspicion she had.

He had begun to go out after supper, always with a fresh shirt and tunic, and when she asked where he was going he would always make some jest about people not having to know more than was good for them. She did not want him to get married. If he brought a wife to this house, she would be the mistress and Esther would have to do as she was told. She knew she had more freedom than most girls her age, and she wanted no changes.

"Shouldn't you be in bed, little one?" said Mordecai, as he helped himself to a dish of meat.

She gave him what she hoped was a withering look as she poured wine into his cup.

"You must stop calling me little girl, cousin," she remonstrated with as much dignity as she could muster. "I'll be fifteen next birthday, old enough to get married and run my own household."

"So now I must do my duty and find you a husband. Yes, I must see to that at once."

"No, no!" She knew he was teasing, for they had been over this ground before, but she couldn't help rising to the bait. "I do not want a husband. Not for years and years. Don't even mention it!"

He grinned, his white teeth flashing. "I think I know just the one for you. Joshua, the innkeeper's son. He would make a fine husband. You would never be hungry and you would always have plenty to keep you occupied. And you could question travellers as much as you liked. Yes, a very suitable match, I would think."

"Joshua is fat and lazy and stupid into the bargain. I won't marry a stupid man!" She glared at him, annoyed at herself for taking him seriously.

"In that case you won't marry at all." He refilled his cup.

"Where are you going to find a man who is smarter than you, little one? I don't think he exists."

"Well then, I shall never marry. That would suit me very well." Abruptly she changed the subject. "What about the king? Why has he come back to Shushan? What is going on at the palace?"

"So many questions! I wondered when we'd get to them." He pulled a stern face. "But I cannot divulge the king's plans. Everything is very secret." He pretended to look solemn.

"I don't want to know the secrets. Just what everyone will know in the market place tomorrow. Please." She looked at him with imploring eyes.

"Oh well, a few facts will do no harm. The king has come back early because he plans a big celebration here at Shushan. He is going to invite all the noble lords, princes and satraps in the empire. There are to be banquets and feasts that will go on for months."

"But what is the celebration for?" she asked, intrigued.

Thinking back over the events of the day, he lowered his voice and began to tell her what had happened, choosing his words carefully so as to give her only the information that would be common knowledge in the city,

*

When the messenger from Persepolis rode into the courtyard with the news that the king would be arriving that night, the administrative staff immediately went into action to prepare for the royal retinue. When they heard that he had ordered the Council to meet the next morning in the Adana, they knew that something very important had transpired. There were all kinds of rumours, but no one knew for certain what he had in mind. Even those closest to the king were at a loss. Mordecai, as Chief Scribe of the Council obeyed the summons and waited as eagerly as everyone else to hear what Xerxes had to say.

For his part, the king knew their impatience, and enjoyed keeping them in suspense, talking first of trivial matters. Finally he came to the point. It was time, he said, for the whole empire to get together for a great celebration. He wanted every province and satrapy to be aware of the wealth and riches of Persia so that everyone would feel proud to belong to such a great empire. To that end, he intended to host a series of feasts here at Shushan and invite all the princes, noble lords, governors, satraps and representatives from every corner of the empire.

"We will make elaborate preparations," he went on, "and plan every detail meticulously in order to impress the guests with all the pomp and spendour of our glorious empire. We will spare no expense in providing the best food and drink and entertainment. It will be a celebration of the magnificence of Persia, the like of which no one has ever seen before."

At last the king stopped and there was dead silence in the hall, while everyone digested this information. Finally Memucan, one of the Inner Council, came forward and spoke.

"My lord king, we of the Council applaud your wonderful proposal, but what of the cost of this undertaking, and what purpose will it serve? Everyone, far and near, already knows the wealth of the empire."

"Yes," echoed a voice from the rear of the hall, "and would it not be better to save our resources to fight our enemies the Greeks?"

At this Xerxes smiled and rose from the throne. Walking along the platform he surveyed the ranks of men standing before him.  A breathless hush descended on the hall.

" Men of Persia," he began, "do not think I will be slow to avenge the wrongs done to my father by the Greeks.  Indeed it is with this in mind that I have put forward my plan, for the banquets will furnish the resources for our attack on Greece."

The men of the Council looked at each other, mystified. What exacly did the king have in mind?

Seeing their blank looks he went on to explain.

"All the princes, lords and satraps of every province of the empire will vie with one another to bring the costliest gifts to show their appreciation and loyalty.  They will fill the coffers of the realm to overflowing.  There will be enough to equip an army, build a navy and launch an expedition against the Greeks."

It was a plan impressive in its simplicity, and when he saw he had their undivided attention, the king continued with a long speech about finishing the work that his father had left for him to do.  Such was the force of his oratory that when he stopped speaking there was no voice lifted in dissent.  Indeed, they were now all fired with enthusiasm and could hardly wait to start putting the plan into action.

\*

"What do you think, Mordecai?  Will the king be success-ful against the Greeks?" Esther asked when he had finished.

Mordecai stroked his beard.  "I have grave doubts.  Can Xerxes succeed where Darius failed?" He was silent for a few minutes and when he spoke again it was as if he had forgotten she was there.  "If anyone could have conquered the Greeks it would have been Darius.  Xerxes lacks certain qualities.  He should consolidate his father's gains, and pay attention to the administration of this vast empire he has inherited. It is one thing to make conquests, but it is another thing to hold them. If only Xerxes could see that that is the work his father left him to finish."

Esther rose to clear the table, and Mordecai suddenly seemed to remember her presence.

"I need hardly remind you, Esther, that you must not repeat anything you have heard. If it were to reach certain quarters, my life would not be worth much. Remember, the eyes and ears of the king are everywhere."

"I would never do anything to harm you, cousin," she assured him. "You are all the family I have in the world."

He smiled and patted her arm. "I trust you to be discreet. You know that we cannot be too careful. Our people are always the first to fall under suspicion." Putting his wine cup on the table, he added, " I have to go out for a while. You'd better get to bed. Sleep well, Esther."

She listened to his footsteps going down the steps, and then, on a sudden impulse, she ran to her room for her cloak and hurried out after him, taking care to be as quiet as possible. Carefully she unlatched the gate and emerged into the street. The moon flitted in and out of the clouds, enabling her to catch a glimpse of him as he turned the corner. Keeping to the shadows she sped after him, following him through the narrow streets and alleyways until he disappeared into a lane that ran alongside a large house. Quickly she reached the corner and peeped round. There was no sign of Mordecai. She crept along the wall until she came to a gate. Looking through the bars she was just in time to see, by the light of the torches on the wall, the face of the woman who greeted him at the door and ushered him inside. She gasped in surprise. She knew that face. It was the woman from the market. Leaning against the wall she thought about this new piece of information

She had often watched this very beautiful, elegantly dressed woman, going from stall to stall followed by her servant girl, and had longed to be like her. Zorpah told her that she was Madam Zinna, the widow of a rich Persian merchant. Zorpah was reluctant to talk about her, and from the little she told her, Esther understood that there was some disapproval of her within the local community, evidently because she had married a Persian. That explained why she did not attend the local Jewish festivals and religious observances. She had never seen her except at the market. And now here was Mordecai visiting her.

She retraced her steps slowly, pondering on this new situation. Was Mordecai going to marry her? He had a good position at the court and he was a loyal servant of the king. He would be a suitable husband for a rich widow. Why then did he keep his connection with her a secret? Why were there no plans to marry? Perhaps it was because she, Esther, was still under his guardianship and he was waiting until she was married and her future assured.

Deep in thought, it was some time before she became aware of the footsteps behind her. Suddenly she realised how dangerous it was for her to be wandering about the city alone at night, something she had never done before. Quickly she reached the corner and glanced back to see a figure hurrying in her direction. She sped up the narrow street, pausing before she turned to the right to look back. The man was plainer now. She could see his face and she had no doubt now that he was following her. She ran quickly along the street and slipped into the farthest corner of a darkened doorway. With breath held and heart thumping, she listened to the footsteps as the man turned the corner and came towards her. Please God, don't let him find me, she prayed. The footsteps slowed down and hesitated. Above the thumping of her heart she could hear nothing. Then she heard the man cross the street, his footsteps receding in the opposite direction. Sighing with relief she waited for a few more minutes before she dared come out of her hiding place. When she finally emerged, the street was empty. Silently she glided along and did not pause until she reached the safety of her own courtyard.

Esther was pleased with her discovery. If Mordecai was to marry, nobody could be more suitable than Madame Zinna. But it would mean a lot of changes, none of which appealed to her. She who had known freedom from an early age, would have to be subject to the new mistress of the house, or if she herself married, be subject to the whims of a husband. Esther saw nothing in the lives of the young married women around her to make her want to share their lot. She vowed she would postpone marriage as long as she could. As for Mordecai, well, he had not mentioned marriage yet, and maybe he never would. Perhaps his work at the palace was such that a wife would only complicate matters. At any rate, she decided she would not worry about it. She went to bed and thought instead of the banquets and celebrations that were to take place at the palace. But before she slept a familiar feeling of longing and frustration gripped her, the knowledge that however much she knew of the life at the court of King Xerxes, she could never hope to be part of it.

\*

The city of Shushan was laid out in districts corresponding roughly to the status of its citizens. Nearest to the palace, the houses of the palace dignitaries and officials spread out on either side of the Processional Way. Next to them lived the exiles, with their shops bordering one side of the large market square, while the rest of the citizens surrounded the other three sides. Esther noticed, as she turned on to the market square, that already the city was busier than usual, with more merchandise for sale and more customers ready to buy. She paused at one of the stalls where an old man sat at work.

"Good morning, Nahum," she greeted him. "Is Jacob about?"

His face broke into a smile. "Good morning, Esther. Yes, Jacob is in the workshop as usual." He would have liked her to wait and talk to him but she had already disappeared round the back of the booth and into a building that served as a forge. As she entered a young man hammering metal at a bench looked up from his work and pushed his brown hair out of his eyes.

"Well, well, it must be later than I thought when the idlers of this world have risen! Did an earthquake get you up this morning?"

"Don't be impertinent Jacob, or I shall withdraw my custom," she replied, trying to look as haughty as possible as she seated herself on the bench opposite him.

He grinned. "Now that would surely ruin us!" He held out the piece of metal he was working on. "How do you like my new design?"

Esther took the circlet and examined it closely. It had an intricate pattern of tiny animal heads, each one subtly different.

"It's exquisite, Jacob. What did you copy it from?"

"It's not a copy. It's my own design. I'm hoping Master Barzai will let me make sets of armlets, pins and brooches, and we can sell them to the men who come to the court."

"That's wonderful, Jacob. You certainly didn't waste time. Did you stay up all night to do it?"

"No, I've been working at things on my own for some time. There are all kinds of rumours that the king will make war on the Greeks. If so, the warriors are going to want all kinds of ornaments like this."

She looked at him with admiration. "You are ambitious, aren't you? Tell me, what else have you heard?"

"Aha! And I thought you came here to enjoy my company." He went on with his work.

"Come on, Jacob," she begged. "Tell me what you know."

"Doesn't your cousin Mordecai tell you all that goes on at the palace? You probably know everything already." He looked at her under his lashes.

"You know he cannot tell me everything. He has to be very careful."

Jacob leaned towards her. "Did you know that all the princes and satraps from every province of the Empire are coming here to Shushan? There will be banquets and entertainments for months. There's even going to be a banquet for the citizens. We are all going to be invited!"

Esther gazed at him open-mouthed. This was something Mordecai had not told her. "Do you mean anyone can go to the palace?"

"Yes, there will be food and entertainments in the gardens of the palace for all. It will last a whole week so that everyone gets a chance to go. It will be a public holiday. It'll be great, greater even that when we celebrated the victories of Darius."

"Don't pretend you were around then! You're not more that three or four years older than I."

"Oh, but I was there, at least at the last one. My grandfather took me. Still, I don't remember much about it. I must

20

have been quite small. It's about time we had some excitement aroung here. Business has been slow for months. That's why I had time to make these," he said, tapping the bronze circlet. "Perhaps, if we make a lot of money, Master Barzai will give me my craftsman's crest, and then I can travel the world."

"He's more likely to keep you here to make more money for him," said Esther. "You ought to put your name on these designs. Otherwise..." she broke off and shrugged her shoulders.

"I would if I could," he said, a sardonic note in his voice, "but that is one thing that was neglected in my education."

"I'm sorry, I forgot," she apologized. "It's just that you seem to know so much. Anyway, you're in good company. They say the king can't write either." Then she leaned over to him. "I can teach you, Jacob. You could learn to write the first letters of your name, so that everyone would know it's yours."

He laid down the piece of metal, his face serious. "I know you told me that Mordecai taught you to write, but I didn't quite believe you. Could you really teach me? It has always been an ambition of mine."

"Come on, Jacob." Full of excitement, she rose and taking his arm, led him outside. She grabbed a stick and began to trace the letters of his name on the ground. "Look, that is your name. Now you try." She held her hand over his and helped him to outline each letter. Then she made him practise it over and over until he could do it quite smoothly.

"I can see the shapes," he said, a wide smile splitting his face. "I didn't know it was this easy."

She took the stick from him. "What was your father's name?"

"Asrak. But, shouldn't I use Master Barzai's name? After all, I work for him."

"No, it's your design. You should write J.A., for Jacob, the son of Asrak."

He looked doubtful, but following her lead he traced the outline again. Then an idea struck him. "I could make this part of my design. Make it so that you would not notice it unless you looked for it. That way I could always have proof of my work."

"Wonderful, Jacob." She clapped her hands, her eyes shining.

Suddenly he grabbed both her hands in his and swung her round in a little dance of triumph. "Thanks, Esther. When I'm rich and famous I'll make gold hairpins for your hair."

She looked at him thoughtfully. "I believe you will be rich and famous. That is, if you can spare the time from drinking in the inn."

"Oh, ho! Been listening to gossip, have we? Yes, I go to the inn, but not to drink the sour ale that Jethro serves his customers. I go to drink in the stories of the travellers, to learn what I can about the rest of the world. I told you I want to travel and see the designs of the great artists of Greece and Egypt, yes, and maybe even reach the lands of silks and spices to the east. That's my dream, Esther, but who knows if it will ever come to pass."

"It will, it must! You are so talented, Jacob. Everyone will want to buy your jewellery, and I will have to marry a very rich husband so that I can afford it."

They both laughed at their foolishness and then Esther picked up her basket. "I must go. Zorpah will create a storm because I'm taking so long." She left him standing there, shaking his head, and looking after her with a wistful expression.

Esther intended to make her way straight home, but when

she reached the square she caught sight of a crowd gathering at the far end. She stopped and watched while more people joined the throng. It was too much for her. She just had to see what was going on and her feet seemed to have a will of their own, leading her forward almost without her being aware of it. When she reached the fringe of the crowd she could see nothing. She pushed forward, making use of every little gap, squeezing under the arms of a fat citizen, forcing herself into each little space until at last she found herself at the front of a circle that surrounded the strangest contraption she had ever seen.

"... all the way from the Orient," the man beside her was saying to his neighbour. Pointing to a long strap that looked like black leather he continued, "See the way it stretches from the pole up there. When they let it go it shrivels up, pulling the poor wretch off the ground and up in the air, with the noose around his neck."

Esther, who had been following his words closely, realized with horror that he was describing the working of a new kind of gallows. As if drawn by a magnet, her eyes fixed on the deadly weapon of death made of poles and ropes, and she listened as he told his willing hearers how he had seen such a contrivance while on his travels in eastern lands, and how it all depended on the shiny black material which could stretch into a long narrow band. When he further revealed that the material came from a tree there was a roar of laughter from the townspeople, who plainly thought that he was spinning them a long yarn. The sound of laughter broke the spell for Esther, who turned to find her way back. At that moment the circle opened and guards appeared dragging a man with bound hands and feet. Immediately the people began to taunt the man.

"Death to all thieves and robbers!" they cried. "Miscreant, criminal!"

Their voices grew louder and louder as they encouraged one another, while the guards went about their business of tying up the man who now began to add his own cries and screams to the uproar. Frantically, Esther sought for a way of escape, but the crowd had surged forward and were pressing tightly together. She closed her eyes and covered her ears with her hands to shut out the noise, and now the pounding of her heart thundered in her head. She tried to swallow but her tongue seemed stuck to the roof of her mouth. Sick with panic, she found herself sinking to the ground, crouched over her basket, while above her the shouts of the crowd reached a new pitch. How long this went on for she had no idea, but finally a loud crack split the air and a loud cheer went up from the onlookers. She remained where she was until, after what seemed an age, the people around her began to disperse, exchanging comments on the effectiveness of the new gallows and speculating on the time the man had taken to die.

She tried not to look towards the gallows but, as if drawn by a magnet, she found herself staring at the limp, twitching figure hanging in the air. With a feeling of revulsion, she averted her eyes and tried to calm herself. It served her right, she thought, for being where she shouldn't be. If only she had gone straight home. She smoothed her dress, and was about to rise when she became aware of men's voices behind her.

"So, the machine worked after all," one man was saying. "That poor devil got sent off quickly to hell where he belongs."

A deep, rich voice answered him. "Well, let's hope the lesson was not lost on these citizens. They must learn who are their masters. None of these merchants will be in a hurry to cheat me, I shouldn't wonder. Hullo, what have we here?"

Esther had risen and turned to face the men. She stopped short, her mouth agape at the rich colours of their dress, the shiny gold trimmings, the sparkle of precious stones on their sleeves. Obviously they were men of the king's court, but she had never before seen such richly dressed courtiers at close quarters. She could not help staring at them, and then it was too late to get out of their way. Before she could gather her senses to move, the nearest man grabbed her chin in a none too gentle fist. She found herself looking what seemed a long way up into a formidable face, a long face with a long nose, and brows as black as pitch. Dark, piercing eyes held her gaze, full of menace that sent chills shivering down her spine. Thin lips stretched over gleaming white teeth added to his sinister air. She made a supreme effort not to show how terrified she was.

"You're a pretty wench," he said with a chuckle. "How old are you?"

Some instinct of self-preservation gave her strength to lie. "Twelve, sir," she answered in a voice surprisingly loud.

"Huh, I'd have thought you older! Oh, well," he said, removing his hand so swiftly that her chin dropped, "You'll keep for a year or two. We've no need to go robbing cradles, have we, Orestes?"

He threw a glance at his companion and Esther took advantage of the moment to scuttle past them and hurry down the street. She could hear them laughing together as they walked on. There would be bruises on her chin tomorrow, where his rings had pressed into her flesh, but that was nothing compared to the escape she had had. She remembered stories of young women being abducted by courtiers. She had no wish to be taken to the palace one night only to be thrown out on a dung-heap the next day.

By the time she reached home her nerves had calmed, although it was many days before she could rid her mind of the images of the gallows and the tall man with the dark visage. Somehow they became linked in her mind, so that they merged into one memory which always evoked a shudder. However, she began to fill her mind with thoughts of the coming celebrations at the palace, where, along with all the citizens of Shushan, she could at last see what was behind those forbidding walls.

# CHAPTER 2

I n the weeks that followed, the city of Shushan vibrated
with activity. Naturally, the chief topic of conversation among the townspeople was the royal
celebration.
Every day they had new marvels to discuss, and more
displays of imperial riches and majesty to gape at. They
watched as craftsmen of all kinds made their way to the palace.
Potters, goldsmiths, sculptors, weavers of fine cloth, carpen-
ters, and masons hurried along the Processional Way, to be
followed by merchants with huge consignments of exotic
foods and spices from all over the world. Every member of the
household staff worked from morning to night, and even the
king threw himself wholeheartedly into the preparations,
anxious not to overlook the smallest detail.

Mordecai found himself constantly at the king's side,
writing down instructions to make sure that all the royal
wishes were carried out. The king was determined to give
each prince and satrap every consideration. He took great care
in matters of protocol, and scrutinized each guest's standing
and rank carefully, in order to avoid any occasion for offence.
The activities of all the nobles during their stay were under the
personal direction of the king himself.

After a few weeks Mordecai, who had by this time
proved his usefulness, was made personal assistant to Carshena,

the chief of the Inner Council. Given sleeping quarters in the palace, he had little time for sleep. The king seemed to be at his most inventive late in the night, and Carshena would send for Mordecai to take down the royal instructions. There was an atmosphere of strain and tension, for Xerxes would not tolerate mistakes. It was only when the king decided to go hunting or chariot-racing, that Mordecai was able to escape to his own house for some peace and quiet.

It was during one such visit that Esther broached the subject of the palace celebrations. She had been questioning him about the preparations, and she mentioned that she would be able to see for herself when it was time for the feast for the townspeople.

Mordecai looked up sharply at that. "I would prefer, Esther, if you did not go the palace," he said.

She stared at him in astonishment. "What do you mean?"

"The palace is no place for a girl like you. Put it out of your mind. I forbid you to go."

Esther was stunned. Mordecai, who had always allowed her so much freedom, was denying her the one thing she had set her heart on. She could not accept it.

"But I don't understand!" she cried. "What harm can come to me among the people? It's not as if I would be alone."

Mordecai rose and paced round the room. "Listen to me, Esther. You were only three years old when your father, my uncle's son, begged me to look after you if anything happened to him on his journey back to Judah. He was a devout man and I promised to bring you up in the tradition of our ancestors. I was only a young man myself, hardly more than twenty-five years old, and it was a heavy responsibility. It was Zorpah who nursed you and brought you up, and taught you the ways of our people. We must never forget that we were exiled from our own land, and we have an obligation to pass on the knowledge of our God from one generation to another. You must not forget that you are a Jew, that God promised to preserve us as a people, even if we are far from our land, and that we are an alien minority here."

"But cousin," she interrupted, "how can you say that? You are a trusted servant of the king. You have worked in the palace all these years."

"I just want you to remember who you are, and what your heritage is."

"I still don't see what that has to do with my going to the palace."

He sighed. "The fact is, Esther, I feel I have not carried out my promise as well as I ought. I should have brought you up like other Jewish girls. Instead I taught you to read and write. You have learned about history and politics and your head is filled with things that perhaps you were better off not knowing." He spread his hands. "But it did not seem fair to deprive you of knowledge just because you are a girl. You always had such curiosity about everything, but I had no idea when I answered your questions, that you would become so involved. Now I see that you have become obsessed with the palace life, a life you can never be part of. It would be better for your own happiness if you could forget all about the palace and concentrate on your life here among your own people."

"But you are part of the palace life, and you are accepted, even though you are a Jew," she countered.

"It is different for a man. Darius himself singled me out when I was a young man because I once rendered him a service, and he arranged for me to be educated so that I would be a useful servant of the palace administration. But there is nothing for a woman at court but to be a concubine or at best the wife of some official. You would be better off married to one of our own people, mistress of your own home, modest though it may be. The palace is no place for an impressionable young woman. It is a place of intrigue and suspicion, filled with unscrupulous men, who will stop at nothing to achieve their ends."

An image of the two courtiers she had met in the city square flashed into her mind and a chill shivered through her. She knew Mordecai was right, but she was not quite ready to relinquish her dream.

"I'm sure you are right, cousin. But it's not as if I would be going into the palace. It is only a garden party, after all. Surely I would come no harm among all the townspeople."

"I do not wish to discuss it further." Mordecai's tone held a note of finality that she had not heard before. "I have made my decision."

She bit back the arguments that rushed into her mind. Now was not the time. Mordecai was tired, and under a strain. She would approach him again when he had rested.

Quietly she left the room, but Mordecai remained thoughtful for a long while. He realised how deeply he had disappointed Esther, but he knew the risks of allowing her to go to the palace. She was not as yet aware of her own beauty, so she had no idea of the way she stood out among other young women. It only needed one of the young men of the court to notice her and he would pursue her relentlessly until he achieved his aim. Mordecai knew very well that in such a situation he would have no power to protect her, such were the ways of the palace. He sighed, and went back to his reading, hoping, however faintly, that he had settled the matter with Esther once and for all.

In the days that followed, Esther went about her tasks with

a heaviness of heart. She spent more and more of her time in the little room on the roof where Mordecai stored his scrolls and tablets. Some of them had to do with the enumeration of artifacts in the palace. Along with each item listed was a little history as to its source and significance, the result of Mordecai's own research into the palace archives. Reading her way slowly through them she learned more about the empire, for many described the conquests of Darius with details of all his exploits. It was a world that fascinated her, but all this knowledge had to remain within her, for there was no one with whom she could share it. Her friend Huldah had no interest in anything but domestic matters, and made it plain on the few occasions Esther spoke about them, that she thought women had no business delving into the affairs of state. As for Jacob, although he might be interested, she felt it would make a constraint between them if she showed herself to be too learned. Instead she lived part of her life in this secret world, even as she worked at her loom or helped Zorpah run the house.

When feelings of frustration or longing threatened to engulf her, she would pick up her small lute and sing the songs of the exiles that Zorpah had taught her, the songs of her heritage. Or, craving companionship of her own age, she would make her way to the Shulman's to talk to Huldah.

There were two Shulman daughters, Huldah, who was sixteen, and Tabitha, who was two years younger. Huldah was betrothed to Giddel, the son of Tobias the baker and the wedding was planned for later in the year. She had a placid nature, with twinkling eyes and a ready smile. Tabitha, on the other hand, was solemn, taking after her mother who was very pious. Mistress Shulman brought up her daughters very strictly, just as if they were living in their homeland of Judah and not as exiles in a foreign land. She observed all the Jewish traditions with care, and did not at all approve of Esther's free and easy ways.

One afternoon, when Esther went to visit her friend, she found her in the courtyard seated at a table under the shade of a tree. Beside her on the table was a pile of brightly coloured material, and her hands were busy with a needle.

"Ah, Esther," she called. "I was hoping you would come today. I'm making a new dress to wear at the palace celebration." She stopped, seeing Esther's change of expression. "What's the matter?"

"I'm not going to the celebration," she stated in a flat voice. "Mordecai won't let me go."

Huldah looked shocked. "But I don't understand. Everyone is going. Why does he forbid you?"

Esther shrugged. "That is the mystery. He wouldn't give me a reason. Just ordered me not to go."

"But he must have some reason," Huldah said. "He must know how much you want to see the palace. You talk of nothing else."

" Exactly. He thinks it is an obsession that I should give up."

"I think," remarked Huldah, "that he should have thought of that before now. After all, it was he who told you all these stories about the palace, from the time you were small." Huldah was unconsciously echoing her mother who frequently voiced her disapproval of the way Esther was brought up.

"Perhaps he regrets it," said Esther. "Especially now that I am almost grown up and he is finding it hard to get me a suitable husband. Not that I mind in the least."

Huldah looked concerned. "But surely you want to get

married?"

"Well, yes," Esther admitted grudgingly. "But life here is so dull. I'd be miserable just keeping house for the rest of my life."

"Hush, Esther! Mama might hear you." Huldah looked round to see if there was anyone within earshot. "You can't mean that. What else would you do?"

Esther laughed lightly. "Who knows? Perhaps I shall marry a rich merchant and travel all over with him, just like Madame Zinna did."

Huldah shook her head and went on with her sewing. "You say some wild things, but I don't believe you mean them. It's just that you have had so much freedom. But a married woman can run her household as she pleases. She has freedom, too."

"Yes, but only so far. It is men who make all the important decisions."

This time it was Huldah who laughed. "You will never change that no matter where you are. Even now, it is Mordecai who decides for you."

"Yes, but there must be a way to change his mind." Then a thought struck her and she leaned over to Huldah, and lowered her voice. "If I were to go with you, as part of your family, surely he would not object to that. Do you think your parents would mind if I came with you?"

Huldah brightened. "Of course not. I'm sure it would be all right. I'll go and ask Mama now." She rose to go, but Esther held her back.

"No. Don't ask your mother. Remember what we just said. It is the men who make all the decisions. Ask your father when he comes home." She knew Mother Shulman would not look favourably on that request, whereas her husband, who had a soft spot for Esther, was more likely to give permission. "If you could get him to tell Mordecai that I will be safe in his care all the time, then there is a chance he will let me go."

So it was decided, and Esther waited impatiently for her little plan to bear fruit. Sure enough, the next time Mordecai came home, Shulman paid a visit, and when he had left, Mordecai spoke to Esther.

" The Shulmans feel that I am being too hard on you, forbidding you to go to the feast. They have offered to take you with them, if I will give permission."

Esther smiled her most radiant smile. "Oh, please let me go, cousin. You know how much I long to see the palace. If I don't get to see it I will always wonder what it is like. It will mean so much to me to see it for myself."

Mordecai heaved a sigh, and thought about that for a little. Then he shook his head with a rueful smile. "But will you be satisfied, little one? I doubt it. However, if you go along with the Shulmans, you can hardly come to any harm. All right, you may go, but you must promise me that you will remain with them at all times."

A radiant smile lit her face. "Oh, thank you, cousin Mordecai, I promise, I promise. And I won't speak to a single pagan Persian!"

He began to remonstrate with her but she had already gone to tell her friend Huldah the good news.

*

On a crisp, sunny day that held a hint of chill weather to come, the wide outer courtyard of the palace was filled with a huge crowd of people milling to and fro. It was the first time ever that the ordinary citizens of Shushan had been allowed within the great golden gates of the palace, and there were many rendered speechless by the wonderful sights that met their eyes. They gazed at the walls decorated with brightly coloured enamelled bricks and the army of warriors marching along them in bas-relief. They made their way slowly round the square, pausing at the marble statues of Darius and Cyrus, until they came to the massive steps of the Adana, the great hall of Darius, where the enormous stone figures of winged bulls guarded the entrance. There the citizens were not allowed to linger too long, for attendants dressed in lavish uniforms ushered them forward to a columned gateway at one side of the square. They found themselves in an inner courtyard paved with blue and white tiles, while along the walls arched alcoves, draped with lavish blue and white curtains, housed long tables filled with all kinds of exotic foods. These were obviously reserved for the most important guests. Couches of gold and silver surrounded a pool bordered with mosaics of white marble and red felspar, while urns of brilliant roses filled the air with their scent, masking the sweaty underarms of the crowds who pushed their way towards the gateway at the far end. On the other side of the gateway they emerged into a wide green park, where white pavilions lined each side, and flights of marble steps led up to the pillared galleries above them.

Here entertainments of all kinds were taking place. There were horsemen, musicians, tumblers, acrobats, dancers and singers. Athletic games and competitions were in progress, young men of the city showing their prowess, and pitting their strength against the seasoned soldiers. Here and there tents were set up with tables piled high with foods of all kinds, roasted meat of lamb and goat, and tiny birds, fish fresh from the river, sweet cakes of honey, figs and dates and pomegranates. The bakers from the royal kitchens vied with one another to produce breads of all shapes and sizes, made with the best flour from the king's mills. Servants served wine in gold cups, on which they kept eagle eyes, just in case any would-be thief might feel tempted to hide one about his person. Slaves carrying trays of food went about replenishing tables, trying to avoid the children who, taking advantage of their parents' preoccupation with the wonders of the scene, chased each other in and out among the throng. People were free to help themselves to the food which they carried off to the marble benches in the shade of the tall trees, to eat their fill and listen to the music of the flute girls.

Esther and her friends moved about, awestruck, marvelling that such splendour existed. The opulence of the palace grounds was beyond everything she had dreamed of, and every detail etched itself on her mind so that even years later she could recall all of them vividly. As they wandered from group to group, the girls exclaimed at each new novelty, and even the sedate Shulmans seemed impressed.

At last, tired out with excitement, they sat down to eat at one of the tables that had just been replenished with trays of food. There were all kinds of meats seasoned with spices, dishes of fruits and vegetables, and bread and wine in plenty. When they had eaten their fill, they sat under a tree, and soon Eli was fast asleep. The girls fidgeted, wanting to see more, until finally Madam Shulman allowed them to wander off, having made them promise to stay together, and to return within the hour.

The three girls set off to enjoy more of the sights, often stopping to exchange a few words with friends and acquaintances from the city, sharing the atmosphere of a high holiday. From time to time they paused at a table to pick up some sweetmeats or fruit. When they came to a crowded spot where some acrobats were performing incredible feats, they sat down to watch. Esther moved a little away from the others in order to see better, and so it was that when Huldah and Tabilla rose to go they could not see her, for the crowd had thickened. After searching around for some time they decided to go back, thinking they would meet her on the way.

Esther meanwhile, having seen all she wanted, looked around for Huldah and Tabilla, but they were nowhere to be found. She was not unduly perturbed, seeing it as a chance to do some exploring on her own. A troupe of dancers caught her attention for a while, and then she moved on. To one side, she noticed a narrow pathway, and could not resist following it, since there did not seem to be a guard around. It led through some bushes to a little lake, beside which sat a small ornamental building. On reaching it she discovered that it was a little bower, the roof resting on carved wooden pillars, its walls made of ornamental trellis. Inside was an elaborate couch of worked silver, covered with silk cushions. Esther entered and sat down, leaning back on the soft silk, enjoying the unaccustomed luxury. This is what it is like to live in the palace, she thought, to be able to walk in beautiful gardens, to sit by a lake and watch the birds as they dived to catch fish. She closed her eyes and pretended she was a royal princess. In no time at all she was asleep.

*

She was awakened by the rustle of leaves stirred by a freshening breeze. She sat up alarmed, not knowing how long she had slept. Looking up at the sun she realised that it had that it had moved round to the west. She must have slept for an hour or more. The others would be worried. Once again her curiosity had led her astray. Quickly she got up and set off the way she had come, hastening her steps as she looked for the opening that would take her to the main courtyard. Coming to a fork in the path she hesitated, trying to recall which way she had taken. She had not noticed the other pathway on her way in, so intent she had been on discovering what lay at the end.

Suddenly she heard a noise behind her, and, turning round she saw a man lurching towards her, obviously drunk. She drew back among the bushes, but he had spotted her and approached her with outstretched arms and a vacant smile on his lips.

"Here's a nice young lady come to meet me. Just what I need!"

She could see by his clothes that he was a workman, probably from the city, and she knew that he would show her no mercy. When he made a grab at her, she swerved and tried to pass him but he was too quick for her. Catching her by the arm he pulled her to him.

"Let me go!" she screamed, struggling wildly to get free. This only added to his enjoyment. With a grin on his face he began to drag her back the way he had come. She continued to scream and struggle but the man was too big and powerful, and she could do nothing against his brute strength. Too late, she remembered Mordecai's warnings.

The sound of running footsteps made her renew her cries, and relief flooded through her when a young man appeared, obviously coming to her aid.

"Let go of Lady Farreda!" he yelled in a commanding voice. "Let go of her at once!" Despite his youth there was a ring of authority in his voice.

The drunk stopped, confused, and dropped her arm. "Who?

Lady ... I, I didn't know. I thought she was a city girl. Beg pardon, sir, I didn't mean to harm her. Just a bit of fun, that's all."

The young man took a step towards him, but before he could say more, the drunk staggered away, mumbling to himself.

Meanwhile Esther tried to recover her dignity. Her kerchief had slipped from her head and her black curls tumbled over her shoulders. She smoothed her hair and dress, aware that the young man was eyeing her.

"Thank you. You saved my life."

She thought he was not much older than herself. Perhaps sixteen or seventeen. He had a handsome face, and his hair curling round his head was light brown, almost blond. Obviously he was a stranger, for his colouring was strange. The fine linen tunic with the silver girdle round his waist revealed his wealthy status. He smiled at her with white, even teeth.

"Well, if not your life, at least your virtue. Glad to have been of service to a beautiful young lady. Are you all right?"

"Yes." She smiled her gratitude at him. "Fortunately you came in time. But I'm not Lady Fareda."

He grinned back at her. "I know. I made it up, to make it sound as if I knew you. By the way, my name is Sarcon." He bowed formally, as if they had been introduced.

"I am Esther."

"Well, Esther, may I ask you a favour?"

Her heart sank. Had he saved her from the drunk only to have her for himself?

"I would be honoured," he was saying, "if you would allow me to escort you wherever you are going."

She was so relieved she gave him a brilliant smile. Then, belatedly she remembered the Shulmans, and her face registered her dismay.

"My friends. I was supposed to meet them in the main courtyard. Near the Adana. They will be looking everywhere for me."

"Come with me. I know a shortcut that will take us there in just a few minutes. Quicker than battling your way through the crowds." Seeing the uncertain look she gave him, he continued. "I've been living here for the the past week. I came with my father for the celebrations. He is the satrap of Idumea." While he talked he led her along the path in the direction of the palace.

"Where is Idumea?" she asked.

"It's in the north. Not as beautiful as it is here. The palace is magnificent. Full of wonderful treasures."

"So I have heard. I would love to see it."

He looked puzzled. "Aren't you staying here? I thought you were in the company of some visiting lord."

That explained his readiness to help her. He had mistaken her for someone of some importance. "I live in Shushan, in the city. I came here for the day with my friends. Now I must hurry, for they will be looking for me."

"I can show you the palace, " he suggested. Well, at least a little bit of it. We can go through the palace to the Adana, and we come out near where you are to meet your friends."

She hesitated. It was the only chance she would ever have, but at the same time she was reluctant to cause the Shulmans any more worry.

"Come on," he said taking her hand, "we'll go through the palace instead of through the gardens. It really won't take any longer."

That settled it. This was an opportunity she could not miss.

"All right, then. But we must hurry."

Leaving the path, they crossed an enclosed garden and made for a flight of steps leading to a terrace. A long, low wing of the palace stretched before them. Two soldiers guarded the entrance to a large double door. Sarcon approached them boldly, still holding Esther's hand, and, after a quick scrutiny by the guards, they passed inside.

"How did they let us in?" she asked.

He pointed to the small crest on his tunic. "This is the crest of our satrapy, and this little crown shows that I am an official guest of the empire. It gives us access anywhere in the palace. Except, of course, the king's quarters."

Esther was somewhat relieved. Shrugging off her feeling of unease she began to enjoy herself. They were passing quickly through a series of halls with brightly coloured mosaic floors and elaborately patterned carpets, empty except for huge urns filled with scented flowers. Some walls were hung with rich tapestries of silk of every colour, or else were of glazed bricks. Still others were of carved ivory, depicting scenes of historical importance. She wished she could linger and examine them in detail, but as they hurried through halls and corridors she had glimpses of life-size statues, mostly of exotic animals, lions with wings, or bulls with human faces. Once or twice they met servants who hurried along showing no interest in them, but there was no sign of courtiers or palace officials.

"Where is everybody?" It seemed strange to her that this vast palace should be almost empty.

"At this time of day they are at the baths, or resting for the banquet tonight. But these are public rooms. The living quarters and guest houses are on the other side of the compound. Here, this will take us to the Adana," he said, ushering her through a doorway.

Esther gasped. The magnificence of the hall was over-whelming. She walked a few paces with hesitant steps, gazing around, completely awestruck, her haste forgotten. Wide and high, it was bigger than anything she could have imagined. Rows of tall columns of convoluted marble with fluted plinths supported the richly decorated roof, and at the top of each pillar, four marble heads of animals looked out in four directions. A gorgeous carpet patterned with myriads of colours stretched down the centre of the hall to a platform on which stood two elaborate thrones of gold encrusted with precious stones. The walls were of carved ivory depicting royal dignitaries and mythical animals, with here and there strips of polished figured bronze that ran from floor to ceiling. At intervals there were inscribed plaques with sayings of the magi. One of these she recognized from one of Mordecai's scrolls. She touched it with her hand and slowly read aloud the words.

Sarcon, who was watching her closely, raised his eyebrows.

"So, you are clever as well as beautiful."

She laughed. "That's the way courtiers talk, is it not?"

"What do you mean?"

"You know how to flatter."

His eyes narrowed. "Is that what you think? Come over here."

Taking her hand he drew her over to an alcove, of which one wall was a sheet of highly polished bronze. There, for the first time in her life, she saw a full-length image of herself. She stared, unable to take her eyes away. Can that be me, she wondered. It was a truly beautiful face that stared back at her, a face of perfect features framed by a rich mass of hair that fell rippling to her shoulders. Her budding womanhood gave promise of a figure of fine proportions, and the whole impression was one of exquisite beauty.

Then she became aware of Sarcon's image behind hers, his handsome face, his virile young body. There was admiration in her eyes as she looked at him, and she saw in the reflection the same admiration mirrored in his. She turned to face him, and they were both suddenly very still. Hardly daring to breathe, they gazed into each other's eyes for what seemed an age, until they were overcome with the intensity of their feelings, and they looked away.

"I must go," she said moving off quickly towards the far end of the hall. "I have wasted too much time already."

He followed silently, trying, as she was, to get back a sense of reality. They emerged through a door in the portico and were immediately engulfed by the throng. She hurried on ahead towards the place where she had left the Shulmans. Sarcon tried to talk to her but they kept getting separated by people. Finally she spotted her friends, and she stopped, waiting for him to catch up.

"Thank you again," she said, tying her kerchief round her hair. "And thank you for showing me the Adana. I will never forget it. Or you."

"Esther, wait." He laid a restraining hand on her arm. "I want to see you again."

"That is not possible. Soon you will go back to your province and I... I will never visit the palace again. It was a wonderful day, and it will always be a wonderful memory. Goodbye."

He said nothing, but his eyes held hers.

She left him standing there, and hurried off to the Shulmans.

"Madam Shulman," she started to say as she approached, "I am very sorry. Please forgive me for keeping you waiting."

43

They all stared at her, their faces showing first relief and then resentment. Then they all started talking at once, their questions tumbling out.

"I got lost, and had trouble finding my way back." She was on the point of telling them about Sarcon, but she stopped herself in time. It would only lead to endless questions and recriminations. Besides, she could not trust herself to speak about him without revealing her emotions.

Madam Shulman got up, looking very displeased. "You promised not to wander off on your own. I thought I could trust you. Why did you not stay with Huldah and Tabilla?"

The two girls added their questions. "Where did you go, Esther? We searched everywhere for you."

"I was watching the acrobats and when I looked for you, you were not where I left you. There was such a crowd of people."

"But that was ages ago!" For once Huldah seemed genuinely upset. "Have you been going about all alone since then?"

"I went in the wrong direction and then I got lost on the way back." Esther looked from one to the other and realized that she could never explain what had happened. Indeed already she was beginning to wonder if she had dreamt it all. "I'm very sorry," she repeated. "I didn't mean to be a nuisance. Please forgive me."

Mr Shulman spoke for the first time. "Praise God you got back safely. Now, let us get home before it gets dark." Taking his wife by the arm he led the way to the entrance.

Following behind, Huldah glanced at Esther. "You will have to tell us sometime what really happened."

"But I told you, I got lost."

Huldah did not look convinced. "You look different. Oh,

I don't know. As if you had seen something very exciting. Your eyes are shining, and your cheeks are quite flushed."

"I was afraid I wasn't going to find you. I ran about in all directions." She was amazed at how glibly the answers came to her. But it was true to a certain extent. She had been very afraid that they had gone home without her, and that Mordecai would have had to come looking for her.

There was nothing more to be said and they walked home in silence. Mr. Shulman insisted that they take Esther right to the gate. Esther apologized again, but he patted her hand soothingly. "Say no more about it. You came to no harm, that's the important thing. We all had a day to remember."

When Esther entered the house there was no sign of anyone. Mordecai must have stayed at the palace. He would not now know of her escapade. But what about Zorpah? She crept quietly along to Zorpah's room and opened the door. She was lying stretched out fully clothed on the bed, snoring loudly. Esther tiptoed off to her own room.

What a day it had been! It had exceeded her wildest expectations. Mordecai was right, she thought. It has turned my head. I will never be the same again.

As she undressed she recalled the moment when she had seen her reflection in the mirror. Surely someone as beautiful as she must be destined for something special. Why else would God have bestowed on her such beauty? Not to be wasted on the son of some lowly merchant, surely. And then there was Sarcon. He was so handsome. What if he were to come and seek her as his wife? But that could not be, he did not know where she lived. Besides, the son of a satrap would be expected to marry a princess or at least the daughter of a nobleman. One day he would probably be the satrap and he would never marry an unknown Jewish girl. She sighed deeply, bringing herself back to earth. Certainly, marrying Sarcon was out of the question.

But I won't marry some local boy, she vowed. I will marry a man of power, someone of great importance, who will value my beauty. Someone in the palace, so that I can live among all the splendid things I saw today.

She fell asleep and dreamed of a prince who came to woo her, and he wore the face of Sarcon.

# CHAPTER 3

Xerxes, the king, was bored. he sat in the banqueting hall, surrounded by all his guests, watching the performance of the dancing toupe. When they finished he applauded languidly along with the rest, but his mind was on other matters. Over the past weeks there had been a surfeit of feasting and entertainment, so that they had begun to pall even on Xerxes, who had a voracious appetite for amusements of all kinds. It was time he was getting down to the business of planning his campaign against the Greeks. With a wave of his hand he motioned to his cup-bearer to refill his cup. At least the wine was good.

The next entertainment turned out to be a re-enactment of one of his victorious sallies against Egypt. The company seemed to enjoy it and clapped vigorously, but even this did little to cheer the king. Instead, he began to drink more and more until he managed to forget his restlessness. His spirits rose again, and when the play was over, he looked around for new diversions.

"I know what we need now," he said to his guests, Nereis, the satrap of Moridia, and Prince Callias of Hyrcania, who sat with him at the table. "We lack women!"

"But my lord king," said Prince Callias, "there is surely no lack of women around here." His glance swept the hall, where dancing-girls and flute-girls intermingled with the guests.

"The most beautiful women you could find anywhere."

"Oh, not ordinary women! I'm talking about the real beauties of the court, the queen and her ladies."

Prince Callias and Satrap Nereis exchanged glances. Just what did the king have in mind?

Xerxes, his speech beginning to slur, pointed a finger at the prince. "You have never seen a woman like Queen Vashti. She is the most beautiful in the whole world!"

Callias forbore to mention that he had already met the queen at the welcoming ceremony when she occupied the throne next to Xerxes, and on several subsequent occasions.

"I don't doubt that for a moment," he put in quickly. "Her beauty is legendary."

But this did not seem to satisfy Xerxes. He turned and beckoned to the chamberlains who stood behind him.

"Send for the queen. Tell her I, Xerxes, request her presence here. Order her to put on her royal robes and her royal crown, and bid her come here so that I may show her off to my friends, that they may see the face and figure of the queen of Persia!"

There was dead silence. It was unheard of for the king to give such an order. All the invited guests at the feast were men. There were no ladies of the court present. It was as if he was bringing the queen down to the level of the dancing-girls and flute-girls who were all servants or slaves.

Then Nehuman, the chief chamberlain, cleared his throat.

"My lord king, it is very late. The queen and her ladies are already in bed."

Xerxes glared at him. "No matter. Bring her here!"

Carshena, the chief adviser of the council, hearing what was going on, hurried forward.

"Sire, it is a most unusual request. The queen..." he

hesitated.

"Well, what about the queen?" growled Xerxes, his eyebrows locking.

Carshena's courage failed him. "Nothing, sire."

The king waved off the chamberlains, who had paused while Carshena was speaking.

"Bring the queen here! That is my command!" He picked up his goblet and emptied it. "Carshena, when I want your advice I'll ask for it."

"Yes, my lord king." Carshena looked subdued.

In the queen's suite, Vashti was preparing to retire. She and her ladies had enjoyed a fine banquet with the wives of the visiting princes and satraps. The entertainments she had organized had been well received, and the ladies had all relaxed in an atmosphere of freedom and jollity. Perhaps she had drunk more wine than usual, but a good night's sleep would take care of that. Her maid was removing the ornaments from her hair which now hung down her back in heavy tresses, when there was a commotion at the door. The curtains swished aside to reveal the chamberlains, headed by Nehuman. For a moment nobody moved. Then there was a flurry of consternation. Ramana, the queen's chief attendant, confronted the men.

"What do you mean, intruding in the queen's private quarters? And at this time of night? This is an outrage!'

Nehuman flung her a look of distaste. It was bad enough being sent on this mission, without having to endure abuse from a mere woman. With a deadpan expression he repeated the king's orders.

Vashti stared at him in horror. "To the banqueting hall? At this hour? To parade before these drunks? He can't mean it. It is unthinkable. I won't do it. Tell the king that Vashti declines."

The chamberlains, however, refused to go away. None of them dared to go back to the king with Vashti's message. Nehuman pleaded with Ramana to prevail on the queen. Ramana pleaded with her mistress to obey the king's command. All to no avail. It seemed the more she pleaded, the more stubborn Vashti became.

"I refuse to be put on display like a slave or an animal in the market-place. How dare the king ask such a thing! My dignity as queen is at stake. He ought to be ashamed to treat me, the queen, in this way. What would the other princes and noblemen think? It would embarrass them as well as me. They would not parade their wives like that. It is unworthy of the king. I refuse to have any part in it. It is a slight on civilized women. Show the chamberlains out, Ramana. I am going to bed."

With that she rose, drew herself up to her full height, and with great dignity she moved to the curtained archway and disappeared into her bedroom.

The chamberlains, realizing that they could not persuade the queen, went back to the king with Vashti's message couched in more diplomatic terms. They braced themselves for the king's anger. It was not long in coming.

"The queen refused?" He sucked in his breath. "She actually refused to come at my command?"

Nehuman spread his hands. He had little sympathy for Vashti. Although the king's request was not in the best taste, no one had the right to refuse the king, not even the highly venerated Vashti.

Carshena, who was, as ever, standing within earshot, acted quickly to save the king's face in front of his guests.

"If it please the king," he began, "there is a man with a

performing bear outside. It would be a diversion for the company. Shall I bid him come in?"

Xerxes nodded, tight-lipped. Then he turned to his guests.

"My lords, a change of programme. The queen we can see another time. Tonight we have a performer who does not often visit our court."

So they brought in the bear, and its antics soon caused the assembled guests to roar with laughter. The incident of the queen was forgotten. Forgotten, that is, by all except the king, who sat looking thunderous, and the men of the Council who were well aware of the king's wrath, and were furious with Vashti for causing it. After all their planning and preparation, it was too bad that the banquet had to end on a sour note. For the king proceeded to get very drunk and finally had to be helped to bed. He was lucid enough, however, to order the Council to meet at noon.

*

Promptly at the appointed time the Council convened, and Xerxes marched into the chamber, his face rigid. They all guessed he was nursing a headache, even though he gave no indication of it, and each one mentally prepared himself to be as alert as possible. It would not be easy to deal with the king in his present frame of mind. There was a distinct possibility that heads could roll.

There were seven officials of the Inner Council, all experts on questions of law and order. Carshena, Sethar and Admatha sat on one side of the table, Tarshish, Meres and Marsena sat opposite, with Memucan at the far end, facing the king.

Xerxes began to speak.

51

"This matter of the queen must be dealt with. I, King Xerxes, sent my servants to Queen Vashti with a command, and she refused to obey it  What does the law say we should do to her?"

Memucan was the first to answer. "Queen Vashti has insulted not only the king but also his officials...in fact, every man of the empire!  All the women in the empire will start looking down on their husbands as soon as they hear what Vashti has done."

"Yes," interrupted Marsena, "they will say, 'King Xerxes commanded Queen Vashti to come and she refused!  If she can do that, why can't we?'  Can't you just hear them?  This plays right into their hands."

Abagtha added his voice.  "When wives of the royal officials of Persia hear about the queen's behaviour, they will be casting it up to their husbands before the day is out.  Wives everywhere will cease to show proper respect for their husbands, and husbands will be angry with their wives."

Memucan felt he had heard enough, and put forward his solution to the problem.  "If it please your majesty, issue a royal proclamation that Vashti may never again appear before the king.  Have it written in the laws of Persia and Medea so that it cannot be changed.  Then give her place as queen to some other woman who is more worthy.  When your proclamation is made known all over the empire, every woman will then treat her husband with proper respect, whether he is rich or poor."  With that, Memucan sat down.

The king looked round his advisers, hoping that there would be other suggestions.  Memucan's sounded too drastic, and was not quite what the king had in mind when he ordered the Council to meet.  Teach Vashti a lesson, by all means, but never to see her again?  I would be punishing myself too, he thought. But he could see that his advisers were taking the matter personally, and it would be impossible for him to back down now. They would take it as a sign of weakness on his part.

"Memucan has spoken wisely. But perhaps someone has another proposal? Is there another who wishes to give a different view?"

No one spoke. They were all hoping the king would adopt this plan of action. It would be a great relief to have the matter settled so easily, and if their wives complained about the harshness of the punishment, they could blame Memucan. He was a widower, and had no wife to berate him.

The king, regarding their faces, saw that they were not going to offer any alternatives. With a heavy heart he spoke. "It seems that we are all of one mind in this matter. Is it agreed?"

They gave their consent one by one, and at a nod from the king, Carshena summoned Mordecai to record the decision. They instructed him to send a message to each of the provinces, in the language and writing of every province, saying that every husband should be the master of his home, and speak with final authority. No wife was to disregard her husband's wishes. This was to be the law of the whole empire. As an example to all, Queen Vashti was to be banished for her disobedience.

The king's herald made the proclamation in the city, and while the men were pleased that their authority was once again firmly established, at the same time there was sympathy for Vashti. The people shook their heads and said that Xerxes should not have put her in such an impossible position. But they took great care not to say it where the eyes and ears of the king might overhear. If the king would not protect his own queen, of whom he was said to be very fond, what chance had an ordinary person to escape his wrath?

After a few days the king's anger cooled down, and he began to miss Vashti. Apart from her great beauty and charm which had delighted everyone at the court, she was very intelligent. She had been very useful for hosting small exclusive banquets, where the king could discuss delicate diplomatic affairs with a few selected princes without offending the others, since the guest list was supposedly the domain of the queen. Often he would ask her opinion of this or that prince, and found she had an instinct for penetrating their defences, and she frequently offered valuable snippets of information, culled from who knew where, which helped him in his dealings with them.

Even now, when he was completing his plans for the Greek expedition, he could have used her to find out from individual lords and satraps what exactly their views were on certain aspects of the campaign. He bitterly regretted his impulsive action in making the proclamation against her, and he vowed he would not be so quick to follow the advice of the Inner Council in future. She had already left the palace, so there was no way he could bring her back without appearing to give in. His advisers began to notice how often his glance rested on the empty throne beside his own, and the brooding look he adopted whenever affairs arose which would have required the presence of the queen. They were not crafty advisers for nothing. Realizing that it would not be long before the king would begin looking for scapegoats (and they knew he would look no farther than the Inner Council), they decided among themselves to bring up the matter of a replacement for Vashti at the next meeting.

Accordingly, when the Council had concluded the usual

business of the day, Carshena rose and intimated that he had a matter for the council to discuss. The king, who had been on the point of leaving, sat forward on his chair and rested his chin on his hand.

Carshena began by referring to the lack of a queen and how this affected affairs of state. Then he went on to lay out his proposal.

"Why does the king not choose a new queen to be by his side when he receives ambassadors and entertains princes and lords? He could choose his queen from one of the six aristocratic families, as was the former tradition of the kings of Persia." It had always annoyed Carshena that Xerxes had departed from that tradition when he chose Vashti as queen. Perhaps that was the reason she had turned out such a disaster.

"No!" The king was emphatic. He drew himself up in his chair, determined that his advisers should not lead him into another fiasco. "I'm not having one of these horse-faced women as my consort. Besides, the best ones are already married. The others remain unmarried because no one will have them. And anyway, there is none of marriageable age. If I am to have a new queen she has to be both young and beautiful."

"In that case," said Memucan, only too ready now to mollify the king over the Vashti affair, "I propose that the king order a search to be made to find some beautiful virgins. We could appoint officials in every province of the empire, and they would search out and bring these beautiful young women here to your House of Concubines. Put them in Hegai's charge and let them be prepared in dress and conduct, and given training in palace protocol. Then the king could choose the one he likes best and make her queen in Vashti's place."

The king was intrigued. His advisers saw that the idea

pleased him, and when he asked for their opinion they all agreed. Abagtha made one suggestion. It was not fitting that these virgins should live with the concubines. He suggested setting up a new house, the House of Maidens, with one of the retired concubines to preside over it, under the charge of Hegai. This was approved. As for Xerxes, he saw it as a way to fill Vashti's vacant place so that he would not be constantly reminded of her.

"Let it be done. It will take some time, and when we return from our expedition, we will make the choice."

He rose, and left the chamber, while the council summoned Mordecai to write down the orders that would set the project in motion.

After this, Xerxes began to concentrate on his plans for his campaign against Greece. Now that the celebrations at the palace were drawing to a close, it was time to prepare in detail. During the past weeks and months he had had many discussions with the princes, satraps, and noblemen, and they were mostly in favour of the campaign. Where they disagreed was in the matter of timing. But Xerxes was determined to proceed as soon as possible, and when he judged that they could all be swung round to his opinion, he called a meeting of the Grand Conference in the Adana.

The Grand Conference opened with all the pomp and ceremony the empire could provide. The princes and satraps of every province paraded in, each one trying to outdo the rest in glitter and show, and took their appropriate places in the strict hierarchy of importance. A fanfare of trumpets and much beating of drums heralded the entrance of Xerxes and his court. The king had gone to great trouble to appear in all his regal panoply. His long robe was of woven gold cloth, the sleeves and neckline encrusted with jewels, as was the dark blue cloak that hung from his shoulders. On his feet were polished leather shoes studded with gems that sparkled as he walked. He wore the imperial crown, with rubies and jacinths set in gold, and in his hand he carried the sceptre of power. With a fine sense of timing, he paused for a moment and surveyed the audience before he took his seat on the royal throne.

The clerks of the Conference began the business of recording the presence of the various delegations, and when all the preliminaries were completed, Xerxes rose to address the company. He began by referring to the recent history of the empire.

"You are all aware of the famous deeds of Cyrus, Cambyses, and my father Darius, and how they added to the empire. I, if I am to be worthy of this illustrious throne, must continue to add power to power. Our whole history has been one of conquest, and we have extended our boundaries from Egypt in the south to Scythia in the north, from India in the east to Macedonia in the west. Some, like the Athenians, sought to conquer us, and they did us great harm when they defeated our army at Marathon. My father, Darius, was preparing to go to war against them at the time of his death, to repay them for the injury they wrought, and I will not rest until I have Athens and burn it to the ground. I propose to build a bridge across the Hellespont and march an army through Europe into Greece. If we crush the Athenians and their neighbours, we shall extend the boundaries of our empire and add Europe to our possessions.

"If you wish to gain my favour, each one of you must volunteer to accompany me on this expedition and present yourself ready and willing on the appointed day. Whoever brings with him the best equipped body of troops, him I will reward with distinctions and high honours. But now I am going to throw open the whole matter for debate, so that you will all have a chance to express your views." With that, he resumed his seat.

Of course, Xerxes was well aware of the views of each one, as he had sounded them out in private, but he was now providing a chance for them to put their views on public record, so that there could be no backing down later on. It was merely a matter of seeing in what terms they would give their approval.

There was loud applause in the hall, although the announcement had come as no surprise. After a few moments Mardonian, brother-in-law of Xerxes, rose to speak. He started by praising Xerxes as the greatest in a long line of illustrious kings. Then he went on:

"My lord king, we are inspired by your words, and we, the whole of the might of the empire, will stand behind you, so that our enemies, the Greeks, who have attacked us without provocation, will be punished. No one will be able to resist the mighty army of Persia."

He stopped speaking and there was silence in the hall. For a while no one dared to put forward the opposing view, until Artaban, the king's uncle, got to his feet.

"My lord," he said, "without a debate in which both sides of the question are expressed, it is not possible to choose the better course. I warned your father, my own brother, not to attack the Scythians, but he would not listen to me. He invaded their country and he left many fine Persian soldiers dead in that land. Our imperial rule there was won at too great a cost. But you, my lord, mean to attack a nation greatly superior to the Scythians, a nation with a high reputation for valour. It is my duty to tell you what you have to fear from them. You said that you mean to bridge the Hellespont. Now suppose—and it is not impossible—that you were to suffer a defeat in an engagement by land or sea, and what if the Greeks destroyed our fleet and then sailed to the Hellespont and destroyed the bridge. We would be in great peril. I know what I am talking about. That very thing almost happened to your father when he bridged the Bosphorus and the Danube. I urge you, therefore, to abandon this plan. Take my advice and don't run this terrible risk when there is no necessity to do so."

He resumed his seat, amid a stir of consternation. Xerxes himself was angry and showed it.

"Artaban," he seethed, through clenched teeth, "if you were not my father's brother I would make you pay the price for that outrageous speech. I forbid you to accompany me on my march to Greece. I don't need your kind of help. If we don't invade the Greeks, they will invade us. That is the choice before us, to fight or be conquered!"

When the king sat down, the applause that followed was not quite as vehement as he would have hoped. There was no doubt that the words of Artaban had cooled their enthusiasm, but no one wanted to be identified as directly opposing the king. The hall was quiet except for a low murmur as people exchanged views on this development. Xerxes stared straight ahead, paying no attention to anyone. Finally Sethar came forward.

"Most noble Xerxes, all the people of Persia know your valour and your brave exploits as a young man in your father's army, and all will acknowledge that your aim to punish your enemies is a worthy one. We are all proud of the empire, and we cannot allow those who attack it to escape with impunity. Those who live on the boundaries of the empire must have the confidence that we will defend the borders from all invaders.

We must avenge the injuries inflicted on us by the Athenians. It is no more than our duty. For this reason alone I move that we proceed with the campaign."

A hum of conversation broke out as Sethar finished speaking. His words had stirred something in them to dissipate the pessimism of Artaban. Here and there a satrap or nobleman got up to voice his agreement with Sethar, and it was obvious that the mood of the Conference had changed again. Finally, Artaban, seeing that no faction had emerged to support his view, rose to his feet.

"My lord king, and men of Persia, I, too, am proud of our empire, and if it is a question of defending its borders, then we are all in accord. Perhaps God, Ahura Mazda himself, will use the Persians as instruments of his justice to punish the Greeks. Even if the unthinkable did happen and we suffered a defeat, we would not need to be ashamed of our efforts to defend the empire. And if we win, we would bring to the vanquished the benefits of our advanced administration. For these reasons, I now withdraw my objection."

The assembly sighed their relief, and since Artaban had been the only one to oppose the war, the whole Conference gave their formal consent and the king then made the declaration: "Prepare for war!"

All the Persian nobles, princes and satraps hurried back to the provinces and began to make elaborate preparations, each hoping to win the reward which Xerxes had offered. Officials scoured every corner of the land for provisions and equipment in order to be ready on the day appointed for the mustering of the army.

At the palace, Mordecai found himself in constant demand, attending to the thousands of details that Xerxes thought up at every hour of the day and often during the night as well.

Day after day, Mordecai had to draw up new arrangements and record them. With the permission of the Grand Chamberlain, he enlisted the help of the scribes and interpreters who came to Shushan with information from the Satrapies, and eventually he had many assistants under his direction. They mapped out the whole campaign in detail, and checked and rechecked the timetable. For bridging the Hellespont, they had to assess the amount of materials required, and order them to be transported to meet with the workmen at the appointed time.

They tried to provide for every conceivable contingency. Xerxes was staking everything on this campaign. It had to be a success. He could not tolerate failure. Day after day, couriers left for distant parts of the empire, their saddlebags bulging with information and orders.

All was bustle, too, in the city. The leather and metal craftsmen had more work than they could handle, and toiled day and night to complete orders before the departure date. When Esther visited Jacob in his workshop, she found him inundated with work, unable to stop and chat even for a moment. He hammered out clasps and fastenings, fittings, chains and instruments of war. No more time for tracing his name in the sand and practising his letters. No time either for the beaded gold work that was his specialty. Master Barzai promised him his craftsman's crest if he completed all the orders on time, and Jacob was determined to do it at all costs. Esther was lonely in those days, missing her conversations with Mordecai whom she hardly ever saw. She saw little of Huldah and Tabilla, who had nothing on their minds but wedding preparations. Instead she helped Zorpah, whose feet were making it increasingly difficult for her to get around, or else she worked at her loom, weaving daydreams of Sarcon as well as cloth. At other times she went up to Mordecai's little room on the roof where he kept his scrolls and tablets and there she spent hours reading painstakingly not only stories of exploits by brave Persians, but even the details of the administration of the empire. She was interested in everything and retained it all in her memory.

It happened that shortly before the departure of the army, Mordecai was busy in the House of Records, supervising the scrolls that were to accompany the troops. Tablets and scrolls holding the records of all the preparations, lay in piles all around, waiting to be stored in the archives. Suddenly the king himself entered, followed by the usual retinue of advisers. Mordecai bowed low but the king did not waste time on ceremony. He asked for a certain scroll to be brought to him, and fortunately Mordecai was able to produce it from the piles almost instantly.

"Aha!" cried the king to his advisers as he unrolled the page. "I knew I was right! There it is for you all to see. Perhaps another time you will take my word without question!"

He handed them the scrolls to examine, and  turned to Mordecai.

"My memory serves me better than theirs."

Then with the affability that came from having been proved right, he went on to describe the point at issue. Mordecai was surprised that the king condescended to speak to him, and he was even more surprised when the king addressed him personally.

"You're Mordecai, aren't you?" Without waiting for an answer he went on. "You have done excellent work for this campaign. I am going to appoint you as Chief Chamberlain to the Inner Council while we are away. The day to day running of the administration here at Shushan will be in your hands. Of course, you will take your orders directly from members of the

Council"

There was a gasp from some of the bystanders, but Xerxes ignored them.

"Haman!" he called to one of the courtiers who was standing at the door with an expression of disapproval on his face. "See to it that Mordecai has everything he needs for his new position."

As the king turned to leave, Mordecai bowed low and thanked him, saying that he would carry out the king's business with the utmost loyalty and devotion to duty.

"If not," replied Xerxes affably, "you will pay with your head."

Mordecai looked after him as he departed with his entourage, just in time to catch the glance of active hostility that Haman threw back at him as he followed the king out the door. Perhaps Haman will go with the army, thought Mordecai. It would certainly make life easier. But there was little hope of that. It was well known that Haman, while he made a great show of displaying soldierly skills in tournaments staged for entertainment, was very much less enthusiastic when it came to using these skills in the arena of battle. Mordecai shrugged the incident from his memory. After all, the palace was full of feuds, imagined and real, and that was only to be expected in a situation where people were always jostling for power. But he found it difficult to understand why Haman considered him a threat.

Xerxes was as good as his word. Mordecai was established as Chief Chamberlain to the Inner Council, only to find that Haman had skilfully manipulated the king into appointing him as a member of the Inner Council to take the place of another who was leaving with the king. This meant that he was in direct authority over Mordecai, who resolved to avoid any possible confrontation. At the same time the matter of succession had to be settled, as was the custom whenever the king left the country on an extended absence. According to law the king could not march with his army until he named his successor. So Xerxes presented his eldest son, Artaxerxes, to the Council, and as he was a well-favoured young man, already proficient in arms but not of an age to take part in a war, the Council duly named him as successor. They then wished Xerxes a campaign of glory and victory.

On a fine spring morning, the palace gates opened and the first contingent of the king's army moved out. First came the Persian Regiment of Immortals, followed by wagon trains of equipment. Then there was a gap in the column so that the infantry would have no direct contact with the Imperial Guard which consisted of the finest horsemen picked out of all Persia. After another gap there followed a troop of spearmen with spears reversed. When they had passed, the ten sacred horses in magnificent harness came into view, and behind them the king, riding in a gilded chariot drawn by white horses. A covered carriage came next, to be used by the king whenever he wanted privacy or shelter from the weather, and beyond it, another regiment of spearmen, this time with spears upright. Taking up the rear was a squadron of Persian horsemen. All were making their way to a large plain outside the city where the rest of Xerxes' army was now mustered.

The townspeople lined up along the Processional Way and the main thoroughfare of the city, all cheering and shouting encouragements to the men who were off to seek glory for the empire. But an incident occurred which the people of Shushan were to recall many times in the years to come. As the king's chariot drew level with the high marble archway at the end of the Processional Way, a voice rang out from the parapet, and all eyes were drawn to the figure of a woman with arms upraised. The king's chariot hesitated for a moment, for the king had recognized Alcytes, the prophetess, and laid a restraining hand on the charioteer. The crowd fell silent and listened intently to the words of Alcytes :

"A king does not win because of a powerful army,
A soldier does not triumph because of his mighty strength;
The steeds of war do not bring victory,
And men are vain who trust in any of them."

There was a hush over the crowd for a moment, and then the king's chariot was on its way again, Xerxes seemingly unaffected by the message. But many pondered over her words, wondering what they meant, if indeed they meant anything. They had to wait for the return of the army before they realized their true significance.

## CHAPTER 4

Esther sat in Jacob's workshop and watched him as he worked. They were discussing the departure of the king and his army that they had both witnessed a few days earlier.

"What do you think, Jacob," asked Esther. "Will the king win the war against the Greeks?"

Jacob glanced quickly at the open door before answering. "Careful, Esther. You never know who might be listening! And it's treason to suggest even the possibility of defeat. Besides, I'm only a craftsman. How would I know anything of these affairs of state? And even if I did know, what good would it do me?"

She made a face at him. "Come on, Jacob, just because Barzai gave you your craftsman's crest, that doesn't mean you should start behaving like a secretive guildsman! Since when did you stop having opinions about everything?"

He grinned at her as he selected a tool from the shelf. "Of course Xerxes is going to win. Think of all the amulets I made for the soldiers. If these don't bring good luck I don't know what will. Yes, Greece will become part of the empire and I intend to travel there to study the art and make beautiful artifacts. I hear the Greeks are fond of gold and silver ornaments. I will become very rich. So you see it is very important for me that the army is victorious. Everything will

66

work out as it should."

Esther looked wistful. "For you, perhaps, but what about me? It will make no difference to me if Greece becomes part of the empire. I will never see it."

"Oh, you are bound to marry a rich merchant who will carry you off on his travels. If not, I shall feel duty bound to come back and marry you myself. I wouldn't want to, mind you, but I would make the sacrifice for your sake." He pretended to be engrossed in the piece of metal in his hand, but he eyed her sideways to see her reaction.

"Such conceit! I wouldn't marry you if you were the last man on earth!"

Suddenly a loud trumpet blast interrupted their banter.

"The king's herald!" They both jumped up and ran outside, joining the throng of people gathering round the royal messenger in the marketplace.

"Hear ye, hear ye, citizens of Shushan! This proclamation is made by order of the most noble king Xerxes, emperor of Persia, to the citizens of Shushan, and to all the people in every province of the empire.

"Be it known to you that whereas Queen Vashti did refuse to obey the king's command, and was banished from the kingdom, according to the laws of the Medes and the Persians, and whereas the king requires a queen to be his consort, the king and his council have appointed officials in every city and every province, to seek out young virgins of great beauty and wisdom. The same will be brought to the palace, to the House of Maidens, to undergo training and preparation until such time as the king will choose one of them to be his queen in the place of Vashti. You have all heard this decree. Let the king's decree be so performed.

Sealed by the king, most noble Xerxes, the twenty second

day of the fourth month, in the fifth year of his reign."

The herald rolled up his scroll and mounted his horse, paying no attention to the crowd which buzzed with conversation. Esther turned excitedly to Jacob and pulled him aside from those around.

"This is it, Jacob! Don't you see? This is my chance to get to the palace! Some way or other, I will be chosen." She jumped up and down with excitement until Jacob caught her hand and led her back to the workshop.

"Esther, you are beautiful enough to be chosen but is that what you really want? What will Mordecai say? Surely he will not allow you to go. Life in the palace would be, well, strange. Different to anything you have ever known."

But nothing could dampen her enthusiasm. "It would be wonderful, wonderful. It's all I ever dreamed of. Oh, do you think I stand a chance? There will be so many beautiful girls."

"I think you're mad, Esther. What do you know about life in the palace?"

"I know more than you think." She stared at him, aware that he did not share her excitement. "Why are you trying to discourage me? I was happy for you when you got your crest."

He looked at her and shook his head. "You're serious about this, aren't you? You really want to go to the palace?"

"Of course," she answered swiftly. It is the chance I have been waiting for."

He turned away and spoke with his back to her. "What if...?"

"Someone else is chosen?" She finished the sentence for him. "No, that will not happen. I knew, as soon as I heard the proclamation that it was meant for me. I will be the one."

He turned to her, shaking his head slowly. "Well, it is possible, and you are beautiful. Come to think of it, if the king has any sense he will choose you. But then you will be lost to us, Esther. If you go to the palace we will never see you again."

"Nonsense, when I am queen I shall send for you to make all my jewels and ornaments. I will make you very rich!"

He laughed. "You do that, Esther, and we will both be on top of the world!"

Relieved that his mood had lightened again, she picked up her basket. "I'm off now. I have plans to make." She left before he could say more.

*

In the evening Mordecai returned from the palace, but she waited until he finished his meal before she brought up the subject.

"When I was at the market today I heard the king's proclamation."

"What proclamation was that?" he asked absent-mindedly, his thoughts on other matters.

"The one about finding a queen to replace Vashti."

"Yes, I remember. I drew it up some time ago, but the king did not want the announcement made until after he had gone. There's plenty of time for them to search the empire for suitable young women. The king will likely be away for a long time, perhaps years."

"How old do these girls have to be?" she asked.

He gave her a keen glance. "As I recall, they have to be sixteen. And even if you were sixteen, which you are not, I would never allow you to go to the palace. So, if you had any thought of it, put it out of your mind. It is not the place for you, a Jew. They want a Persian girl, not an exile."

Esther was silent. It was not going to be easy to get

69

Mordecai's permission. But that would not stop her. She would find a way.

*

The arrangements for Huldah's wedding went ahead, and Esther threw herself heartily into the preparations. She helped sew dresses and household goods, and spent many hours setting up the little house that Huldah's bridegroom had bought for them. It was a happy, light-hearted time, yet behind it all, Esther wrestled with the problem of how to get chosen for the House of Maidens. When Huldah and her friends teased her about finding a husband, she parried with evasive comments, convinced as she was that her destiny would be very different.

The wedding feast was a joyous occasion. The Shulmans were a popular family, and many friends and relatives gathered to celebrate the marriage. Esther mingled happily with the guests, conscious that she made a pretty picture in a blue linen dress that accentuated her fair skin and dark hair. She was aware of many admiring glances from the young men, but none of them could wipe out the memory of Sarcon, even though it was now more than a year since that memorable encounter. At one point during the festivities, she noticed that Mordecai was deep in conversation with Kenaiah, one of the city merchants. She would not have found this remarkable had not Kenaiah summoned his son, even as she watched, and the three of them became engrossed in what was very obviously a serious discussion. At once she suspected that Mordecai was trying to arrange a marriage for her. It was the custom at weddings, when families got together, for the elders to look over the young men and women and start negotiations over suitable matches. It was not surprising, after all. Her next birthday would be her sixteenth, and most young women were betrothed at sixteen. She bit her lip and pondered how she could get out of it. If she had not had other plans, marriage to Meres might have seemed attractive. He was handsome, with dreamy, dark eyes that somehow did not fit in with the life of a merchant in Shushan. He was more like a desert tribesman. She knew the other young women considered him the best match, a fact which would make it even harder for her to refuse him, if she had any say in the matter. Suddenly the wedding celebration turned sour for her.

Yet, in the months that followed, when Mordecai made no mention of a betrothal, she convinced herself that she had been mistaken.

*

The blow, when it fell, came unexpectedly. On one of Mordecai's visits home, Esther came in to find him discussing the arrangements for her sixteenth birthday feast with Zorpah. While they were talking about the guest list, Mordecai mentioned Kenaiah. Immediately, Esther was on her guard.

"Why are you inviting him? You haven't invited him before."

Instead of answering, Mordecai got up and paced the floor. "Esther," he began, "when you were left in my care I promised that I would always take care of you. Now you will soon be sixteen and I feel the time has come to safeguard your future. If anything happened to me you would be very vulnerable. In any case, I will not live for ever, and I want to see you provided for. A woman needs a man to protect her."

Esther jumped up. "Wait, cousin, don't say any more. I

don't want to hear it. Nothing is going to happen to you. Why not leave things as they are?"

"Esther, I'm not talking about now, but about the future. Nothing is going to change overnight. But you have to get used to the idea that things change. That's the way of life. It is for this reason that I have arranged a betrothal between you and Meres, Kenaiah's son. We would like to have the betrothal ceremony at your birthday feast. He wanted it months ago but I managed to delay it because I did not think you were ready for it. Now, you don't have to marry him right away. You can wait another year if you want. I don't want to rush you."

"No, no, please Cousin, don't ask me to do that!" pleaded Esther. "I can't do it, I just can't." She saw the disappointment in his eyes and felt a pang of remorse, but it was not enough to make her change her mind.

"Come now, Esther, you must be reasonable. Besides, marriage is not so bad! Look at your friend, Huldah, as happy as a little lark."

Esther's face had gone pale. "Why can't you understand? I don't want to marry anyone. I don't want to be a perfect Jewish housewife!"

Moredecai smiled. "You can be any kind of wife you want. I'm sure Meres won't mind. He is fond of you. It was he who approached his father to make the arrangements. Besides, he is the most suitable husband for you among our people. You will be well provided for. Kenaiah has promised to build a house for you and Meres. I insisted on that, knowing how much you like your own ways, and what a tyrant Kenaiah's wife is. You won't even have to live with them."

Still Esther shook her head. "I just can't do it."

"What is this, Esther? You are not making sense. Surely

it is what every young woman expects, to have her future settled. I don't understand. Do you object to the young man, is that it?"

"No, it's not that. I don't want to be betrothed to anyone." She stopped, hoping that Mordecai would let the matter rest, but the look in his eye told her otherwise.

"This is nonsense, Esther." His voice became business-like. "I have gone to great lengths to make a good choice for you. Meres comes from a good family and seems a fine young man. I know that many parents would like him for a son-in-law, and if we put him off now, he will look elsewhere. Surely you just have to get used to the idea of marriage. I thought all girls of your age thought of nothing else."

Esther thought of the many times she had daydreamed about marrying Sarcon whose face she had kept alive in her memory. Would she feel the same if he asked her to marry him? But what about her destiny? No, it was all the same. She must not thwart her destiny by marriage. Of that she was quite sure. Even if it meant disappointing Mordecai, who had always been so good to her.

"Well, let Meres look elsewhere. I hope he finds someone else. I know, cousin, that you are trying to do your best for me, but I will not be betrothed to Meres, or anyone else."

Mordecai's face was a picture of dismay. "Then what is to become of you? I don't want to force you into a marriage that would make you miserable, but I must make some provision for you. My duties at the palace are becoming more onerous every day. I don't know how long I will be able to maintain this house. So we must plan for the future. Esther, if it is not to be Meres, then who else?"

She had to muster all her resources to resist his entreaty. "I appreciate all you have done for me, and what you are doing now, but I do not wish to marry anyone."

"Then what is to become of you? Have you thought of that?"

She remained silent while he waited for her answer. At last in exasperation he grasped her shoulders and forced her to look at him.

"This is ridiculous. How can a girl of your age know her own mind? I am your guardian, and you will do as I say. It is not for you to decide these matters. I thought you would be pleased, but you seem to have changed, Esther. This last year you have not been yourself. Every time I come home I find you dreaming, staring into space. And now you disregard my wishes. I tell you, I am more than a little disappointed." He dropped his hands and turned away.

"Please, cousin, I don't want to disappoint you. But I have this ... feeling, I don't know how to explain it, that my destiny lies elsewhere."

"Elsewhere? What do you mean?" A thought struck him and his tone became icy. "You are surely not thinking of the palace! Put that idea out of your mind. I will never allow my ward to become one of the king's concubines!"

Esther's temper flared. "I have no intention of becoming one of the king's concubines! But I am not going to be married off, just so that you can marry Madame Zinna!" Then ashamed of her outburst, she hid her face in her hands, but not before she had seen the startled look Mordecai gave her.

There was complete silence for a few minutes. Then she felt Mordecai gently removing her hands from her face. Taking her hand in his he led her to the bench and sat down opposite her.

"My child, I am not trying to get rid of you. But you know nothing. I cannot marry. It was a condition of entering the king's service that exiles such as I would devote our whole lives to the king's service. Only in very special circumstances would the king grant his permission. So you see, I am not trying to get rid of you. I'm merely trying to protect you, in case something happens to me."

"But what could happen to you, cousin? You are not an old man, you have many years to live yet."

"Life at the palace is uncertain. There are always those who would make trouble."

"But I don't understand," said Esther, puzzled. "People think very highly of you, and the king commended you and promoted you to a higher position."

"It's not the king. There are some high-born Persians who resent minorities like us having high positions at the court. They know I am a Jew, because I don't try to hide my religion."

"Will it be different when the king comes back?" she asked.

He shrugged. "In the presence of the king no one must be seen to act unjustly. As long as one can appeal to the king there is a chance for justice, but in his absence..."Mordecai paused, and spread his hands. "Anything can happen. That is why I do not want you to go to the palace. It is full of intrigue and jealousy and jostling for power. I would be very much afraid for you, what would become of you."

"You may think this is fanciful, cousin, but I am sure it is my destiny to go to the palace. When I heard the proclamation, I knew beyond a doubt that this was meant for me. All my life I have thought about the palace and imagined myself there. Here is my chance, the only chance I'll ever have. I will be queen. I know it. Will you help me?" Even as she spoke, she found a new confidence, as if stating it aloud gave credence to what until then had been a creature of her imagination. Now she believed it implicitly.

Mordecai listened with growing dismay. "Esther, my dear girl, you don't know what you are asking! How can I help you? It would be a disaster if they connected you in any way with me. How could a Jewish woman ever be queen of Persia? This whole notion is nonsense. Put it out of your mind, I beg of you, and get back to reality. This is a daydream, a mere fantasy in the mind of a young girl."

"No, cousin, I will not put it out of my mind. No matter what you say. The king has to choose someone. There is no reason why I should not be the one. No one needs to know that I am Jewish." A small doubt entered her mind. "Unless, perhaps I am not beautiful enough, as beautiful as the other women at the palace?"

Mordecai shook his head. "It isn't that at all. You are very beautiful now, and you will be even more beautiful as you get older. Besides, there is a sort of shine about you that makes you stand out. If you wore rich clothes there is not one woman in the palace to equal you. But that is not the point."

"Then what is your objection?"

"Your heritage, your people, Esther! Have you forgotten who you are?"

"I will still be the same person. I won't change. Why do I feel that it is the most natural thing in the world for me to go to the palace? When I was there at the celebration, I felt at ease, just as if I were at home."

Mordecai stood up. "I knew it was a mistake to let you go there! That is where all this trouble started. I've had enough of this, Esther. I'm going out. I hope when I come back you will have come to your senses!"

*

When he reached Zinna's house, he almost forgot about Esther in the pleasure of seeing Zinna again. She offered him a glass of fine wine and his vexation soon began to dissipate in the tranquil atmosphere and the elegant surroundings. They had been friends for years, and because they knew each other so well, he couldn't hide the fact that he was upset about something. He found himself telling Zinna about the confrontation with Esther. Zinna listened and said nothing. At last he stopped, and waited for her comments, expecting that she would voice agreement with his attitude.

"Well," he urged her, "what do you think? Surely you cannot approve of her intentions? Here she has the chance to marry a fine young man and she is ready to throw it away on a whim!"

Zinna chose her words carefully. "Have you thought of the possibility that she might be chosen queen? What it would mean to have one of our people in such a position?"

He stared at her, completely taken aback. "Well, no. It did not occur to me for a moment. Besides, I think it very unlikely, considering her background."

"I think Esther is right. It is the chance of a lifetime for anyone brave enough to do it. Look at our history as a people. What about Joseph in the court of Pharaoh? You know how he was able to help his people."

"But that was different, he was a man."

Zinna laughed. "You men think nothing was ever achieved except by men! What about Sarah, or Rachel, or Rebecca? Or Abigail, or Ruth?

Mordecai laughingly lifted his hands in a gesture of surrender. "You are right. Sometimes women have played their part. But you are not suggesting that Esther...?"

"Why not?" she countered. "She is a beautiful girl and if her character matches her beauty she will be a woman to be reckoned with. And you told me she can read and write. That shows she has a quick mind. Surely she has more chance than some unlettered girl from the provinces."

He pondered this for a little. "I am so afraid that the palace would ruin her. You know what it is like. How can I be sure she would be safe? I would never forgive myself if anything happened to her."

"But surely these young women are well looked after. It is not, after all, a life of hardship. And if it is God's will, he will protect her."

"But can we be sure it is God's will?"

"No, we can't. We can only go by circumstances. Here is a beautiful, talented girl who would be an asset at any court. Why should she be restricted to an ordinary life where her talents would be wasted? Are you going to stand in her way?"

"You amaze me, Zinna. You of all people know what court life is like, and yet you want me to give Esther my blessing."

"You could keep an eye out for her, and if she is unhappy, you could bring her back home."

"But that is the problem. If anyone were to associate her with me it would kill any chance she might have. They would not accept a non-Persian. And she is bound to give herself away in some little ways. They would be very suspicious."

"Maybe I can help there. Having been married to a Persian who was a constant visitor at the court, I learned a great deal about their ways, their thoughts, their ideas, their customs and habits. I could teach Esther all I know." She leaned forward, her face lit up with enthusiasm. "Tell her to come and visit me.

We will have a talk."

"It is hard for me to resist you, Zinna. However, I have grave misgivings. I will not give my permission, but she can come and see you and perhaps you will change your mind.

"Perhaps," smiled Zinna.

"But what am I to do about the betrothal? Kenaiah is very eager to settle the matter."

"Tell him you have another proposal to consider. He must give you some more time."

"It seems I have little choice." He rose to go. "A man is supposed to be master in his own house, and here I am being dictated to by two women."

"For a man who has neither wife nor daughter, you are doing very well," laughed Zinna as she escorted him to the door.

"You are a good friend. How many times have I come here with the burdens of the world on my shoulders, and by the time I leave, you have lifted them."

"You know you are always welcome," said Zinna. "Don't forget to send Esther to me."

\*

Esther wasted no time in presenting herself at Zinna's house. She was delighted that she had found an ally, and was eager to get to know the woman whom she had admired for so long. Zinna welcomed her warmly and led her to the enclosed garden where a pair of carved wooden chairs and a table were laid out under the shade of the tall trees.

"Mordecai told me of your desire to go to the palace," said Zinna in her direct way. "Are you absolutely sure this is what you want?"

"I have thought of nothing else for a long time now," replied Esther. "I just did not know what to do. And then when the proclamation was made, I knew it was meant for me."

"You are very fortunate, to know your mind, to be convinced of your destiny while you are yet young." Zinna sounded wistful, as if perhaps thinking of her own youth with a hint of regret. Then she went on briskly, "I may be able to help you. But first, let us have some refreshments."

She clapped her hands and a servant appeared, bearing a tray filled with all kinds of fruit, which he placed on the table. Esther chose some apricots, while Zinna picked out a fig.

"I don't know how much Mordecai has told you about me," began Zinna. "I was married to a Persian merchant, and we lived in different cities of the empire, Babylon, Persepolis, Ecbatana, while he carried on his trade in gold and silver and precious stones. When we lived in Persepolis, I had a friend who was one of the queen's ladies. I often went to the palace and joined them in their amusements. Queen Vashti was very fond of entertainments of all kinds. In this way I became very familiar with the customs of the court and with Persian customs in general. You would be surprised now much value they put on what would seem to us to be very trivial details. Now, I can share with you what I know of their attitudes and habits, because it is very important that you do not appear ignorant of them, if you are to pass yourself off as a Persian."

"But, many of the other girls will be from the provinces. They are not likely to know about court life either."

"Ah, but think what an advantage for you, to know these things when you go there. I well remember how inept I felt when I first moved in Persian society. Knowing these details can make all the difference for you at the palace, and perhaps save you some embarrassing moments, and from unwittingly giving offence."

"You are very kind to take the trouble." said Esther, grateful not only for the advice, but because at last someone was taking her seriously. "I am eager to know all I can about life in the palace."

Zinna smiled, her eyes lighting up with pleasure. "I am doing this for Mordecai's sake. He has been a good friend to me since I came back as a widow to Shushan, accepting me when others would not have anything to do with me. It is largely through his help that I have been able to make a life for myself here."

Esther could no longer keep back her curiosity. "Did you ever visit the queen here at the palace?"

"No. When my husband died I did not feel like becoming involved in court amusements. Then Vashti was deposed..." she broke off. After a moment's silence she went on, " It is not an easy road you are choosing, Esther. There are many risks. But, I know what it's like to feel compelled to follow a certain course. My parents disapproved of my marriage. They did not arranged it, you understand, but for me there was no question. I did what I had to do. Which is why I now live here quietly."

She stood up and held out her hand to Esther. "Come, let us go into the house, and I will show you some of the mementos of my past life. They will remind me of all the things I have to tell you."

\*

Mordecai was very uneasy in his mind about the turn of events. He hoped that when the time for Esther to go to the palace she would change her mind, but so far she seemed more set than ever on her course of action.

Meanwhile, he was preoccupied with his own situation. His work took up most of his time, but what troubled him more than anything was the open hostility he faced from Haman. No matter how hard he worked, and how careful he was over details, it seemed that Haman found some cause for complaint. Anything that went wrong at the palace, with regard to the day-to-day administration, Haman would ultimately trace its source to Mordecai. Many of his complaints were patently without foundation, but Haman was careful to bring them up when there were no witnesses around, so that no one else was aware of the extent to which he interfered. If there was an unusual occasion when Mordecai or his underlings might be held responsible, he made sure everyone heard of it. It was a very difficult situation, and Mordecai's only solution was to keep out of Haman's way as much as possible.

Esther spent part of every day with Zinna, learning Persian ways. Although she would be taught all about palace protocol if she were to be accepted, there were nuances of custom and tradition that Zinna was able to teach her, giving her an understanding of the undercurrents of court life, so that no one would be able to take advantage of her inexperience. She also taught her to weave fine linen cloth of subtle merging colours. They made dresses in the Persian fashion, with cunning seams to show off Esther's figure to best advantage. Together they decided what she should wear when she went to the palace in order to make a good impression. As they worked and planned, Zinna told amusing anecdotes about court life, which helped to remove some of Esther's misgivings. She was very glad of Zinna's company, for her friendship with Huldah had cooled off considerably.

At Esther's birthday celebration, when no one mentioned

a betrothal, a puzzled Huldah took Esther aside.

"Where are Kenaiah and Meres?" she asked. "Are they not coming?"

"There is not going to be a betrothal. Why then should they be here?" countered Esther.

"No betrothal!" Huldah gasped. "But you told me Mordecai had arranged it! What happened?"

"I did not want to marry him, or anyone else." said Esther, in a matter-of-fact voice. "That's all there is to it."

Huldah stared at her friend "What then will become of you?"

It was then that Esther told her that she was hoping to go to the House of Maidens. She knew that Huldah would find it difficult to understand, but she was not quite prepared for the strength of her reaction.

"I can't believe that you would do this! Become like a Persian! What about your heritage? How can you give up being a Jew, change to Persian ways, and live the life of a courtesan? I'm amazed that Mordecai will allow it. You should be ashamed to think of it. Here you are, with the chance to marry a fine young man, and you chose instead to go among pagans! You will never see your friends again. Oh, why are you doing this?"

"Because I feel that this is what I am meant to do. It is my destiny." Esther's voice was subdued but firm. She knew she was fighting a losing battle. Huldah would never understand, not in a lifetime.

"Destiny?" Huldah cried shrilly. "I never heard such nonsense! You are mad. All that reading and writing has spoiled your brain. Mamma always said no good would come of it. And I always stood up for you. But I see now that she was right."

"I am sorry that I disappoint you, Huldah, but I will not change my mind."

"And what if they refuse you at the palace? You will never find a husband here after that."

"They will not refuse me." Esther sounded a good deal more confident than she felt.

"Well, then," said Huldah, "there is no more to be said." She turned and left.

Esther looked after her, sad at losing her friend. Somehow her future did not seem quite as shiny. Yet she knew that in order to follow her destiny she would have to overcome opposition and give up people who were dear to her. It made her appreciate Zinna's help and friendship all the more.

*

As the year drew to a close there was nothing but good news from Xerxes' army. All so far had gone according to plan. The new bridge across the Hellespont enabled the army and the navy to gather at Abydos, where Xerxes held a grand review of all his forces. Hopes continued to ride high into the new year, and when news came of the victory at Thermopylae, and then of the capture of Athens, there was great rejoicing. There were celebrations in the streets of Shushan, and the people praised Xerxes, saying that he was a great conqueror, greater than his father, Darius.

Hard on the heels of this, however, came the news of the battle of Salamis, and the complete rout of the Persian fleet. There were fears for the life of the king, and rumours continued to fly all spring. First one courier would announce that the king was safe, only to be followed by another who said the safety of the king was still in doubt. Finally, by the end of the summer, it was more or less certain that Xerxes was on his way home with the remains of the army.

Spirits were at a low ebb in Shushan. The only one who did not share in the general depression was Esther, who could think only of the test she must soon face. Mordecai had reluctantly agreed to smooth her path by speaking to Hegai, who promised to look out for her and present her to the officials in charge of choosing the young women.

The day before she was to leave for the palace, Esther made her way to the market for the last time, stopping at Jacob's workshop. It was here that the plan had first taken shape, when she had won him round to her point of view.

"So, you are ready to take the palace by storm It will never be the same again!" he teased her.

"Life will never be the same for me. I admit I am a bit scared."

"Come now, you mustn't get cold feet. You know I am depending on you to gain me an entrance to the palace."

She laughed, a trifle sadly. "I'm going to miss you, Jacob. It will be hard, not being able to run down here and talk to you."

He walked over to a shelf and picked up a small object which he placed on the table in front of her. "Look, I've made a ring for you. To make sure that you do not forget your friends."

It was made of gold strips, delicately woven together, and in the centre was a tiny crown studded with minute slivers of rubies, emeralds and sapphires. It was an exquisite example of perfect workmanship. Esther gazed at it in awe.

"It's the most beautiful ring I've ever seen," she whispered.

"Try it on," urged Jacob. "I hope it fits."

She slipped it on her finger. "Perfect." she said, looking up at him. "How did you know the size?"

"I guessed." He smiled at her, happy at her reaction.

"But I could never accept it, much as I would like to. It is far too expensive."

"Of course you must accept it." He seemed quite unperturbed at her refusal. "As to cost, it was made from scraps left over from a very large order from a rich merchant who provided the gold and gems. Barzai was so pleased with his huge profit that he said I could do what I liked with them. And I do have a motive in mind. When you go to the palace wearing that ring, I'm hoping that others will see it and ask who made it. Then you only have to tell them, and I will be swamped with orders. It is merely a sample, to publish my skill abroad. It is my ambition to create beautiful jewels for those who can afford to pay me. Who knows, one day I may be the court jeweller!"

She got up and embraced him. "When you put it like that, then I'll be proud to wear your ring. But what if I'm turned down at the palace? All your efforts will have been wasted."

He shook his head. "I don't believe that, any more than you do. You are going to be queen, Esther. I know it, and so do you. Don't ever doubt it."

"Bless you, Jacob, for your faith in me. I will wear the ring always, to remind me of a faithful friend who truly believes in me."

Jacob said nothing. There was no more bantering and teasing. They both suddenly realized that she would never visit the workshop again. Their eyes met and held for a long moment. Then silently she took her leave, not trusting herself to speak.

In the evening she prepared a special supper for Mordecai,

who had come to spend the night so that he could escort her to the palace in the morning. As they sat down to eat, Mordecai said, "You look just like your mother with your hair pinned up like that."

"Tell me about her, cousin. What was she really like?" She had heard the story many times but never tired of it.

"I did not know her very well, because at the time of Simeon's marriage, I was travelling a lot in the king's service. She was beautiful and charming, and they were very happy together. And when you were born, their happiness increased. It was only a short time after I was appointed permanently to the palace that she took ill and died. Simeon could not adjust to life without her. That's why he decided to go on the expedition to Jerusalem. He was desperately looking for something that would put meaning back into his life. So he left you with me, for three months. But two months later he was killed in a skirmish at the walls of Jerusalem."

"Did you ever wish you had gone with him?"

"No. I did not think it was wise at the time, even if I had been able to get leave from the palace. The reports that came back from those who had gone before were not good. They did not find the Jerusalem of their dreams, and many of them were disillusioned. Instead they found the walls broken down, and the Jews living in poverty. Those who remained had to struggle for existence. Anyway, Judah is still just a province of Persia, so one might as well be here as there. Perhaps some day Jerusalem will be restored to its former glory. It is what we all hope and pray for." He was silent for a moment. "I am afraid your father would not approve of what you are doing, and no doubt he would blame me for allowing you to go. I only hope you are not putting yourself in some danger."

"I can take care of myself, even if I am only a woman. But

a woman has power too, a different kind of power. There are ways she can protect herself. Especially if she is the queen. And I mean to be the queen."

Mordecai scanned her face anxiously. "I hope for your sake you are right. But the palace is a dangerous place. Nothing is certain. Don't ever tell anyone that you are a Jew. Refer to me only as your guardian. And whatever you do, don't get involved in palace intrigues. Above all, remember your heritage, and keep faith in our God"

"Don't worry, cousin. God will take care of me. See how well he has smoothed the way for me already. And don't blame yourself. Whatever happens, it is the life I have chosen."

*

Esther dressed carefully, helped by Zorpah and Zinna. Her gown of fine cream linen had a bodice embroidered with silk flowers and sleeves that fanned in tiny pleats from shoulder to wrist. The gold earrings and the chains around her neck were a gift from Zinna, who when Esther protested, said it was time they were going back to the palace. She wore fine cream leather shoes, with gold filigree clasps, and she covered her head and face with a gauze scarf edged in gold.

"My word, you are just like a princess," said Zorpah, and burst into tears.

Esther put her arms round the old woman. "Don't cry, Zorpah. Remember, you made me a princess, since you brought me up. But you will have news of me through Mordecai, and he will give me news of you, and if you get tired of looking after him I will send for you to come to the palace and be one of my ladies."

At that thought, Zorpah could not help smiling. But she wondered that Esther could be so calm. She showed not a trace of nervousness.

"You look like you belong in the palace," were Mordecai's words when he saw her. He was anxious to get going, and ushered her out, scarcely giving her time for farewells.

As they walked up the Processional Way, Esther could hardly contain her excitement. She would have liked to run and dance, and shout out to passers-by that she was on her way to the palace, but that was out of the question. Instead she paced sedately beside Mordecai, her eyes downcast, her veil over her face. It won't be long now she promised herself, but it seemed an age before they were entering the palace grounds by a side entrance. She recalled the day she had visited the palace and her meeting with Sarcon. If only he were still here, she thought. It would have been comforting to have a friend around her own age.

They crossed a courtyard and then walked through a garden to a building off to one side. There were fine statues and fountains cascading into pools, but Mordecai would not let her linger. He hurried her on to a side door and into a small chamber.

At once she noticed the heavy scent of roses mixed with other spicy fragrances that she could not identify. Looking around she saw that the room was hung with heavy silk tapestries embroidered with vividly-colored stylized trees and flowers. On one wall was a frieze of carved ivory and the floor was of blue and white mosaic tiles.

Mordecai took both her hands in his. "Are you sure you want to go on with this? You can still change your mind."

Esther shook her head. "No, cousin. My mind is made up. This is what I want, what I have dreamed of."

"I will come by the gardens of the House of Maidens every day. Hegai has arranged it. If there is anything you need, or if you are not happy here, you must tell me. I will see that you don't come to any harm." His voice sounded confident, but his eyes betrayed his anxiety.

"Don't worry!" She removed her veil and patted her hair into place. "Do I look all right?"

"You look perfect." He could not help smiling. She was more concerned about her appearance than anything else at this point. He reached out and drew her into his embrace. "I will miss you, Esther. Never forget who you are, but never reveal it."

"Thank you for all you have done for me, cousin. Who knows, some day I might be able to repay you." Despite her light tone her eyes filled with tears.

Mordecai drew away before he should be forced to wipe his own eyes, and quickly walked from the room.

Left alone, Esther felt a moment's sadness. From now on she was on her own, her childhood left behind. Yet her mood soon changed when she looked around her. Two huge urns were filled with flowers, the source of the scents she had noticed on entry. She walked over to the wall to inspect the ivory carvings and saw that one held an inscription. Moving closer to study it, she recognized a quotation from one of Mordecai's scrolls. Slowly she read the words aloud:

Wisdom calls out. Reason makes herself heard.
On the hilltop, near the road, at the crossroads
                    she stands.
At the entrance to the city, beside the gate she calls.
I appeal to you, mankind. I call to everyone on earth.
Learn wisdom.

Suddenly sensing she was not alone, she turned and found herself being watched by a man dressed in the uniform of a court official. He was middle aged, beardless, with greying hair and of a heavy build. He came forward to greet her.

"I am Hegai, chief eunuch, and keeper of the House of Maidens. And you are Esther. Let me look at you."

She stood still while he studied her from every angle, sizing up every detail of her appearance. Then he nodded, seemingly satisfied.

"Mordecai did not exaggerate. You are as beautiful as he said. He also tells me you can read and write a little. Did you know that piece?" he asked, pointing to the inscription, "or did you really read it off just now."

"I had read it before, in one of Mordecai's scrolls."

"Well, perhaps we will be able to use your talents at the palace. But for the time being, do not boast of your accomplishments. It would cause jealousy and make things difficult. It is enough at present to be able to sing or play the lute a little."

She nodded, uncertain how to address him. He was much too imposing for her to treat him as a servant.

"But first you must pass the admission test. Come, follow me and I will take you to the admission officials."

Hegai led the way through maze of corridors and halls until they came to a pavilion that jutted out into the garden. Several men seated at a table looked up as they approached.

"My lords," said Hegai, drawing Esther forward, "I present to you Esther, a virgin of the city of Shushan. I have looked into her credentials and found them to be in order. She is sixteen years of age, and has been carefully brought up by a guardian, a man with whom I am personally acquainted. She is well educated and talented, and her beauty speaks for itself. I recommend her highly and leave the rest to your decision."

He smiled encouragingly at Esther and left her with them

The men stared at her, but she purposely avoided meeting their gaze. She stood very still, resisting the urge to adjust her veil which now hung down behind her back. She held herself tall, as they scrutinized her from top to toe. Then they asked her to walk to the window while they surveyed her carriage and poise. She felt calm and at ease. Surely the outcome must be favourable.

They asked her to approach the table again, and this time they asked her questions about her life, which she answered carefully as she had rehearsed with Zinna. Suddenly one of the men farther down the table, addressed her. "Young woman!"

She turned and found herself looking straight at a tall dark richly clad man and her heart almost stopped. This was the man from the hanging in the square. She could never forget that long thin face, those dark piercing eyes. Involuntarily she started, and he must have noticed her reaction, for he now looked more closely.

"You look familiar. Have I not seen you somewhere before?"

Before she could answer there was a fanfare of trumpets, and all the men jumped up, gathering their robes about them. One of them turned to her and said abruptly, "We will let you know later of our decision. Meantime, we must attend the king."

They all filed out, leaving her alone, with knees still shaking, all kinds of thoughts racing through her head. Did that man really recognize her? Would he make inquiries about her? How could she explain being in the square alone that day? Would all this jeopardize her chances of being accepted? It was a decidedly less calm Esther that awaited the return of Hegai.

## CHAPTER 5

Esther looked down from her vantage point on the terrace to the garden below, where the other girls were practising a dance to the music of the flute. She was altering a dress for a play that the House of Maidens was going to present when the king returned, and as she plied her needle she savoured the unusual experience of being on her own. In the months since she had come to the palace she found that what she missed most was time to be alone with her thoughts. As it was, every waking moment of the day was taken up with some activity or other, for the girls had to follow a strict routine.

Every morning they went to the baths for a series of beauty treatments. First they soaked in goat's milk and then the eunuchs would massage their bodies with oil of myrrh. Their hair was washed with special preparations of herbs and then brushed with scented oils. The ladies of the court taught them little tricks to enhance their beauty, but all had to be done discreetly, to give no hint of artificial aid. Even their food was strictly supervised, and they fed on the choicest meals from the royal kitchens.

In the afternoons, the Mother Adviser, who looked after the welfare of the girls, taught them the arts of entertaining the king, and the fine points of palace dress and etiquette. Later on they learned from her the role of the queen in royal ceremonies, as well as the protocol of the day-to-day life at the

93

court, including receiving ambassadors and presiding over banquets and entertainments. As a break from the classroom, they worked at various crafts according to their talents and inclination. In the evenings, instructors came to give lessons in singing, dancing and playing musical instruments. By the time bedtime came, with all its attendant beauty rituals, the girls were more than anxious to lay down and sleep.

Esther had no time to be homesick. Looking back, she marvelled at how her life had changed since she came to the palace. That first day, when Hegai found her in the pavilion, she had almost convinced herself that he was going to send her home immediately. When he told her that she had been accepted, she could hardly believe it. In her elation she forgot all about the tall man with the dark looks. Hegai took her to the House of Maidens, and handed her into the care of Xaniada, the Mother Adviser, who greeted her kindly and showed her around her new home.

The compound known as the House of Maidens was built in a rectangle surrounding a garden with a tiled pool in the centre. Two long buildings housed the living quarters, while the two shorter buildings at either end held the administration rooms for Hegai and his staff, and the vast bathrooms. An arched walkway ran all round the interior of the rectangle and gave access to the garden. The whole complex itself lay at right angles to the main part of the palace, and was surrounded on three sides by another garden, called the Garden of the Elms, because of the many large elm trees that grew round the perimeter. Pathways threaded through the garden leading to the different buildings in the palace grounds. The young women were forbidden to go beyond the outer gardens, unless for a special reason, and then only under the strictest supervision.

Hegai assigned Esther to the Windflower Pavilion which housed fifteen young women. A flight of wide stone stairs rose from the kitchens on the ground floor to the living quarters above, which consisted of a long chamber, furnished with brightly-patterned carpets and rich embroidered hangings. There were curtained alcoves along one wall, each containing a low wooden pallet piled high with quilts and cushions, and a chest bound in polished brass. During the day, when the curtains were drawn back the room became a sitting area, the beds serving as couches. On one wall was a huge mirror of highly polished bronze.

Xaniada showed Esther her assigned alcove, and pointed out the chest where she could keep her personal belongings. At the far end of the room two young women were unpacking a case of materials and placing them on the shelves. Xaniada introduced them as Kalifa and Marajani, and asked them to look after Esther.

The two girls welcomed Esther with warm smiles. She was struck at once with their natural beauty, and their unself-conscious poise. She began to realize that it would not be easy to stand out among such fine looking women. Her morale was shattered even further a few minutes later as they made their way out to the garden to join the others. On the terrace was a young woman so beautiful that Esther could not help staring at her. Kalifa called to her: "Isandra, here's a new girl. Come and meet Esther."

The other girl made no move. Slowly she looked Esther over from head to toe. "Well," she drawled, "wherever did they find you?" Without waiting for an answer she turned on her heel and disappeared down the stairs.

Esther was taken aback. She felt overawed by Isandra's polished appearance and manner. How could she hope to compete with such a ravishing creature, whose piled-up hair, painted eyes, ornate jewels and rich gown gave her and exotic air? Suddenly she felt let-down, out of place, in her simple linen dress and plain gold jewellery. She looked again at Kalifa and Marajani. They too had a polished look. Her heart sank even further. She must have been dreaming to imagine that she could outshine such beauties.

Kalifa, noticing her crestfallen expression, tucked her arm into Esther's. "Don't take any notice of Isandra. She says things like that to everyone."

"But she is so very beautiful!" protested Esther.

Marajani laughed. "Surface beauty! She scorns anyone who might be a rival. You ought to be flattered that she thought you worth an attack. Anyway, we remember when she first came here from one of the provinces up north somewhere—she was all homespun clothes and an accent you could cut with a knife. She lost no time in getting rid of both. They are very good to us here. We have freedom to chose our own dresses and ornaments so that we can develop our own personalities. They want us all to be different. Thank Ahura Mazda that there is only one Isandra."

Esther noticed that Marajani had given God the Persian name, and was grateful to Zinna for making it known to her. Otherwise she might have asked about it and so betrayed her ignorance of things Persian. She felt that the palace was already full of pitfalls for the unwary, and she reminded herself that she must not be provoked by Isandra's insulting behaviour. Mordecai did warn me, she thought. I had better get used to it.

She forgot the incident in the excitement of meeting the other young women who quickly initiated her into the routine of the House of Maidens. Each pavilion, she learned, was run by a eunuch known as the House Officer, and by the Mother Adviser who was usually one of the queen's ladies now in retirement. The House Officer had the oversight of the compound, making sure that the servants kept the house in order, and provided meals on time. The Mother Adviser looked to the welfare of the young women, making sure they followed their routine, as well as imparting to them, both formally and informally, her vast knowledge of the workings of the palace, and of the idiosyncrasies of the king.

At first Esther enjoyed the company of the young women of her own age. They were a happy lot, always laughing and chatting, and for the most part, they all got on well together. At this stage, when there was as yet no question of competition, since the king was still away at war, they did not see each other so much as rivals as companions in a great adventure. They had come from all parts of the empire, and very few, if any, had enjoyed such luxury before. They revelled in the constant pampering, the ever-present servants to do their bidding. It was the Mother Adviser's firm belief that if the young women were busy and happy, they could not help but impart that happiness to all around them, all the way up to the king. As a strategy it seemed to work, for there was an atmosphere of harmony which the girls were encouraged to cultivate at all times. Isandra, to be sure, never lost an opportunity to put the others down, but she was clever enough to hide her animosity whenever the Mother Adviser or any court official was present.

Every day Mordecai walked in the Garden of the Elms so that Esther could slip out and meet him for a few moments. In the beginning he questioned her anxiously, but as the days went by, and Esther, far from showing signs of stress, bloomed before his eyes, he relaxed his concern somewhat and reduced his visits to two or three times a week.  To Mordecai it was evident that the life at the palace suited her, and he marvelled that she seemed to have put her past life behind her without a qualm.  He had to admit to himself that she did not seem to need his protection, although he still exhorted her to be vigilant at all times.

The one aspect of her new life that Esther found difficult was the lack of privacy.  After a few weeks of constant companionship she longed to be able to get away on her own.  She especially missed not being able to go to Mordecai's library and lose herself in the reading of a scroll.  There were no tablets or scrolls to be found in the Windflower Pavilion.  It was taken for granted that none of the girls could read or write.  Sometimes she entertained the other girls with stories she had read and they wondered how she had learned so many stories of Persian heroes, not to mention Greek and Egyptian ones.  She passed off their questions lightly, saying that she had a very special nurse who had taught her many things.  Which was true as far as it went.  Because she knew many Jewish songs that she had learned from Zorpah, she was always in demand to entertain the company.  She became popular with the others, chiefly because she tried always to maintain a good humour.  It was part of her strategy.  She knew that the Mother Adviser watched each girl all the time to see if she would make a suitable queen, and she sensed that one of the requirements was the ability to add lustre to the throne.  She never lost sight of her goal.  She was lucky that she was enthusiastic by nature, and she threw herself into every activity with a zest that endeared her to all.

So it was, as she sat sewing, that she felt very content that matters had turned out so well.  She was pleased that she had managed not to react to the vicious attacks that Isandra directed at her. Indeed, now she did not even need to say a word, for the others would rush to her defence. But an unforeseen event was soon to shatter her complacency, and put her resolve to the test.

From her vantage point on the terrace, Esther could see the fields that stretched along the river bank, and her eye detected what she thought was a pool of blue water. She focused her attention on it for a few moments until she realized it was a field of irises in full bloom. This gave her an idea and she immediately went in search of the Mother Adviser.

"Mother Xanadia, it is soon to be the spring festival. Would you give us your permission to go down to the fields to gather the lilies to decorate the Fire Temple?

"Well," said the Mother Adviser, "we will consider your request. How many of you want to go?"

"Oh, all of us, of course, " replied Esther, sure that the others would all be eager to go.

"I shall put the matter to Hegai. He will decide," said Mother Xanadia.

Esther thanked her and left. It would not do to appear too assertive.

The next day, with Hegai having given his permission on certain conditions, the young women set out for a day of unaccustomed freedom, and wandered about in the meadows, accompanied only by their maidservants. Guards were posted along the road by the river for their protection. Esther was delighted at the success of her idea. She revelled in the fresh breeze on her face, and sniffed the wild flowers and the river smells that she had known since childhood. It came home upon her how much she had given up. She was virtually a prisoner at the palace. No longer could she come and go as she pleased. Her life was not her own. For the first time she asked herself if it was really worth it.

Thinking these thoughts as she gathered lilies into her basket, she absent-mindedly wandered away from the others. It was when she came to the trees and bushes that lined the river bank that she realized she was alone. She looked round. The others were some distance away, bent to their task, and chattering away to each other. Suddenly she could not resist the temptation. Slipping through the trees she made her way to the bank of the river and seated herself on a rock.

Out in midstream a fisherman was lifting his nets. Watching his little boat, she dreamed of setting out on a voyage to far-off lands. If she had been born a boy, it would have been a natural thing to do.

A noise behind her startled her, and she turned quickly, uttering a gasp. Coming toward her was a light-haired young man. At first she thought she was dreaming. He looked like Sarcon. It was Sarcon! She could not mistake his smile. With an effort she found her voice.

"Sarcon! What are you doing here?"

"Esther! You remembered me! I was afraid you wouldn't. I'm sorry if I startled you. I was following you, hoping I would get a chance to speak to you."

"But how...?" She could not begin to put all her questions into words. She stared at him. His was still the face of her dreams but older, more mature.

"Come, sit down and I will tell you everything. It is a long story. When I went back to Idumea I could not forget you. I begged my father to get me a position at the court here, supposedly so that I could learn the laws of administration. It took a long time, but eventually I was so persistent he had to give in. I came here about half a year ago, and at once I began searching for you in the city. I questioned many people, but

I had no luck until one day I stopped at the goldsmith's workshop. A young man, Jacob I think he said his name was, heard me asking for you. He was suspicious of me at first, but I finally managed to convince him that I meant you no harm. Imagine how surprised I was to discover that you were here in the palace all the time! I was very discreet," he put in quickly, as he saw her face darken. "At no time did I disclose to a soul that I knew you. Sometimes I caught a glimpse of you in the Elm Garden, but there was never a chance to talk to you until today. From my room in the palace, I saw the procession of young women coming down here and I took the chance. I've been watching you from the trees and I could hardly believe my good luck when I saw you leave the others. Oh Esther, you are more beautiful than ever!"

"You should not be here. What if anyone sees us? You must know that I am one of the aspirants." Esther's protestations sounded feeble even to her own ears. She could not deny the surge of happiness that enveloped her when she saw him.

"Oh Esther, never mind about that. My life is nothing without you. It is the thought of you that has kept me going all these months." He took her hand and spoke earnestly. "I want you to be my wife. We can marry and go back to Idumea. My father is satrap and will give me a high position in his staff. Also I inherited a fine estate from my uncle. Even if it is not a palace I will treat you as a princess." He raised her hand to his lips.

Esther gazed at him in amazement. To think that he had gone to such lengths to see her again. She thought of the weeks and months, yes and years, that she had woven fantasies about him coming back to find her. She wanted to throw herself in his arms, to respond to his depth of feeling with matching emotion. Her eyes must have betrayed her, for the next instant his arms were around her, his mouth on hers. She yielded to the sheer excitement of his touch, returning his kisses with a rising passion that she had not known she possessed. For a few blissful moments she merged her desire with his, until reality hit her. This could not be! With a tremendous effort of will she pushed him away.

"Don't, Sarcon!" she pleaded. "I cannot do this. I am committed here. I cannot marry you. Go away and leave me alone." She looked round fearfully, but there was no one in sight.

He stared at her, puzzled. So taken up was he with seeing her again and the success of his mission, that it did not occur to him that she would refuse him. Besides, she had kissed him with real desire.

"I don't believe that is what you want. I took you by surprise. I should have given you more time. There is a special feeling between us, that you cannot deny."

She shook her head. "What is this feeling but the urgings of nature." She had learnt a lot about the the urgings of nature since coming to the palace. "You are the son of a satrap, and you know that you must marry for political reasons. I am sure you did not tell your father about me." She saw by his expression that she had struck home. "You want to bed with me, that's all."

"No, no, Esther!" he protested. "I love you. I remembered everything about you, your hair, your face, the way you laugh. I will never want another woman but you. When my father sees you, he will agree to our marriage, I am sure. I dreamed of you for so long. Did you never think of me?"

Hearing the wistful tone of his voice, she felt herself softening. It would take very little to sway the balance. Desperately she steeled herself, regretting the pain she was causing to them both.

"Of course I thought of you. But these were fantasies. My life is here at the palace. If it were not so, I would gladly accept your offer."

He leaned forward and spoke earnestly. "I can give you everything you have here, except a crown, but is that so important to you? I would love and cherish you always. Even if you do become queen, Xerxes will not love you."

She heaved a sigh. What he said rang true, but she could not afford to listen to him "For years this has been my goal. It is as if I always knew I belonged here. I can't give it up now. I would not be true to myself if I did."

Rejection made him angry and his words hit out at her.

"And what if he chooses another? Would you rather be a king's concubine, favoured for a while and then discarded, than the respected wife of a governor? That is where your ambition is leading you!"

"I won't be just a concubine," she countered vehemently. "I will be queen!"

"How can you be so sure the king will choose you? Xerxes is not an easy man to please."

She sighed again, weary of arguing. "I have this conviction deep within me. I am convinced that it is my destiny to be queen of Persia. I can't explain it It is something that has grown within me. It is as if I am being called of God." She turned to him, her eyes glistening with tears. "Don't make it harder for me, Sarcon," she pleaded. "Go away and forget all about me."

"No, I won't go away. I won't give up hope. Not until I see the crown on your head."

She picked up her basket. Her resolve was strong again.

"There is nothing more I can say. I must get back The

others will be wondering where I am." Again she cast her eyes along the bank to the trees. There was still no one to be seen. They might have been alone in the world. "It is better that we are not seen together. You go ahead and I will follow."

He looked at her sadly, feeling helpless in the face of her determination. "If Xerxes has any wisdom at all, he will choose you as queen. Only, I still hope he doesn't. But promise me, if you ever need help you will send for me. I would serve you any way I can."

She nodded silently, and with one last look he walked off up the bank and disappeared among the trees.

When she reached the open field there was no sign of the others. Her heart sank. Now there would be trouble. How was she going to explain her absence?

She hurried along, reaching the Garden of the Elms without meeting anyone, but she had no illusions about being unobserved. The eyes and ears of the king were always vigilant and there were many windows of the palace that looked out on the meadows. Still, Sarcon was nowhere in sight, and with luck no one would remark on her walking out alone. She slipped into the Windflower pavilion as quietly as possible. Immediately Marajani and Kalifa ran to meet her.

"Where were you, Esther?" cried Kalifa "We looked everywhere for you! Then we thought you must have come back with some of the others, but when we got here, they said they hadn't seen you. We were so worried, we were just about to go for help."

"I'm glad I got here before you started sounding alarms. Did anyone else notice I was missing?" she asked anxiously.

"No, I don't think so." This time it was Kalifa who spoke. "Nobody paid much attention because a pedlar arrived in the courtyard and everyone went to look at his wares. But where were you? What did you do all the time?"

Thank God for the pedlar, thought Esther. Aloud she said, "I just went down by the river bank and sat there for a while. I forgot about the time."

They accepted her explanation without question, much to her relief. She went off cheerfully with the others to add her flowers to those already in the Fire Temple.

Her relief, however, was short-lived. Later, as they were all together taking their evening meal, a servant summoned Esther to Hegai's office. As she rose, they all turned to look at her, the unspoken question in their eyes. All, that is, except Isandra, who turned away to hide a smirk, and Esther knew then who had informed on her.

There was a heavy weight in the pit of her stomach as she followed the servant. Isandra must have seen me and told the guards, she thought. Now they will send me home. They will think I had an assignation with Sarcon, and I won't be able to make them believe otherwise. This is the end of my dream.

Hegai's face was stern, and his voice peremptory as he dismissed the servant. Ordering Esther to follow him, he led her out to the garden, and stopped beside the fountain.

"We are alone here, and no one can hear our conversation. Now I want you to tell me everything. I had a report from one of the guards. It seems someone alerted him to the fact that you went away from the others. You knew my strict orders. Why did you disobey them?"

She was tempted to say nothing about Sarcon, and merely give the explanation she had given to the girls. But then she told herself that she had nothing to hide. She was not sure how much Hegai already knew. It would be all the worse for her if he thought she had deliberately tried to conceal the facts. His eyes never left her face as she told him all that had happened. She omitted nothing, not even her first meeting with Sarcon. Hegai listened without interrupting, his face like a stone mask.

"And when he asked you to marry him, what exactly did you answer?'

"I told him I could never marry him."

"Why did you say that? Did you not think that sometime you might marry him, perhaps if another was chosen queen?"

"No, it is out of the question. My life is here at the palace. I'm sure of that." Or was, she added to herself. Now I am more than a little confused.

"Did you make it perfectly clear to this . . . Sarcon?"

She nodded.

"And how did he react?"

"He accepted it, finally. I told him he must not speak to me again."

"Hmm." Hegai stroked his chin. "I could have him removed, but that would mean disclosing the matter to others. No, we will deal with the matter another way. I must say, Esther, I was shocked and disappointed to learn of your disobedience. And you went against my orders in straying from the others. The other matter, your meeting with Sarcon, I knew nothing about. You did not have to tell me about it, but you did, and that shows that you are honest."

Hegai's voice softened somewhat as he went on. "I took an interest in you for Mordecai's sake, and I have been watching you for some time. I have high hopes for you, but this could damage your reputation, if others chose not to believe your word. Especially if that young woman who reported you wanted to make a big issue out of it. She does not have any love for you, that one. She hinted at things that I know are not true of you. Now, this is what we will do. I will

106

remove you from the Windflower pavilion." At this Esther gave a gasp, but he went on: "You have talents that I can make use of. You can be a help to me checking lists and so on. These are not onerous duties, only requiring to be done at set times. There are rooms next to the administration building where you can live with your own servants. You will be free from the malicious taunts of Isandra and I will be able to keep an eye on you. We will let it be known that I want you under my surveillance, and the others will deem it a punishment for disobedience. But I want to protect you and keep you from other incidents such as today's, because I feel that you are the special one. However," he warned, "I am not the king, and I cannot say whom he will choose, but I will do all in my power to promote your cause."

Esther stammered her grateful thanks. This was the last thing she had expected, that Hegai, the Keeper of the Women, would single her out for special protection. It was a subdued young woman who went back to the Windflower pavilion.

"What did Hegai want to talk to you about?" questioned the Mother Adviser.

"I can't tell you without his permission. You must ask him," replied Esther, knowing well that the Mother Adviser would never dare.

Hegai was as good as his word. The next day she moved into the apartments at the end of the compound, together with seven personal maids to attend her. The others thought that it was her punishment for disobeying the rules, and commiserated with her at being watched all the time. Esther did not enlighten them. She had more freedom than they had, now that she had her own household. She joined the others in all their activities, except on the occasions when Hegai would summon her to his office to help with his records. It was a joy to Esther to hold a scroll or a tablet and read off the words, even if the subject was merely a household inventory.

Also, she was free from the taunts of Isandra, a fact she was thankful for, because she knew that one day she would have been provoked beyond her endurance, and then do or say something she would regret. Such an outburst would ruin her chances of ever becoming queen. The one attribute prized more than any in a woman was self control.

Sometimes she felt depressed when she realized how slender was the thread on which her future hung. External influences over which she had no control, could easily influence the course of events. At these times she would bring into mind the assurance she felt when she had declared her destiny. God had smoothed the path for her thus far. He would bring it to pass. With these thoughts she encouraged herself, and gradually the somber mood would pass and her confidence would be restored.

Esther continued to see Mordecai occasionally in the Garden of the Elms. There was a small secluded bower behind her new apartment where few people ever came, and they could talk in private. Sometimes he had business with Hegai in connection with records and at these times he would arrange a meeting. However, even he had to be careful.

"People are beginning to notice my frequent visits in this direction," he told her. "If it should come to Haman's ears he would use it against me. And I don't want you linked with me. I will find some way to keep in touch, but I daren't come here often."

Esther thought for a moment. "There is a young man called Sarcon, from Idumea, who would help. He is trustworthy, and he would never betray me. Ask him to keep an eye on me. If I ever need to talk to you I will wear a black scarf on my head, and if you need to talk to me, he should wear a black sash. Then we can meet here and talk. That way he has no direct communication with me."

Mordecai looked at her quizzically. "How do you know this young man? How do you know we can trust him?"

"It's a long story, but what I say is true."

He smiled and shook his head. "It hasn't taken you long to adapt to palace ways. Already you have secrets from me."

"It's not that I want to, Mordecai, but you yourself told me we cannot be too careful."

"Well you are right. We'll see how this works. If I hear nothing from you I will assume that all is well."

So it was arranged. Esther walked in the Elm Garden every day. Once or twice she thought she caught a glimpse of Sarcon, but she could not be sure. The daily routine went on, with the House of Maidens preparing constantly for the day when the king would return.

# CHAPTER 6

As the summer wore on, the news coming from the Persian forces gave rise to expectations. Xerxes was now in Abydos, on his way home, but he had left part of the army, including his regiment of "Immortals" with his commander Mardonian, in the hope that he could still overcome the Greeks with his land forces. However, even these hopes were dashed when couriers arrived with the news of the rout of the Persian forces at Plataea. The Greeks were now victorious on land and sea. So it was with little enthusiasm that those at the palace prepared to welcome Xerxes and the army back to Shushan. The council had to exercise great care in arranging the ceremonies, for there could be no great celebrations for an army returning in defeat, but at the same time they must make an effort to retrieve some kind of honour from the campaign.

Every day messengers arrived from Xerxes with orders for the Council, and left again with despatches for the king. Although he had not yet returned, his presence was already being felt at the palace, and the pace of life began to quicken. As the army, now much smaller since the troops from the satrapies had already dispersed, drew nearer to Shushan, anticipation began to build up in the city, and merchants appeared seemingly out of nowhere, to be ready with their wares. Commerce, which had been sluggish in the absence of the king, began to revive again.

The House of Maidens buzzed with excitement. There was a constant flurry of activity as the girls had last-minute fittings for dresses and sandals, and they went to endless rehearsals preparing their entertainments for the king. All they had learned since coming to the palace would soon be put to the test. An undefined tension that evidenced itself in little spats among the girls, and a sharpening attitude on the part of Mother Xaniada and her helpers, began to prevail. Esther found herself thankful when Hegai called her to assist with his lists of inventories. It was a welcome relief from the endless chatter and speculations of the others. She was glad too, that she had her own rooms where she could withdraw with her own ladies when she felt the need of peace and tranquility.

When the day finally arrived on which the king led his troops into Shushan, the whole population of the city turned out to greet him. People, dressed in their best clothes, lined the main street, from the outskirts right up to the palace gates. All workers left their posts, glad of the excuse for a holiday, and prepared to make the most of it. It made no difference to them that the army was returning in defeat. All they wanted was to enjoy the spectacle.

A troop of cavalry with pennants flying led the procession, followed by drummers and trumpeters playing martial music. The regiment of spearmen came next, and after them, the king's guard, splendid in their fine uniforms. There was a short pause and then the king's chariot came into view, at which a huge roar erupted from the crowd. Their king was safe, and they welcomed him enthusiastically, even if he was not carrying trophies of war.

Xerxes, standing in his chariot, acknowledged the cheers of the citizens with a wave of his hand, but his face remained impassive.  Whatever his subjects were thinking, for him it was not the triumphant homecoming that he had envisioned when he set out.  The procession moved on, with more spearmen and cavalry taking up the rear, until they came to a halt in the market square, where a platform had been erected.  The city governor and other dignitaries went forward, bowing, to greet the king, and escort him to the platform where they made speeches of welcome on behalf of everybody and gave thanks for his safe return.

Then it was Xerxes' turn, and when he stepped forward to speak, the cheering of the crowd was deafening, and lasted for several minutes.  A number of times he raised his hand in a motion to stop them, but they would not allow him to speak.  He gave no indication that their warm welcome affected him in any way, and his expression remained stolid.  At last the roar died down and he began his speech.

"Citizens of Shushan and people of the mighty Persian empire, I thank you for the warm welcome you have given to the army and to me today.  And we thank Ahura Mazda, our wise spirit lord, who brought us safely home to Persian soil.  We do not return with the victory we hoped for, but we return, knowing that our enemies will not lightly provoke us again.  We have shown them the might of the Persian empire, and they will remember it for generations.  Such an undertaking as we embarked upon entailed great risks, but only by great risks can we achieve great results.  If the results are not as great as we hoped for, still, much has been achieved  We have made new allies of the nations that border our empire in Asia Minor, and we have shown the world the greatest army it has ever seen.  We inflicted many blows on our enemies, but it was with the loss of many of our fine soldiers.  It was in order not to lose any more of our Persian manhood that we decided to return.

We deeply regret the lives that were lost and we sympathize with their families. My own family did not escape unscathed. However, we can take consolation from the fact that they acquitted themselves bravely, like true heroes. It is an honour to die for one's country."

He paused, looking round the people, and then continued.

"Men of Persia, our enemies will not trouble us again for a long time. We are glad to have accomplished that. We look forward to the fruits of peace. We are glad to be back home."

More cheers greeted his speech, although half of the audience had understood little of what he said. It was enough for them that he made a rousing speech that sounded appropriate, whatever it meant. They continued to cheer him as he mounted his chariot again. The procession moved on to the palace where another welcoming ceremony took place.

A large crowd had gathered in the large courtyard in front of the Adana. Every element of the palace organization was represented, from the household staff to the stable grooms, from kitchen workers to gardeners, from bakers to blacksmiths. Lining the steps to the Adana were the officials, their wives and families, while the royal children with their nurses, together with the women from the harem, filled the portico. Esther along with the other aspirants stood to one side of the balcony. They were all avid for their first sight of the king.

When the king's chariot rolled into view, the courtyard rang with cheers and shouts of acclamation. All watched as he dismounted and slowly mounted the massive stone staircase. Even at a distance he seemed to exude an aura of power, his whole demeanour proclaiming the confidence of the mighty emperor. Esther and the others who were seeing him for the first time gave a gasp of awe as he reached the platform and turned to face the crowd. He was, indeed, a lion of a man, his broad shoulders making him seem large and imposing, even although he was of average height. His dark hair and beard were thick as a mane and precisely curled, while his long straight nose added strength to a face that was softened only by the fullness of his lips. But it was his eyes more than anything, which arrested Esther's attention. They were dark grey and piercing, topped by thick black brows that were almost a straight line, and it seemed to her, as his glance swept over the assembled company, that he took in everything, that he was aware of everything. This was a formidable man, and his queen would have to be a woman of tremendous inner strength and resourcefulness. She wondered if she, or any of the other aspirants, could meet his demands. It was common knowledge that he liked women, and treated them well. Still, it was another thing to be his queen. Look what had happened to Vashti. She felt a tremor of apprehension. He certainly did not look approachable, though that was to be expected in a man dressed for war. Even with all the lessons she had learned, it would not be easy to entertain such a man. For a fleeting moment she thought of Sarcon, and how much easier her life would be if she were to marry him. But the moment passed, and she strengthened her resolve. She was determined to meet the challenge, however formidable it was.

After a formal greeting from the members of the Inner Council, Xerxes addressed the company in much the same manner as he had spoken to the citizens. They cheered his words and chanted his name, but his expression remained sombre. He raised his hand in acknowledgment a few times and presented his officers to receive the applause of the people. Then with a final wave he turned and began to make his way towards the massive doors of the Adana. It was at that point that Alcytes, the prophetess pushed her way to the front of the crowd, and raising her arms she declared in a ringing voice:

"The spear of Persia was thrown into the distance
and did not find its mark. One day it will return
and find its mark in the heart of Persia."

Then she disappeared back into the crowd. There was a stunned silence. Xerxes, who had hesitated long enough to hear her words, tightened his mouth into a thin line, but made no comment, and quickly strode inside. The people, somewhat subdued by Alcytes' prophecy, dispersed slowly, pondering on her words, talking among themselves, and recalling the words she had spoken before the army had set out. These words, ambiguous at the time, now took on new meaning and everyone was now convinced that she had foretold the disastrous campaign. Xerxes should have silenced her, was the general opinion, but even the king would not act against the prophetess. It would be like trying to silence God himself.

The king's homecoming had an immediate effect on the palace. In the days that followed the king's advisers realized that the war had taken its toll on Xerxes. He seemed continually to be in a foul temper, and no one dared to cross him. Not only that but he spent hours alone, brooding, and would not attend the many entertainments put on in his honour.

In the House of Maidens the atmosphere was uncertain too. The time of preparation for the girls was almost over, and soon they would be presented to the king. But the weeks passed and they heard nothing. The uncertainty began to put a strain on the whole house, and the tension was now stretched to breaking point. Madam Xaniada, her patience sorely tried, brought the matter to Hegai, telling him that something had to be done, if she was to keep the peace in her household. Hegai promised to do what he could.

The trouble was that the king showed no interest in the matter, whenever one of his advisers broached the subject. Memucan and Sethar had tried on several occasions, but they could only go so far.

"What is wrong with the king?" Memucan asked. "He was never like this before. He seems to have lost interest in ruling his empire. He spends his time racing his horses instead of attending to matters of state. Something has to be done."

"It's true he is depressed because of the failure of the Greek expedition," said Sethar by way of an answer. "And don't forget, he lost some of his family too."

"Yes," agreed Memucan. "They say he stood on the hill above Salamis and watched the defeat of his fleet. His two nephews were among the dead that day. His sister's only sons. It must weigh heavily on him. But we have had our time of mourning. He should put it behind him now."

"Well, it can't go on much longer," said Sethar, shaking his head.

"What can't go on?" asked Hegai, who had come in search of them, and had overheard Sethar's words.

They both turned to him.

"This behaviour of Xerxes." Memucan was plainly perturbed. "It is time to put things behind him and get on with ruling this empire."

"Can't you find some woman to divert him, Hegai? Surely there is some woman in the harem who will lift his spirits."

"That's what I wanted to speak to you about,' said Hegai. "The king shows no interest in his concubines. There is talk that he is nursing a broken heart because of some woman he met in Asia Minor." Here he looked expectantly at the other

116

two, but they made no response. If they knew anything they did not intend to divulge it to Hegai who was the keeper of too many secrets as it was. Hegai let it pass. "Something has to be done about the aspirants. They are becoming restless, and with the soldiers back home, there are not a few who would be quite happy to take up an offer from an officer. If we are not careful we will lose them, and the king will not have many to chose from."

"But what has this to do with our present problem which is to get the king back into action?" wondered Memucan

"It might rouse him from his lethargy. These beautiful fresh young women are a sight to behold. I don't believe the king, even in his present mood could resist them."

"You do what you can, Hegai. At this stage we are desperate enough to try anything."

At the earliest opportunity, therefore, Hegai himself approached the king and suggested that he should see the girls and make his choice. With the utmost tact he reminded Xerxes that he would need a queen to entertain the visiting dignitaries who would soon be visiting the palace. He even managed to hint delicately that the Inner Council were threatening to make their own choice from among the aristocrat families.

"All right, all right, Hegai. You are right as usual. But I don't want to be troubled now. Certainly you know my likes and dislikes better than anyone in the Inner Council. You pick out a few."

Hegai heard the note of indifference in the king's voice, but he was determined to push him a little further.

"There is to be an entertainment tonight, in the House of Maidens. If it would please your grace to be present you would have the opportunity to assess the girls and make the choice yourself."

"Yes, yes," Already the king was bored by the whole subject. It was obvious he would agree to anything to get rid of Hegai.

"It will be an honour for me to present myself to escort your majesty," said Hegai, knowing he had gone as far as he could go. He bowed and left before the king had managed his wave of dismissal.

The aspirants had been rehearsing their entertainments for the king for many weeks. They had been accustomed to performing ever since they came to the palace both individually and in groups. Some played instruments, some sang, some danced, and they all took part in a pageant celebrating the might of the Persian Empire. When Hegai announced that they were to perform for the king, there was an outburst of nervous energy, and it was all he could do to settle them down enough for the performance, which was to take place in the torchlit courtyard of the House of Maidens. At the appointed time Hegai presented himself at the door of the king's quarters. He listened as the chamberlain relayed his message to the king, and was dismayed to hear the king say, "I don't feel up to it tonight. Tell Hegai I will come some other night."

Hegai thought quickly. He knew if the king did not come tonight he would not likely come at all. When the chamberlain came to relay the king's message, Hegai went forward to meet him inside the door, and said in a loud voice so that the king would hear, "His majesty is not expected to be present publicly. We have made arrangements for him to watch the performance from a curtained alcove on the terrace."

He waited with bated breath for the king's reaction. After a moment's silence, the king himself appeared at the door. There was just the faintest smile on his lips. "I know you of old, Hegai. You are determined to have me there, and I might as well get it over with. All right, let's go."

"I assure your majesty you will not regret it. It will be an evening of great entertainment."

Having seated the king behind a carved trellis that gave him a plain view of the garden beneath, Hegai gave the signal for the performance to begin.

The girls were all dressed in identical dresses of white silk, and as they danced and sang, the flickering torchlight aided by a pale translucent moon surrounded them with ethereal light. Between them the girls created a magical atmosphere, and Hegai, watching in the shadows, thought that the king must surely be affected. At the end of the performance the singers and dancers seated themselves in small groups as had been arranged and waited for the king's verdict.

"You were as good as your word, Hegai," said the king, when Hegai appeared. "An excellent entertainment, especially with such beautiful young women. Now, one of them I especially took note of. The tall one, a very striking beauty with long black hair." He moved over to the trellis and pointed out the one. "That one, Hegai. Send her to my room. I will join her presently."

"At once, sire," said Hegai. He descended the staircase and dismissed the girls, all except the one the king had asked for. Her he escorted to the king's quarters. "Goodnight, Isandra," he said as he left her.

Esther had watched, deeply disappointed, as Isandra left smiling with Hegai. She knew of course that the king would not base his decision about the queen on the strength of watching a performance, but nevertheless, Isandra had been the first one to catch the king's eye. But she had realized before that many factors would enter into the choice. I was naive to be so sure, she thought. I thought I could make it happen just by wanting it so much. I prepared as best I could, I did nothing to spoil my chances, and yet there is something else that I can not control. Is it destiny? Or is it God who decides? There came to mind the stories of David that Mordecai and Zorpah had told her of. He became king against all the odds, even though king Saul tried to kill him. But he was a man. Did God concern himself with women too? She had no answers. She slept fitfully, dreaming all sorts of jumbled dreams of running about the palace.

In the morning she went to the baths as usual, only to find everyone in an uproar. The other girls told her what had happened. It appeared that Isandra had failed to charm the king and after only a short time, had sent her to the house of concubines. Here she had run amok, throwing everything she could lay hands on, cursing everyone at the top of her voice. The custom was that any woman having been to the king's quarters, was sent to the harem, but she wanted to go back to the House of Maidens. It had taken three eunuchs to restrain her, and they sent for Hegai who tried to explain to her that the king might send for her again. But Isandra felt she had been rejected and nothing would calm her. At last Hegai promised to find her a husband of high standing at the court if she would wait in the harem, and with that she had to be content.

Esther could not help feeling a sense of relief. One of her rivals was out of the way. Yet, as she listened to the others speculate on what had happened, she realized again that Xerxes would not be easy to please. There was talk of the king sinking into a deep depression, despite all the efforts of his friends and the Inner Council. She searched her mind for ways to stir his interest, so that she would not suffer the same fate as Isandra.

Memucan was pressing Hegai again. "Isn't there one

aspirant who will interest the king? Surely all the effort and expense we put out on these girls is not wasted."

Hegai looked at him. "There is one who is rather special. But the king did not choose her. What am I to do?"

"The king is not in a fit state to choose wisely. You chose the one you think will make a difference, the one who is most fitted to be queen. Oh, I know," he lifted his hand as Hegai made to protest. "You can't make the ultimate choice, that is up to the king, but you could save us all a lot of trouble. I know Xerxes. Once he gets fixed on a woman, life is easier for everybody. It's just a question of finding the right one. So, find her, or we will all be in trouble."

"I'll do what I can," said Hegai. He remained deep in thought as the others left. He wanted to keep Esther until the king was in a better mood. He had no doubt that she was the most suitable candidate for queen. Certainly there were others who matched her in physical beauty, but she had something extra, a kind of radiance about her, a projection of her personality that was almost physical. She had the innate grace and dignity so necessary for a queen, and an ease of manner that was most pleasing. Besides, he had grown fond of her, and wanted her to be queen. If only he could be sure that the king would choose her. He had hoped to wait for an opportune time, when the king would be in a good mood, and amenable to his suggestions, but to send her to him when he was in such an unpredictable frame of mind might ruin everything. He shook his head. It was a big risk to take.

He sought out Arieste, the king's favourite concubine, to get her opinion on the king's mood. She was not encouraging.

"He seems to have lost interest in women," she reported. "No one has had any success with him since he came back from the war. It is so unlike Xerxes."

Having listened to Arieste, Hegai decided that he had no choice. He would have to take the risk and send Esther to the king. She had much to lose, but the situation was desperate. Something had to be done. He sent his slave to fetch her.

*

Esther knew at once when Hegai's summons came that it was to be her turn to go to the king. She felt her excitement growing. This was to be the culmination of all her hopes and dreams. She hardly listened when Hegai warned her of the consequences of failing. She would not fail like Isandra! How could she, when she knew that destiny had brought her to this moment? However, she took note of what he said about the king's moods. She needed to be armed with as much knowledge as possible.

"For instance," he was saying, "when the king is irritated he has a habit of twisting the ring on his little finger. Watch out for that. Also, don't be put off when he draws his eyebrows together. He looks formidable, but often it is just an act. And whatever you do, don't act as if you are afraid of him. Xerxes fears weakness in himself and despises it in others. One has to judge how far one can go with the king. It is possible to get close to him, but only as he allows it. I am asking you to walk a tightrope." Then Hegai smiled at her. "But you are different to the others, because of your background and learning. Xerxes will appreciate that."

"I hope so," said Esther. "I will do my best to please you and the king."

Hegai laughed. "By Ahura Mazda, not in that order! Now, call your ladies and we will go and choose what you will wear."

They made their way to the wardrobe room in the Windflower pavilion where all the dresses were stored. Here there were seamstresses who sewed continually, creating the fine silk and linen gowns for the girls, and decorating them with gold and silver embroidery and all kinds of precious stones. Shelves were filled with shoes and headdresses of every description, belts, girdles and veils—in short, everything needed to complete an outfit. One whole wall was a mirror of highly polished brass.

The servants brought out an array of dresses and laid them out for Esther to choose. On an impulse she turned to Hegai.

"You know the king's taste and what is most suitable. Please, will you choose for me?"

Hegai raised his eyebrows. He was surprised and pleased that she should leave that decision, a woman's special prerogative, to him. Yet pleased as he was, he appreciated her astuteness in acknowledging his vast experience of the king's taste. It was yet another of these gestures that had singled her out from the beginning. She seemed to have an intuitive knowledge of doing and saying exactly the right thing. What a queen she would make!

He set about looking for a dress that would attract the king's attention, choosing those made up in the style he had in mind. He tested the colours against Esther's complexion, and finally found three from which to make the final choice. As Esther tried them on in turn, he ordered the servants to bring accessories which were carefully matched. When they had settled on one dress, and he was totally satisfied with her appearance, he called the seamstresses to make some adjustments necessary for a perfect fit. Then he sent her to her room to rest and prepare for the evening ahead.

"I will come myself to escort you to the king's chambers,"

he told her. Don't worry. Your ladies will see to it that you are ready at the appointed time."

Impulsively she went to him and took his hand in both of hers. "I want to thank you for all you have done for me," she said.

Hegai smiled, his hand resting lightly on her shoulder.

"Just make sure you please the king. That is all the thanks I want. Now, go and prepare your mind, which is the most important thing. Much depends on you tonight, perhaps even the future of the empire!"

A shadow crossed her face, until she saw the twinkle in his eye, and she understood that he was teasing her. Her ladies exchanged glances. It was remarkable how Hegai relaxed his usual stern attitude when Esther was around. Could she soften the king in the same way?

Esther's first thought when she returned to her room was to get word to Mordecai and let him know what had happened. Taking her walk in the garden at the usual time, she donned a black scarf to give the signal to Sarcon. After a while she saw Mordecai making his way along the pathway. Taking Bilkah, she left her attendants and went to meet him. They were aware of her rare meetings with Mordecai whom they recognized as an important palace official. She had told them that through him she sent news to her family and friends. Most of the aspirants had similar clandestine networks and they had no reason to suspect that Esther's contacts were any different.

Telling Bilkah to keep a lookout, she entered the little arbor and was joined a few moments later by Mordecai.

"You look well, Esther," he greeted her. "I do believe you grow more beautiful every time I see you." When he had embraced her he held her at arm's length and scanned her face. "You have something to tell me?"

"Cousin, I go to the king tonight!" Her voice trembled with excitement.

He looked at her intently. "This is truly what you want? It is still not too late to draw back," he reminded her.

"Of course this is what I want!" she said vehemently. "This is why I came to the palace. I am not afraid. I really feel that I am to be the one."

"If God wills," he murmured. He had to accept that she would not change her mind.

"Yes, if God wills," she repeated. "Pray for me, Mordecai, that the king will like me."

"I have never ceased to pray for you, Esther, that God would keep you safe." He gave a rueful smile. "If I did not believe that he protects you I could not live with myself."

She laid her hand on his arm. "Thank you for all you have done for me. I have always felt safe here because you are here too. You made it possible for me. You will let Zinna know?"

"Of course. All your friends are anxious to know how you are getting on. But you must be very careful, now more than ever. From now on you will be on your own. You will no longer be under Hegai's protection. It will be harder for us to meet. Remember what I told you. Don't reveal to anyone that you are connected to me. They must never know that you are a Jew."

"Don't worry, I won't. Nobody has any idea. What about you? Are you still having trouble with Haman?"

He shrugged. "Nothing changes. I try to keep out of his way, and he is too busy working his way up in the palace. An ambitious man."

"Well, let us not waste time talking about him. Tell me about Zorpah, and Zinna."

"Zorpah misses you. It is hard for her to imagine that the

child she reared from infancy is now living in the palace. Zinna visits her from time to time. At first she was a bit suspicious of her, seeing her as a threat, but now she looks forward to each visit. Poor Zorpah. It's lonely for her without you."

"I miss her too. She was like a mother to me. Sometime I hope I can repay her for all her care. Tell her I think of her, especially when I sing the songs she taught me."

"I'll give her your message. By the way, the Shulmans want to be remembered to you." Mordecai smiled. "They seem to have got over their disapproval."

The rest of the conversation was taken up with talk of their friends in the city. Finally, it was time to go.

"Take care of yourself, Esther." Mordecai's eyes were full of concern. "I don't know when I will be able to see you again, once you have gone to the House of Concubines. God be with you."

"And with you, Mordecai." Tears welled up in her eyes, but she smiled and waved to him as he left. She felt a sadness creeping over her, and doubts crowded in. She could still be living at home in Mordecai's house, free to come and go as she liked, instead of living here a virtual prisoner, watched at all times. Then she shook free of these thoughts. Nothing stays the same. My future is here. I would rather be where I am.

She set her mind to the evening ahead. This was her chance, and she must do everything in her power to make the most of it.

*

She spent the rest of the day in preparation. After soaking in a special herb bath, her body was massaged with fragrant oils so that her skin was soft as rose petals. A servant brushed her hair until it shone. Bilkah came with a tray of food, but she was too excited to eat. Her ladies fussed around her so much that at last she could stand it no longer and she sent them away, saying she wished to sleep.

Alone, she lay down on her bed and thought about her meeting with the king. Nervous tremors assailed her. Would she be able to please the king? Perhaps he would not like her appearance, or her voice. Who knew what whims influenced a mighty emperor. She reminded herself of the confidence and assurance with which she had started out. Surely she had not been mistaken in her sense of destiny. Zinna had told her that she believed God had chosen her to represent her people in the palace, and at the time she had taken Zinna's words lightly, more as a confirmation of her own desires. Now she wondered if it was true. If so, it was an awe-inspiring thought. She could not fail if she was part of God's divine will. With these thought she fortified her resolve until she felt her confidence returning. She called for her ladies and began the elaborate ritual of dressing.

Her dress was of pale saffron-coloured silk, the bodice embroidered with gold thread. The wide sleeves were trimmed with gold filigree embedded with tiny topazes. The same gold filigree and gems decorated the neckline and the hem. The dress was simply cut, and sewn with cunning seams so that it flowed over the curves of her body and fell in folds behind her as she walked. She wore earrings of gold, long pendants in the shape of a lion's head, its mane studded with topazes, and on her arm were bracelets of gold and topaz. On her feet were leather gold-thonged sandals. Her maid dressed her hair carefully, drawing it back with gold pins, and letting it fall over her shoulders in thick curls.

"You are smiling, my lady," said Bilkah. "You must be pleased. I have never seen you look so beautiful."

"Pray God it will be enough to satisfy the king," she murmured. "Yes, I'm smiling, Bilkah, because I can hardly believe that that person in the mirror is me. It is just like a dream, and I am afraid I will wake up and all this will be gone."

"It is no dream, my lady. We are all proud of you. The king cannot help but be pleased with you."

For a moment, Esther's preoccupation with herself slipped, and she turned and hugged Bilkah and her other ladies. "You have all helped me. It is thanks to you I look so beautiful."

When Hegai arrived he ordered her to stand before him so that he could have a last critical inspection. He regarded her for some minutes, taking in every detail of her appearance.

"Yes," he said at last. "But there is something missing. Boy!" he beckoned to a slave who was standing at the door. "Bring the chest here."

He opened a large box and took out a small half circlet of gold worked in the form of a chain. This he placed on top of her head and fixed it with pins in her hair. Then he stepped back to admire the effect.

"You look just like a queen!" exclaimed the ladies and clapped their hands in admiration.

"Perfect," said Hegai, regarding her with a look of satisfaction. "Are you ready?"

"Yes—no, wait. There is something I forgot." She went into her bedroom and from a small box on the table she took the small gold ring that Jacob had made for her. "Wish me luck, Jacob," she whispered, slipping it on her finger.

It was like a marriage procession, that walk along the torch-lit corridors with Hegai at her side and her ladies following behind. The king's suite was on the opposite side of the palace, and as they passed from one building to the next, she recalled the first time she had seen these walls, when she had followed Sarcon with awe-struck wonder. How could she have imagined then what the future held? And Sarcon, what about him? She wished that it was he she was going to meet. A momentary pang struck her, but she brushed it away. She must put personal feelings behind her. From now on she must concentrate on pleasing Xerxes and make sure that he chose her as queen.

The guards at the huge double doors of the king's chambers recognized Hegai, and the doors swung open as they approached. Hegai gave her an encouraging smile which she returned with a sudden confidence. This was her moment of destiny. She could feel it coursing through her veins. They entered a wide high-roofed hall with massive marble pillars. She had scarcely time to glance around before Hegai led her up a short flight of stairs to a room furnished with silk-cushioned sofas and low tables. Hegai motioned the ladies to remain there, while he and Esther turned to the left, through an archway hung with blue tasseled curtains. They were now in a large room which at first Esther thought was empty. Then as her eyes became accustomed to the muted light she noticed, at the far end of the room, near the tall windows, the figure of a man seated on a chair. His face was turned away towards the garden, and if he heard them he gave no sign.

Hegai, motioning Esther to stay where she was, went forward and stopped a few paces from the king. He bowed.

"My lord king, it is I, Hegai, keeper of the House of Maidens, come to present to you the lady Esther. May she find favour with you.'

He turned and beckoned Esther to come forward. As she

advanced she kept her eyes fixed on the king. He did not even look in her direction.

"My lord king," said Hegai again. "The lady Esther."

She did a low obeisance and raised her eyes. The king gave her a slow stare from dull eyes, and then turned to the window again.

There was a moment of silence; then the king spoke.

"All right, Hegai. You may go."

His voice was low and resonant, but Esther was quick to notice the listless tone. This was not what she had anticipated. It was obvious that the king was in a very depressed state of mind.

She threw a glance at Hegai who nodded reassuringly, before bowing again and leaving.

She was alone with the king.

# CHAPTER 7

For a few moments there was silence. She looked round the room. It really was fit for a king. Gorgeous silk hangings lined the walls, carpets of brilliant colours covered the tiled floor, and urns filled with sweet scented blossoms stood in the corners. There were gold chests, one piled with musical instruments, another with carved wooden ornaments of bakir, the favourite indoor game of the Persians. Her eyes continued to survey the room until they rested on the king, and she became aware that he was watching her.

"Come up here," he said, "where I can see you."

She walked towards him, up the two steps to his chair and sank down in a low bow.

"Stand up."

His tone was peremptory. He might have been speaking to a soldier, she thought.

She stood up and looked straight at him. His piercing dark grey eyes fixed on hers, and then he slowly looked her up and down. She remained perfectly composed, as she had often rehearsed with the other women in the Windflower pavilion. When his eyes again rested on hers she read in them an expression that told her quite plainly that he approved. It's this dress, she told herself. I'm glad I let Hegai choose it for me. She held his gaze with confidence. Then suddenly, his expression changed. Abruptly he turned his face away, but not before she saw that the brooding look had returned.

Rejection! Could it be possible? It hung in the air, almost tangible. Was it for this she had prepared for almost two years? She had been so sure that she would succeed where others had failed. She refused to accept it. She hadn't mistaken that gleam in his eye a moment ago. What then? She was confused, wondering what she should do. She looked at him, and followed his gaze through the window. She saw that he was staring at the memorial arch, erected in the courtyard to honour the nobles who had perished in the war Even as she watched, the pennants bearing their colours and badges fluttered in the breeze. In a flash of inspiration, she understood.

"My lord king," she began, a little amazed at how strong her voice sounded. "They would not begrudge you joy and happiness. You do not need to feel guilty."

As soon as the words were out of her mouth she regretted them. No one spoke to Xerxes like that, least of all a young woman of no consequence.

Slowly he turned to look at her.

"Guilty," he repeated flatly. "I, Xerxes, guilty." He considered it for a moment. Then his voice sharpened. "Why would I feel guilty?"

"Because you are alive and they are dead."

He continued to stare at her until she began to feel very uncomfortable. She had no idea what he was thinking.

"I see. But you do not think I should feel guilty?"

"No, sire." She wished she could disappear into the air. Why on earth had she started this? But since she had, she decided to put on a brave front. What was it Hegai had said? If Xerxes frowns don't be intimidated. Well, there was no doubt about the frown. She went on:

"They knew when they went to war that the outcome

might cost them their lives, but they gave them gladly in the service of the empire. If you are to feel guilty, then all of us in the empire must feel guilty also."

At that the corners of his mouth began to twitch, and soon he was chuckling, his shoulders shaking visibly.

Esther felt her face begin to redden. She had made matters worse. Now he was laughing at her. She hid her embarrassment by saying with a smile, "At least I made you laugh, sire."

"You did indeed!" he said, composing himself again. "It is a long time since I felt like laughing. The idea of a beautiful young woman having to feel guilty because men were foolish enough to go to war was just too much for me. Your pardon," he said, sounding not in the least sorry. He smiled, showing his white even teeth. "Well, you have my attention. What else do you do to entertain your king, besides scolding him for his lack of perspective?"

"Would you like me to sing for you, sire?"

He gave a slight movement which she took to mean consent, although she sensed he was a trifle disappointed. Perhaps he had expected something more novel from her, but she did not have the experience to gauge what it could be. She went over to the chest and picked up a lute. Plucking a few strings she found it in perfect tune, and seating herself on a low stool, she began to play and sing. Her voice was soft and low, with a soothing quality that suited the words of the song:

> Cool grey the lake
> In the morning mist, and
> Sighing of leaves in the dawn breeze
> Birds call in the far distance,
> Waves lap in a fish wake;
> The quiet place under the trees.

Deep blue the lake
In the bright sun glistening
Haze of heat on the still water.
Motionless is the bird, listening
To the hum the insects make,
Unaware of the silent watcher.

Dark black the lake
In the cool of evening,
Secret sounds in the tall reeds.
Perfume of flowers in the night air weaving,
Life at rest till the day break
In the peace that stillness breeds.

She was so caught up in the song that she quite forgot she was in the presence of the king. When she finished, she raised her eyes and found him watching her. She returned his gaze, waiting for him to speak.

"You sing pleasantly. Your voice is soothing. Sing something else."

She stroked the strings, and this time she did not choose a Persian song, but one that Zorpah had taught her. It was one written by David, the Hebrew king. He had known deep depression, and the song began with expressions of hopelessness, to be followed by recollections of God's goodness and the times he had known victory with God's help. The despair in the song gave way to hope and it ended with the assertion that he would yet perform great deeds. While she sang, Esther was aware of Xerxes getting up from his chair and pacing to the window. When she finished he remained for a few moments with his back to her. Then he turned.

"Where did you learn that song?"

"My nurse taught it to me. It was a song of her people." She felt quite safe saying that because the servants of the Persian upper classes were often drawn from the different ethnic minorities that had been captured at one time or another.

He nodded, moving over to the couch where he stretched out at full length, and then beckoned to her.

"Come, massage my temples."

She knelt down beside him and stroked his forehead gently.

"That song—I remember hearing a song like that in a camp, somewhere." He sighed. "It was a long time ago. What is your name?"

"Esther, sire."

"Esther. That's an unusual name. You intrigue me. Tell me about yourself."

"I have lived all my life in Shushan. My parents died when I was small and I was brought up by my guardian."

"And are you happy at the palace?" His question had a sardonic ring to it.

"Yes, sire. Who wouldn't be? The court of the king of Persia is the hub of the whole world."

He smiled at her naiveté, and sighed. "Alas, I thought I could make it so but I failed. He rose abruptly and pointed to the wall where a huge ivory relief carving depicted the victories of Darius. "Look at my father!" he exclaimed bitterly. "He was a great conqueror. He carried on the work of my grandsire Cyrus. They extended the borders of our country and made Persia a great empire. I failed to carry on their work. I failed ... " His voice trailed into a whisper. He continued to stand there staring at the wall, a bleak look on his

135

face.

Esther watched him, aware that he had quite forgotten her presence. To him she was nothing, a young virgin of no standing, who knew little of the affairs of men. It was of no consequence that he revealed his weakness in front of her. But he was just a man, vulnerable in his defeat, needing consolation. She forgot the lessons she had learned about not asserting herself in any way. Stepping forward to his side, and looking at the images on the wall, she spoke as she had often heard Mordecai speak.

"They were men of their times, and they had to conquer these nations who were always making war on the land. You yourself conquered Egypt, and quelled the uprising in Babylon. You have not lost any lands that were handed down to you. But you have done more. You have united all these nations into one powerful empire, under one powerful government. Throughout the land people live in peace and are prosperous. You have made just laws and the people repay you with great loyalty. These are not the fruits of failure, my lord king." She stopped, realizing that this time she had gone too far. Who was she to lecture the king on affairs of state?

She turned to face him. He was staring at her with smouldering eyes. She expected him to dismiss her instantly.

Again the short laugh, but there was no amusement in it.

"Well, well! I should appoint you my spokesman. What advice would you offer, then, in my situation?"

She knew he was teasing her, but she answered earnestly.

"My lord king, it is easier to conquer other lands than to govern one's own wisely."

This time he laughed out loud. "By the gods, you are full of surprises! Where did you learn to quote the words of the great philosopher?"

"My guardian taught me to read," she replied.

He raised an eyebrow. "Did he, indeed! " Placing his arm around her shoulder he led her back to the couch. "Isn't that an unusual occupation for a ... well, a young woman in your position?"

"Yes, but I begged him so much that in the end he gave in. I have read many books of history and the writings of the ancients."

"I suppose he must be a rich merchant, to be able to afford all these books. A man like that is bound to have opinions. Tell me, what does he think of King Xerxes?"

"He thinks you are a brilliant administrator," she replied boldly, quoting Mordecai. "He thinks you are just what the empire needs to hold it together."

"This guardian of yours sounds like a discerning man. But, no more politics. Let me lie with my head in your lap, and tell me about your life in Shushan.

Madame Xaniada had mentioned once that Xerxes liked to hear about the lives of his subjects, so she began telling him about growing up in the city. At first she was hesitant, but then she remembered amusing little anecdotes that she had shared with Jacob. However, she was careful to omit any reference that might connect her with the Jewish exiles. When she talked about the colourful characters she knew in the city, the king was vastly amused, and she blessed the curiosity that had led her to find out so much about her fellow citizens. After a time she saw that he had closed his eyes, but when she stopped he ordered her to go on. Eventually, his breathing became deeper. He had fallen asleep. She continued to sit perfectly still so as not to wake him up. She studied his face, much more handsome now that it was in repose and not wearing a frown. She gently touched his dark curls, noting the traces of grey at the temples, and feeling an upsurge of compassion for him. He is only a man, she thought, with so many burdens to bear. So powerful, yet so vulnerable.

She lost track of time. The lamps burned low and she began to feel cramped, but still she did not move. She thought of all the times she had imagined her time with the king, but it had never entered her head that it would be like this. She felt wide awake, riding a crest of excitement, as if she were in command of the situation. They had shared a communication that was more than just superficial. Surely she had made an impression on him. The night wore on, but for her time seemed to stand still. She felt no need of sleep as she watched over him. It was hard to believe that she, Esther, was sitting with the king's head in her lap while he slept soundly.

Eventually, as the sky began to lighten, the king stirred and sat up.

"Have I slept long? Yes, I must have. It's almost dawn. I haven't slept so deeply in weeks, no, months." He rubbed his face and turned to her smiling. "You must have cast a spell on me. I feel very much restored." He stretched lazily, and then rose and walked to the window. He paused, looking out.

"You stirred up many memories in me," he said. With his back to her he began to talk, describing scenes from his campaigns. He spoke, not of great events, but of trivial incidents that seemingly had little significance. He told little anecdotes, going from one to the next as if he didn't want to stop. He paced slowly back and forth, reliving aloud moments of time, and as she listened, mesmerized, he evoked for her the atmosphere of the army camp, the camaraderie, and the superhuman efforts of men trained to follow duty in the midst of drudgery and deprivations.

At last he paused, as if suddenly aware of his surroundings.  He glanced round and found her watching him.  He looked at her for a long time.  Then he came to her, and taking her hand he pulled her to her feet.  He laid his hand gently on her cheek.

"You have the most beautiful eyes," he said. "They shine like stars.  What delights they seem to promise me!"

His long fingers feathered lightly over her wrist and palm, and deep within her a new sensation shivered and was gone. His arms went round her, drawing her close, and his mouth on hers was gentle but decisive, claiming her for himself.  She responded gladly, thankful and relieved that she had managed to dispel his gloom, even for a little while.

He drew away from her and smiled.

"Go and make yourself comfortable," he said, waving his hand in the direction of the royal bedroom.  "I will join you presently."

*

When Esther woke up some hours later, Xerxes had already gone.  The sun was trying to penetrate the thick hangings at the tall windows leading to the terrace.  She stretched lazily, savouring the luxury of lying on the huge bed, surrounded by silk cushions, and draperies of gold and purple. The room was full of the scent of roses.  The night had been so different from what she had expected.  Somehow the long hours, when he had slept with his head on her lap, had bonded her to him in a peculiar fashion, so that when he took her to bed, he was not a stranger, but someone to whom she felt very close.  She forgot her ambition to be queen, forgot that she was on trial.  He had treated her with great tenderness, which had surprised her, for it was not something she had expected in the king. She felt a rush of gratitude towards him. Even if he never sends for me again, she thought, I will always remember last night with great happiness. She sighed with contentment. The last thing she recalled before she went to sleep was him reaching over and covering her with the silken bedcover. Who would have guessed that the warrior king could be so gentle?

She heard a movement in the room, and saw Minna her servant, approaching, carrying a robe of soft wool.

"I heard you stirring, my lady, and I brought your robe. Do you wish to go to the bath-house now?"

"Yes, Minna, thank you." She yawned and stretched and with reluctance left the bed. Her night with the king was over. There was no way of knowing if he would ask for her again. Kings were capricious in that respect. She donned the robe and slipped her feet into leather sandals. After a last glance round the room, she walked through the doorway leading to the terrace, down a wide flight of stone stairs and across the courtyard to the bath-house in the Women's Palace. Behind her trailed Minna, carrying the beautiful silk dress, the gold sandals and the jewellery, all to be stored in Esther's new wardrobe.

*

Xerxes, meanwhile, was in the chamber of the Inner Council, attending to the affairs of state. For nearly two hours he had been listening to his ministers giving reports, bringing everyone up-to-date on each jurisdiction of government. His attention began to wander. Zarusan was droning on, lost in the precise details of his own department. The king who had got the purport of it in the first few sentences, let his mind drift back to the early hours of the morning.

He had awakened feeling refreshed for the first time in many months. Something of his former zest for life had returned. How was it, he asked himself, that a few hours in the company of a young virgin had affected him so profoundly? He smiled to himself. Esther! She didn't have the sophistication of his favourite concubines, and yet she had made him forget his depression in a way that they were unable to do. She was so fresh, so exuberant, so original, and at the same time she had a vulnerability about her that was very appealing. She evoked a tenderness in him that he had not experienced since the days of Vashti. He was touched by her response to him, as if she sensed his every need. There had been an unreal quality about the whole evening, as if she had transported him to a strange country. He was amazed at his own emotions, for it was not like him to idolize women, and yet he felt a kind of reverence for her. She had surprised him. Perhaps that was her attraction, and the fact that she appeared to have a maturity beyond her years. He was eager to see her again, to find out whether she really was as desirable as he remembered.

At this point he became aware that all the faces of the Council were turned towards him, obviously expecting a response of some kind. Resolutely, he put all thoughts of Esther out of his mind.

"An excellent report, Zarusan." He looked round the table. "Does anyone wish to discuss it further?"

The business of the empire continued.

Afterwards when the king had left, one or two of the members commented on the marked improvement in the king's mood, and that he had at last attended a meeting of the Council. They speculated on what had lifted his depression.

"Whatever or whoever it was," said Memucan, "we are all thankful to see the king back to his usual self."

\*

The Women's Palace stood opposite the King's Palace, on the north east corner of the king's courtyard. It was similar in plan to the House of Maidens, although larger and much more lavish in decoration. The upper floor was divided into two-room suites, one for each of the women.

Esther spent the day getting to know her new surroundings. She met some of the other women who were friendly and warm towards her. They were all of them rivals for the king's attention, yet there was no trace of competitiveness in their behaviour. This surprised her, for she had heard stories of ongoing feuds, but unknown to her Hegai had made sure that she had only the most trusted women about her. She also met Madame Lila, an older woman who had once been the favourite of King Darius, and was now in charge of the concubines. Esther was able to have her own ladies with her, and she was especially glad to have Bilkah, Kenida and Marista close at hand.

She was given two large rooms looking on to the courtyard which had a pleasant aspect with shady trees surrounding a blue tiled pool. Glancing across at the king's palace she tried to locate the room where she had spent the night with the king. She wondered whether he would send for her again. She could only wait and see.

A little later a servant to tell her that a eunuch wished to speak with her.

A tall beardless man, dressed in the white robe of the king's household staff, quickly delivered his message.

"The king requests that you dine with him tonight in the king's palace. I am instructed to escort you there at dusk."

142

Hardly waiting for her acquiescence he bowed and left. Naturally it would have been unthinkable for anyone to refuse the king's request. He must be well used to delivering messages that required no reply.

A smile lit up Esther's face. "Minna, come. We must decide what I will wear tonight."

A few hours later she sat in the outer hall of the king's palace waiting for a servant to summon her to his presence. Strangely enough, she felt more nervous. She felt that the king might be disappointed when he saw her again, that the rapport that they had the night before might have dissipated. Rising from the chair she walked slowly across the room to the window. Her dark blue dress embroidered with tiny precious stones, rustled as she walked, the pleated skirt fanning out with every movement. Her hair was piled up on her head and from her ears hung long silver earrings sparkling with jacinths. Having spent hours in preparation for the evening, she knew with a feeling of satisfaction that she was looking her best. I know I can please him, she told herself, in an effort to calm her nerves.

Suddenly she sensed that she was not alone, and she turned to find the king watching her from the doorway. He had come to fetch her himself, his sandals making no sound on the thick carpet. She stared back, seeing the broad shoulders in the purple caftan, his hair still damp from his bath. A tremor fluttered inside her as she sank down in a deep curtsey. When she raised her head he was beside her, reaching out to draw her up and raising her hand to his lips.

"I watched you silhouetted against the night sky, shining like a star. You are well named Esther. A star! My star!"

With his arm round her shoulder he led her through to the king's private dining hall where tables were laid with all kinds of dishes.

"We will eat first, and then you can tell me more of your entertaining stories," he said. He sat her down at one of the small tables while he himself took his seat at another small table facing her. She knew that no one was ever allowed to dine at the same table as the king, but she noticed that the tables had been pushed as close together as possible without breaking the law.

Xerxes now clapped his hands and six servants appeared with more trays of food. She chose her favourite, vine leaves filled with spicy meats, and slivers of roasted fowl meat, together with a sauce made of dates, figs and almonds. There were little bread cakes and bowls of olives, cucumbers and melons, and sweet cakes filled with butter and honey. When the servants had filled the gold goblets with wine, the king signaled for them to leave.

They ate their meal leisurely, Xerxes talking about the hunt and chariot-racing, his two main pastimes. She sensed that he kept talking to put her at her ease, and she was grateful, because it was daunting to dine alone with the king, an honour accorded to very few. Even when his council were invited, they were usually seated in the adjoining room. She blessed Zinna for teaching her the small items of Persian etiquette, without which she might have betrayed her origins, and she soon forgot her shyness, asking questions as her curiosity was aroused. Xerxes was happy enough to discuss his favourite subjects, looking into the eyes of the young woman who had captivated him.

"Have you enjoyed your meal?" he asked at length.

"I have never eaten such a wonderful meal." she replied.

He smiled. "Spoken like a courtesan. But you don't have to flatter or pretend, Esther. I will always accept the truth from you. Don't ever forget that."

She looked at him, wondering. He spoke as if he intended a long relationship. What would he say if she told him she was a Jew? That was one truth she would not risk telling him.

"It was the truth." She smiled at him. "I hardly ate all day. I was very hungry."

He smiled back at her. "If you are finished, there is something I want to show you. Something I think will interest you."

He escorted her from the room, and through a sequence of halls, until they came a large room lined with shelves stacked with piles of scrolls and tablets. This was the palace library where the books and archives were stored. Along the walls were statues, and above them plaques and carvings in bronze and ivory. As they passed each one, Xerxes gave her a short commentary on it.

"This is Sores. He was a valiant commander in battle, in the reign of King Cyrus, my grandsire, he led the Persian army by brilliant strategies out of certain defeat at Mares, and turned it into a triumphant victory."

"And here," he went on, "are the Marpenes. Their craft was handed down from generation to generation, using the same symbols. The statue in the corner is of Lacon, who was responsible for many effective changes in the judicial system that amalgamated the laws of the Medes and the Persians." He broke off, turning to face her.

"Do I weary you with all this?"

"Not so, sire," she protested. "I remember everything you said." With a mischievous gleam in her eye, she repeated all he had told her.

He raised an eyebrow in disbelief. "By the gods, you learn fast."

145

"No," she confessed. "It's just that my guardian told me these stories many times when I was growing up."

"Ah, yes, your guardian. He seems to have had a profound influence on you. Well, from now on, you are going to be under my influence."

He spoke lightly, a smile on his lips, and she told herself not to read too much into it. She looked wistfully around.

"How I'd love to come here again. There are so many interesting things."

The king smiled indulgently.

"You can come here whenever you want. I will arrange it."

"Oh, thank you, my lord king. It will mean so much to me."

"I do believe you mean it," he said. "You know, Esther, you're a strange young woman. You are so different. Just what is your secret?"

"My secret?" she echoed, uneasily.

Xerxes drew her close. "Come now, all women have a secret, some magic spell that they weave. What's yours, Esther?"

She relaxed. He was, after all, just flirting with her. She returned his smile. "If I told you, it wouldn't be a secret, would it? And then it would lose its magic."

"Then keep your secret, Esther," he chuckled. "Whatever it is, it's good for me. Now come," he added, curving his arm round her waist. "There are sweetmeats and wine awaiting us in my chamber."

As they left the library she could not help wondering what his reaction would be if he ever found out that she was not Persian. It was no small thing to deceive the king.

# CHAPTER 8

T here followed for Esther a time that she was to remember as the most carefree of her life. She had much more freedom than when she was in the House of Maidens. With certain limitations she could wander about the palace and the gardens more or less as she pleased, as long as she had her ladies with her. Occasionally the king took her with him to watch the chariot-racing, and sometimes he attended the informal evening entertainments provided by Esther and her ladies.

Palace gossip had it that Xerxes was infatuated with her, and no longer spent his time drinking with his courtiers. Esther paid no attention to the gossip, taking nothing for granted. In the forefront of her mind always was the thought of the queen's crown. She would not let anything spoil her chances, especially now that the king was showing a marked interest in her. He never singled her out for special attention at public events, but he made it clear that she must always be at his disposal whenever he sent for her. However, there was so much secrecy in the life of the court that she had no way of knowing whether she was the only one enjoying his favours. After all, he had the other aspirants to choose from.

Meanwhile Mordecai followed closely all that was happening to Esther. A few days after her first visit to the king, he arranged, by way of Sarcon and Bilkah, to meet her in the rose arbor behind the Women's Palace. With Bilkah posted as a look-out, they were able to speak privately.

"Esther!" he greeted her, embracing her warmly. "I don't need to ask how you are. You look better than ever."

"Cousin Mordecai, it is so good to see you. Yes, I am very well. I suppose you know that I am often with the king?"

"I heard. A concubine. I wanted more for you than this."

A shadow crossed her face. " I still hope to be chosen queen. He has not yet made his choice, but he likes me, I know, and treats me very kindly. He is only a man, after all, just like other men."

"No, he is not like other men. He is not a king for nothing. He can be very ruthless when he pleases."

"Don't worry, I take care to please him all I can. Now, what about you?"

He sighed. "My responsibilities seem to be increasing and my day becomes busier than ever. But it means I can move around the palace more as my work takes me to different departments. It makes it possible to see you, although not too often. No one must link my name with yours."

When she told him that the king had given her permission to use the library he said, "That's good. Sarcon is often there to search the archives. He will be our go-between if you need to send a message. But be careful. The eyes and ears of the king are everywhere."

"You can be sure I won't do anything to harm us or Sarcon."

"Well, now that I am assured that you are fine, I must go." He looked round but there was no one to be seen except Esther's ladies at some distance. "God be with you, Esther." He embraced her briefly and left.

It was shortly after this encounter with Mordecai that Esther came face to face with Sarcon in the library. The telltale colour flew to her face. They had not spoken since that fateful day on the riverbank. Now the memory of that meeting hovered between them. Her heart pounded, but always there was the fear of eyes watching them from the carved wooden screens that surrounded the room, and with a mighty effort she struggled to appear unconcerned.

"Sarcon," she greeted him politely, her voice as neutral as she could make it. Why did he have this effect on her, she wondered. After all, she was now one of Xerxes' favourites, with more to think about than a girlish fancy.

"My lady." He bowed and waited for her to speak.

She looked round quickly. There was no one in the room except Bilkah, who always accompanied her, but still she could not be sure that she was not observed.

"I am looking for the writings on Cambyses' campaign against the Egyptians. Can you tell me where it can be found?" Her tone was one she would use to address any court official.

"Yes, my lady. Come this way." He led her to an alcove among the shelves, and after searching among the scrolls he picked one out and handed it to her.

She thanked him and was about to turn away when he said in a low voice: "They say you please the king well. That I can well imagine. What about you? Does the king please you? If you want to change your mind now I can still get you away from here, without anyone knowing."

She shook her head. She looked round again but they were well hidden from prying eyes in this corner.

"The king treats me kindly. I have no wish to change my life." His eyes held hers as she laid her hand on his arm. "Thank you for your concern, but there is no need for it."

He looked crestfallen, as if he had really hoped she would change her mind.

"I will always be concerned for you, Esther. Remember you can trust me."

She smiled and nodded. Although their conversation had lasted only a few moments, to prolong it any longer was risky. Taking the scroll she left the alcove and made her way across the main area of the library to where she had left Bilkah.

"I got it, Bilkah, the scroll . . . " her voice trailed off as she noticed the man who had just entered. The tall dark man from the market square. She had not seen him since her first day at the palace. He had seemed to recognize her then. Would he recognize her now? Her hand trembled.

"Is something the matter, my lady?" whispered Bilkah, her eyes following Esther's glance.

"No, nothing." Gathering all her strength she struggled to act normally. Out of the corner of her eye she was aware of him staring at her. "Come, Bilkah, let's go."

Assuming an air of indifference she led Bilkah towards the door, deliberately ignoring the man who was now leaning against a pillar watching them. With a feeling of relief, she gained her own room.

"That man in the library, Bilkah. Do you know who he is?"

"That's Lord Haman, my lady. He's very handsome, isn't he? They say he is a great man for the ladies."

Haman. Mordecai's enemy. No wonder she had such a feeling about him. And if he ever connected her with Mordecai he could ruin them both. What if he had seen her talking to Sarcon? The thought brought her out in a sweat. Any doubt cast on her integrity would ruin her chances of ever becoming queen. She made up her mind to be extra careful, and to keep out of the way of Haman.

That night the king sent for her. They dined together and then she entertained him, playing her lute and singing. He seemed quite content in her company, much happier than the first night she had seen him, a ready smile on his lips. When he took her to bed, though, he suddenly became serious.

"Esther, you know the king has duties to perform that are not always of his choosing."

She wondered what was coming next. Did it have anything to do with her conversation with Sarcon?

"This business of the aspirants," he went on. "I cannot delay much longer. So, if I do not send for you so often, for a while, you will understand?"

She let out her breath and gave him a brilliant smile. It had nothing to do with Sarcon. At the same time she felt a stab of disappointment. He had not yet made his choice.

"It is as my lord the king pleases."

"No," he said with some exasperation. "It is not as the king pleases. That's what I'm trying to tell you. You look relieved. Can it be that you find me wearisome, and are glad to be free of your duty?"

Once again she realized that Xerxes missed nothing. He could read people's faces like a book.

"Not so, sire," she protested. It's just that I am happy you told me, that you should give me a reason."

He appeared taken aback. "Yes, I'm surprised at myself. I don't usually feel it necessary to explain my actions. But it's important that you understand."

Understand what, she wondered. She was more confused than ever, but she dared not ask him what she meant. She might not like the answer.

As if he saw her doubt, he put his arms around her, drawing her close. He spoke over her shoulder.

"You have a strange effect on me, Esther. You please me. You please me very much. And it is important that you should find me pleasing too." He drew back and looked at her, one eyebrow cocked. "You do find me pleasing?"

"Of course, my lord king."

"Of course my lord king," he echoed, and frowned at her.

There was a moment's silence. Her voice when she spoke, was hardly more than a whisper. "What more can I say?"

His eyes gleamed. "You know my name."

"Xerxes, I find you most pleasing." She was staggered at her own boldness. If she had misread him it was the end of everything.

He laughed heartily as if at some private joke, and then bent to kiss her. She closed her eyes with relief.

Esther was called to the king's suite three or four times in the next month. There was some talk in the harem that the king was seeing the other aspirants, but none, it seemed, for a second time. She began to feel a little more confident. Sometimes when there were foreign ambassadors at court the ladies were present to provide entertainment. Esther and her attendants often sang and played their lutes in the great hall. On these occasions she was sometimes aware of the king's eyes on her, but he made no attempt to speak to her. It was only when she was alone with him that he dispensed with formality. He often talked to her about events in the empire, and because of her background knowledge, she could listen with understanding and even discuss some issues.

One night he told her that the court was to move to Persepolis for the summer months.

"I shall miss you, Esther," he said. "With the spirit of Ahura Mazda leading us, when we return we will settle the matter of the queenship."

Was that a hint that it would concern her, she wondered. On an impulse, she removed the ring Jacob had made for her and put it on the king's little finger. "Let that remind you of me until you return."

"Do I need anything to remind me of you, Esther?" he asked with a smile. "I do not think you are easy to forget." He examined the ring closely. "An intricate design, and very well made too. Where did you get such an unusual ring?" he asked.

"There is a young goldsmith in the city. He is a real artist. His name is Jacob Asrak and he works with Barzai. See," she pointed, "here are his initials worked into the design."

"Interesting," remarked the king. "We will have to get him to do some work for the palace. I like to promote craftsmen. The empire needs them."

There the matter rested, but Esther was satisfied that she had done something to help Jacob.

After the king left with his entourage, life at the palace settled into a quiet routine. From time to time, Bilkah would come and tell her that Mordecai waited in the garden and she would go and talk to him. With Haman out of the way with the king in Persepolis, he was much more relaxed. Esther asked about her friends in the city, Zorpah and Zinna, Huldah and Tabitha, and of course, Jacob. It meant a lot to her that she still had a link with her previous life, because it reminded her that she was here in the palace for a purpose. She must never lose sight of that.

News came sometimes through messages sent from Persepolis. Couriers arrived several times a week and it was not long before little snippets of information filtered through from the servants who always seemed to know what was going on before anyone else. The couriers would exchange information for the choicest food as kitchen staff attended to their needs.

According to reliable sources, Xerxes was intent on completing the huge palace begun by Darius many years before. While about three-quarters of it was now in use, there were still buildings to be added to the complex, and Xerxes himself liked to oversee the work. Esther heard rumours too, from the women, that Xerxes was amusing himself with a certain lady who was a favourite of long standing and famous for her charm and wit. She surmised that the rumours were true. She had no illusions about the king, and she expected that he would have women in attendance, but always before her was the image of the queen's crown. A concubine of many years was not a likely rival in that context.

She had been so certain all along that it was her destiny to be the queen, but now, when Xerxes was away so long, and had sent her no message, doubts began to surface in her mind. She concentrated on filling her time with activity, sharing in the work with the other women, playing her lute, and reading in the library. Sometimes she met Sarcon, and they exchanged a few words when it was safe to do so, each being careful not to endanger the other. Their eyes communicated unspoken thoughts, and love flowed between them in momentary flashes, but only if they were sure there were no witnesses. Once their hands touched as he handed her a scroll. She started back, eyes wide, as if struck by lightning, and turned away before anyone could notice, amazed that he still had this effect on her, even though she was bedazzled by the king. On occasion he would go out of his way to do little things for her, unobtrusively, but she noticed and she would silently convey her thanks. She found his constant concern comforting in the midst of the uncertainty of her situation.

At last the summer was over, and preparations began at the palace for the return of the court. Esther could hardly contain her excitement. She remembered the king's words to her before he left. He was going to choose a queen. Who would it be?

*

The cavalcade rested at midday, at one of the official royal outposts on a hilltop overlooking the plain of Keresh. They had ridden hard since they left Persepolis some days before, hoping to cover as much distance as possible while the weather was good, and since it showed no sign of breaking, they were able to ease up, knowing that they would reach Shushan the next day. After dismounting and partaking of their midday meal, all the company lazed in the shade of tall trees. Xerxes, wishing to stretch his legs after a long spell in the saddle, walked over to the next ridge, followed only by two bodyguards. He was happy with all he had accomplished in Persepolis. He had received delegations all summer, presided at top councils of governors and satraps, and performed the usual rituals and traditions of the empire. Petitions had been received, and demands expedited, policies reviewed and revised. As well, he had been able to supervise the additions to the palace which now served as a testimony to the splendour of the Achaemenid empire. Begun by his father, Darius, and now completed by his son, Xerxes, the palace was also a symbol of his dedication to carry on the work of his predecessors. This was one task that he had been able to bring to a satisfactory conclusion.

He was glad to be going back to Shushan. It had become associated in his mind with Esther. How he missed her! He wouldn't have believed it possible. There were women enough to satisfy him in Persepolis, but compared with Esther's freshness and innocence, their sophistication seemed jaded. She was the one who made him forget for a while the burdens of being king, yet she never overstepped the boundaries of propriety. She treated him like an ordinary man, without losing the respect and deference that were due to him. Once he thought of writing to her, but writing did not come all that easily to him, and he was too cautious anyway. A letter could easily fall into the wrong hands, and he wanted to safeguard her from any danger. She could so easily be used by an unscrupulous faction. He amazed himself with his concern for her. He had vowed after Vashti that he would let no other woman into his heart. He had always regretted the pain he had caused his former queen by sending her away, all the more because he had suffered so much too. He must protect Esther from a similar fate, for she had become indispensable to him. The long absence over the summer merely confirmed what he already knew. He must have her as queen. Now, longing for the moment when he would see her again, he retraced his steps and signalled for the cavalcade to move on. The sooner he reached Shushan, the better.

\*

Esther and her ladies watched from the high terrace as the king's bodyguard trotted into the courtyard. Early in the morning the messengers had confirmed that the king's retinue would return that day, and now with the late afternoon sun streaming over the battlements, they watched for the arrival of Xerxes himself. They had not long to wait. The white charger bearing the king clattered into the courtyard, and drew to a halt in front of the huge pillars guarding the palace entrance. The king dismounted. Handing the reins to the waiting groom, he strode quickly towards the stone steps. Suddenly he stopped, and turning, looked up to the terrace where Esther and her ladies were standing. For a moment he paused, and then, raising his hand in a greeting, he hurried inside.

Esther's ladies could hardly contain their excitement. "Did you see that, my lady? The king waved to you!"

Esther maintained a cool expression. "He waved to us all. You know how he always acknowledges the presence of ladies."

But she, too, felt excited. Could it be that the king really singled her out? It wouldn't be wise to start imagining things. Where Xerxes was concerned she could take nothing for granted.

"Come, my lady," said Bilkah. You must get ready in case the king sends for you."

"There's no hurry, Bilkah. The king will want to bathe off the dust of travel before he sees anyone. Besides, he may not send for me tonight."

"I think he is in a hurry to see you. There's no harm in being prepared."

Esther allowed herself to be persuaded. She was hoping that the king would send for her. It would indicate how important she was to him, if he wasted no time in seeing her after a long absence. She decided to wear one of the fine new dresses that had been made for her over the summer. It was a gossamer silk, woven in patterns of blue and green, plainly cut but with plenty of material, so that it swirled around her as she walked. Her earrings were of silver, studded with jacinths and emeralds, and on her wrists were matching bracelets. She wanted to make a special impression, to present a regal appearance, but in a subtle way. She sat and mused while Minna dressed her hair. A hint of kohl round her eyes, a dusting of powdered roses on her cheeks, and a slight tint of vermilion on her lips, all served to enhance her beauty, so that in the light of the myriad lamps she looked irresistible. The air about her, when she moved, was filled with the scent of roses and sweet spices.

She was hardly ready when a servant of the king's personal staff brought the summons. The king required her to attend him immediately.

"There now, my lady," said Bilkah in triumph. "What did I tell you? Isn't it good that you took my advice?"

"But then, you always give me good advice, Bilkah," laughed Esther. She could afford to be magnanimous. Her spirits soared as on wings and her feet hardly touched the ground as she made her way to the king's palace, escorted by the servant.

He was waiting for her as she came through the door of his private hall.

"Greetings, my lady Esther," he said formally, as she sank in a low obeisance.

She murmured a greeting in reply, but he was already dismissing the attendants, and as soon as they were alone, his face broke into a warm smile, and he pulled her close, folding her in his arms.

"By the gods, Esther, I've missed you! Let me look at you. More beautiful than ever." He studied her with satisfaction. "Did you miss me at all?"

"Every moment, my lord king."

"Xerxes."

"I missed you every moment, Xerxes."

He laughed delightedly, hugging her to him again.

"Now we must make up for lost time. Over dinner I will tell you all that I've accomplished in Persepolis. All my plans are being carried out and I left everything in order. Now I am free to devote myself to all that needs to be done here. I cannot tell you how happy I am to see you again. Oh, and here is your ring. It served its purpose, but now that I have you I don't need it any more."

She had never seen him so exuberant. He was like a man twenty years younger. A complete change from the man she had first met. She set out to match his mood, and the evening was a great success.

At one point he held her face in his hands and gazed at her intently.

"You are wise beyond your years, Esther. How old are you, anyway?"

"I will be eighteen on the fifteenth day of this month," she replied.

"Indeed! So young. We must celebrate your birthday in a special way. A coming-of-age banquet. Yes, I will give a great banquet for you. In the great hall. We will invite the whole court. You must invite anyone you want. Your guardian, perhaps? I would like to meet him."

"I will ask him," said Esther, "but I do not know if he will be able to attend." It was no more than the truth. Her mind, though, was more on the implication of what Xerxes had said. He would not put on a banquet for her unless he intended to make her queen. Her heart sang. The long absence, far from spoiling their relationship, had actually enhanced it. There was no doubt that he esteemed her highly.

Xerxes was as good as his words. The whole palace began to ring with preparations for the feast. Esther and Bilkah had long discussions about what she would wear and had still not come to a decision when a messenger arrived with rolls of blue and white material, sent by order of the king himself. The significance of this was not lost on Esther—blue and white were the royal colours. She called for her seamstresses and they started to work immediately. She wished she could ask her friends, Jacob, and Huldah and Tabitha, but it would draw attention to the fact that her friends were Jewish. She never forgot Mordecai's warning. She could risk nothing, because of Haman. He was sure to be invited to the banquet.

At last the day of the feast arrived. The huge banqueting hall was a myriad of lights and colourful hangings. Musicians and dancing girls entertained the crowd. Tables piled high with food of every description lined the walls, and servants circulated filling the goblets of the guests from their flagons of wine.

Esther had prepared with the utmost care. As she entered the hall in the company of her ladies, she held herself proudly. This was her banquet. Xerxes had organized it specially for her. Although he had not mentioned the queenship, she had it in her mind that he meant to announce it tonight. Now the members of the Inner Council came forward to greet her, just as if she was queen, with obvious goodwill towards her. She was unaware of the secret meeting of the Inner Council that had taken place earlier in the day.

Xerxes had called the Council to meet in the small embassy room at noon. As soon as they were all seated, he reminded them of the decision taken before he went away to war, to find a replacement for Queen Vashti. He described the beautiful young maidens that they had found from all over the empire, and he commended them for the diligence with which they had carried out the mandate. Then he went on:

"The time has come to choose a queen. Of all the aspirants, my choice has fallen on Esther. In my estimation, she has all the attributes of a queen. She is beautiful, charming, and kind, and she has the dignity and poise to adorn the throne. In addition, she is discreet, and wise beyond her years, and lastly, she pleases me. She is the best suited to be queen in Vashti's place. Now, I would like to hear your views." This he did as a matter of protocol. He was going to have Esther as his queen no matter what they said, but he allowed them as usual to have their say.

The announcement came as no surprise to his listeners. They had known how matters stood between Esther and the king, and they had made it their business to find out everything about her, and even to have her watched. In all the months of the king's absence, there was never a whisper of indiscretion on her part. No one spoke ill of her, and her behaviour was exemplary. Some of them did not hold with the idea that she could read and write, and spent so much time perusing scrolls in the library, activities which according to their way of thinking should be the sole domain of men, but since Xerxes had given her permission, they could not very well object. However, Esther had charmed them all, treating them always with the right amount of deference due to them as the king's Inner Council, so there was no real reason to go against the king's choice. As usual, Memucan was the first to speak.

"It was the decision of the Council to search for a new queen, and the king has wisely followed the advice of his Counsellors. It was always understood that the final choice should be left to your royal majesty. If the king is satisfied that Esther is the most suitable, then I think we should concur with his choice."

Carshena agreed, saying that the king needed a consort to help him on royal occasions and the sooner there was a queen the better for the empire. Enough time had been given, and he believed that the king's choice was a good one. Privately, he thought that already the king had spent too much time and money on something that was of no great significance to the empire. The queen was only a figurehead, after all. Any woman would do as long as she was beautiful, obeyed the rules and followed the traditions.

Abagtha also gave his consent, saying that the king's choice was above question. Esther was known throughout the palace as a woman of dignity and integrity, as well as being a great beauty as befitted the queen of Persia. It was well known that she was learned in the writings of the ancients, which was an advantage when dealing with foreign ambassadors. She could be relied on to uphold the traditions of her Persian ancestors. She would make a good queen. There was nothing in her conduct since coming to the palace that would suggest otherwise.

Artaban, the king's uncle, rose to his feet. "There is something that must not be overlooked," he began.

Xerxes' head lifted sharply and there was a faint murmur among the members of the Council. Surely Artaban was not going to raise an objection at this stage, just when everything was settled?

"My lord king, we in the Council know how much you suffered over the losses of the Greek campaign, and how you were temporarily unable to carry on with your noble work as king. We all know too, how near you were to despair. Who was it that lifted you out of your depression? Was it not Esther who turned the king's sadness to joy?" He looked round at the others. They all nodded.

"We will always be in her debt. As we all saw the effect she had on your royal person, Sire, we rejoiced that the good spirit, Ahura Mazda, had sent someone to uplift you. Not only do we acquiesce in your decision, we bless you for it."

Sounds of approval greeted Artaban's speech. They were glad that he had mentioned these things, although it was only the uncle of the king who would have dared to bring them up. Xerxes did not like to be reminded of his weakness and failures.

Xerxes said nothing for a few moments. He had forgotten, so far was he removed from those depressing times, just how much Esther had changed his life. He realized more than ever how right and proper it was that she should be queen. He had called this meeting as a mere formality, to approve his choice, but as it turned out, he appreciated the unreserved confirmation he had received from his advisers. He thanked them briefly, and left in a thoughtful frame of mind.

*

Esther moved around the hall speaking to her friends. The aspirants from the windflower pavilion were there, closely escorted as usual, and she was especially glad to talk to Kenaida and Marista whom she had not seen for a long time. They congratulated her on being chosen as queen.

"But nothing has been decided," protested Esther. "The king has made no announcement. Yes, I am in favour with him, but that does not mean he has chosen me to be queen."

The two looked at her wistfully, each wishing that she had been the chosen one. Kenaida said, "You must be the only one that doesn't think so. Everyone in the palace is talking about you and the king. He couldn't wait to see you when he got back from Persepolis. And he is giving you this feast. What more can it mean?"

"I hope you are right. I just don't want to assume anything that concerns the king. If it is true, what will you do?"

"Oh, you don't have to worry for us, Esther. We can have our pick of husbands. Already we have been getting admiring glances. This is our first really public appearance, another reason to think that our time as aspirants is over. Hegai tells us he has some offers for us, but we cannot make any plans until the queen is chosen. So we are just as anxious for the matter to be settled. And we are truly happy for you. For my part, I found the king intimidating. It won't be easy to be consort to King Xerxes."

With that, Kenaida moved along and left Esther with her thoughts. The tension mounted inside her and she longed for Xerxes to appear. Looking round the hall she became aware of a pair of eyes regarding her with more than unusual interest. With delight she recognized her old friend, and beckoned to him. In a moment he was by her side.

"Jacob! I can hardly believe it is you. You look so handsome, and dressed like a prosperous merchant, too. What has happened?"

"Thanks to you, Esther, I was commissioned by the king to make a number of gold ornaments. It was your doing, I know. Already I have more orders than I can handle. I thank you with all my heart."

"No need to thank me, Jacob. Your work spoke for you. That ring you gave me. The king noticed it and asked who made it. Your craftsmanship did the rest. He obviously admired your work."

"You remember how we planned it all these years ago? You were to become queen and I was to become rich with all the commissions I would get through you."

"I am so glad for you, Jacob. But I am not yet queen," She

stopped. "What is it? You looked as if you were going to say something?"

"No, it's nothing. I must go. Perhaps we will be able to talk again."

When he left, she looked round, wondering what had caused him to hurry off, and there leaning against a pillar was Haman. Even as she caught his eye, he straightened up, and giving her a small bow with just a hint of a smile on his lips, he moved off. A knot tightened inside her. He had been watching her talking to Jacob. She wondered if he had overheard what they said. Could he make trouble for her?

A fanfare of trumpets interrupted her thoughts. The king entered the hall, a bevy of court officials clearing his path. He was finely dressed in a robe of purple cloth, with a gold-linked chain at his waist. Beams of coloured light flashed from the gem-studded circlet on his head. He strode forward, looking every inch the powerful monarch that he was, acknowledging the bows and applause of all. Esther's throat constricted with excitement as she watched. Now the king was on the dais, and the crowd fell silent, waiting for him to speak.

"Friends and loyal subjects," he began, in his resonant voice, "We are gathered here to celebrate the birth day of the Lady Esther. Since coming to the palace, she has impressed everyone with her beauty, and she has won the hearts of us all with her radiant personality." He looked over the heads of the listeners until his eyes met hers. "Come forward, Esther."

With two of her ladies in attendance, Esther stepped forward and faced the king, sinking in a low curtsey.

The king smiled at her and continued.

"You have brightened our lives, Esther and we hope you will continue to do so for many, many years to come. May this anniversary of your birth day be a happy one."

There was loud applause and shouts of "Happy birth day," which she acknowledged with a smile. When the noise subsided, the king went on:

"In keeping with our tradition, I will present my birth day gift to the lady Esther." He stepped down and came towards her, while a servant bearing a small chest appeared behind him. Xerxes opened the chest and there was a loud gasp from the onlookers as he lifted from it a crown of gold set with jacinth and white adamants, the royal colours of Persia. Motioning Esther to kneel before him, he held it above her head, with these words:

"Esther, you have proved yourself worthy of this crown. It is with the full consent of the Council I now confer on you the crown of the consort of the Emperor of all Persia."

He placed it on her head, and, taking her hand, he raised her up and leading up on the dais, presented her to the people. Now she could stand on the same level with him, as queen. The people clapped and cheered and the whole hall reverberated with the sound. There was a roll of drums and the trumpets blared again as a salute to the new queen.

Esther was in a kind of daze, quite overcome with the swiftness of events. She raised her hand and smiled, holding tightly on to Xerxes with her other hand. She felt unreal, as if it was all happening in a dream.

At last Xerxes signalled for silence.

"In order to fulfil the laws of the Empire, and to follow the tradition of the Achaemenids, I now call on the priests to come forward and perform the rite of marriage."

Esther caught her breath. She had hoped for this moment for so long, and now that it was here, she could hardly take it in. Xerxes must have planned it all himself, she thought, — the elaborate dress in the royal colours of Persia, the birth day feast as the excuse to have everyone present without knowing what was to take place. And she, not daring to hope too much, had been more in the dark than anyone.

Xerxes was still holding her hand, and as the priests prepared to perform the ceremony, he whispered to her:

"I hope this is all in accordance with your wishes?"

As if there could be any doubt. But she appreciated that he had come even that close to asking her consent.

"It is, my lord king," she replied with dignity. She hardly heard the words of the ceremony. This was it, the pinnacle of her ambition, the achievement of her goal, the fulfilment of her destiny. She felt intensely happy. It was hard to believe that she, a Jewish girl, was now queen of Persia. The thought sobered her a little. No one knew her origins, and she wondered how much would change if anyone was to find out.

But she could not think of the future as she acknowledged the cheers of the people. She looked around the faces for a sight of Mordecai, and there he was, applauding with all the rest, his face beaming. Beside him stood Jacob, and as she caught his eye he gestured, pointing at his head and then at himself. What was he trying to tell her? At last she understood. He had made her crown. She touched it, and then laid her hand on her heart. She saw him nod, and raise his fist in a sign of triumph. It was a great moment for them both. Their dreams really had come true.

Xerxes and Esther made their way from the hall in stately procession, stopping every few paces to accept the good wishes of the courtiers and officials. At last they reached the entrance, only to find Alcytes the prophetess barring their way. She wore a loose white gown and as she raised her hands the wide sleeves billowed out like wings on each side. She fixed her eyes on Esther.

167

"Enjoy the sunshine while you can, but be prepared. There are dark days ahead for us all," she pronounced, before disappearing down a corridor.

"Take no notice of Alcytes," Xerxes reassured Esther. "She loves being a prophet of doom."

Esther smiled back at him, determined to let nothing spoil this night. But the incident stayed at the back of her mind, as if waiting for the moment when the truth of her words would be revealed.

# CHAPTER 9

Esther's life changed dramatically when she became queen. She never went back to the Harem. Instead she was housed in the Queen's Palace, a separate building set in a beautiful garden. In one wing of the palace were the family rooms where all the royal children lived, in another were the servants' quarters and the kitchens and laundries that served the household. The queen's suite took up most of the main wing, and comprised two levels, part of the upper one being a terraced garden. From there a wide flight of stone stairs led down to a tree-lined courtyard which gave access to the King's Palace.

Esther felt a greater sense of isolation because the palace was a self-contained unit. She was no longer part of the camaraderie of the Harem, and her life became more circumscribed. At first she was not aware of it. She insisted that her ladies, Bilkah, Arista and Kenida remain as her attendants and she chose as her servants some of the young girls from the families of Jewish exiles. She spent much time with the king. He wanted her with him all the time, and he gave very little attention to the work of the government. It was of course understood that the marriage season be observed, and it was no surprise that the king neglected to review his troops or spend his time in administration. Instead there was a succession of parties and feasts, entertainments and pageants, and a general air of relaxation prevailed in the palace. Esther was in the king's bed every night, except when he went hunting, for then he liked to go to bed early and rise before dawn and because of that he preferred to sleep alone.

Their relationship was an easy one. Although in public, Esther behaved with the utmost decorum, in private she quite lost her awe of him. They talked about all kinds of subjects , and her curiosity knew no bounds. He often teased her about her questions. There was one question, though, that she longed to ask him, and one night her curiosity got the better of her.

"What was it," she asked, " that made you chose me from all the others?"

A lazy smile curved his lips.

"What others?"

"You know, the other aspirants."

"There was never any question of the others once I found you."

"But I thought . . . " She bit her lip. That was best left unsaid.

"You thought I treated them all the way I treated you?" He chuckled. "You have a highly exaggerated view of my powers! Flattering, but not true." He lay back, his hands clasped behind his head. "I saw them, of course, but that was a mere formality. When I came back from the war and was faced with making a choice . . ." He shook his head. "I regretted that I had ever consented to the arrangement." Turning to her he played with a lock of her hair, teasing her. "Then you came along, and I knew it was my duty to tame you before you wreaked havoc on all the men in the palace!"

"So that was why you chose me!" she said. "Now I know."

"I chose you, my star, because of your secret."

A sliver of panic flicked across her mind but she held it

down.

"My secret?"

"Your magic secret," he said, looking deep into her eyes. "When I am with you, for a few precious moments snatched from time, I forget that I am carrying the burdens of the empire."

*

Esther got to know the royal children, although the older ones tended to keep to themselves. She saw very little of Artaxerxes, the eldest son and heir, and on the few occasions they met, he was polite but distant. Once, at a banquet, she caught him staring at her, with an expression in his eyes she could not read, and he did not respond when she smiled at him. As for the younger children, they loved listening to her as she told them stories from history. For this reason she spent much of her free time in the library, looking for stories that would interest the children, and writing them down in a simplified form. Her freedom of access to the archives was one aspect of her life that she valued. There was a huge collection of books amassed in the days of Darius, and Xerxes was diligent in ensuring that the library was always being extended with new acquisitions. She and the king would often pour over manuscripts together. It was one interest that they had in common.

Her life settled into a new routine. If she missed the incessant chatter of the women in the Harem, she was kept in touch with their daily lives through Bilkah, who was always ready to pass on little items of palace news.

Xerxes continued to treat her with respect and affection. Indeed it was the consensus in the palace that he was besotted with her, and they speculated on how long his obsession with her would last. Xerxes had never been known for his constancy, but now, it seemed, he had no thought for any other woman. As the months went by and there was still no lessening in his preoccupation with the Queen, the men of the Council began to be concerned.

"He does not pay as much attention to the empire as he used to," complained Carshena to Memucan. "Of course, the government is sound, and the affairs of state go on as usual, but situations change and require adjustments, new polices. At present Xerxes is content to leave things to carry on as they are, merely giving the royal assent to the orders that the Council devises. It isn't enough! There has still to be vigilance, or the affairs of State will deteriorate imperceptibly until at some stage a crisis will emerge and we will be ill prepared to deal with it. A king neglects his kingdom at his peril."

Memucan and the others agreed with Carshena. None of them, though, was prepared to face the king with these matters.

"What about you, Memucan?" Abagtha asked. "You are the most senior adviser. Would you make an approach to the king?"

Memucan prevaricated, saying that they all remembered the problem they had when Xerxes was depressed, that it was better that he enjoyed a spell of relaxation with his new queen, that eventually he would want to take up the reins of government again.

Seeing that Memucan was reluctant to speak they let the matter rest. Another month went by without any change in Xerxes' behaviour. At last Memucan was forced to take action.

When the king arrived at the next weekly Council, the only

172

one he now attended, he went through the business with the usual dispatch, but this time, when he rose to leave, Memucan was ready for him. He quickly intimated that he wished to speak privately with the king. The members of the Council filed out quickly, only too eager not to be part of the confrontation.

"My lord king," began Memucan," Your loyal subjects all rejoice in you, that you have a new queen who is most beautiful and pleasing in every way."

Xerxes grunted, barely listening to him.

"We of the Council realize that both you and the queen required a time to yourselves, to adjust to each other, to spend the marriage season together, and we have endeavoured to lighten the burden of kingship in order to enable you to devote time to the queen." Realizing that Xerxes' attention was wandering, he spoke a little more sharply.

"We of the Council think that the king must now devote himself to the affairs of state, and resume leadership of the Empire."

Still Xerxes said nothing, but now he was staring at Memucan, who began to feel less than comfortable.

The king's frown became more pronounced. "What is it you want to know?"

"We would like to know," he said lamely," when the marriage season will end, and when we can look forward to your decisions concerning the polices we will be pursuing as regards our allies and the vassal states."

Xerxes rose and went to look out the window.

"Thank you, Memucan," the king said, without turning round. "I will advise the Council at the appropriate time. Meanwhile, you will carry on your duties as you have been doing."

Memucan bowed. "Thank you my lord king." Realizing that was the only response he was going to get, he silently left the room.

Xerxes went in search of Esther, and found her seated with her ladies on the terrace.

"Come with me," he said. "I need some distraction." He led her back to his quarters,

Sensing that he was upset, Esther asked, "Did something happen at the Council ?"

"Oh, forget the Council! he answered irritably. "I've had enough of them for one day!" He caught her to him and embraced her, resting his face in her hair.

"Tell me what is bothering you," she pleaded gently. "Perhaps I can help."

He smiled at her. "You already have."

"But there is something wrong," she persisted.

He took her hand and let her over to the couch. "Just these interfering busybodies on the Council! They think I spend too much time with you."

So that's it. Aloud she said, "Perhaps they are right, my lord. I have been monopolizing your time when you should have been attending to your duties. Please don't neglect them because of me. You have been very kind to me, and I have been happier these last months than I ever thought possible."

He smiled and stroked her hair. "You have made me happy too, Esther, at a time when I never thought to be happy again. But don't spoil it by nagging me about my duty! It's enough to have the Council doing that! Besides, why should I spend my time with them when I can be with most beautiful woman in the world." He laid his head on her breast, and closed his eyes. "This is where I want to be!"

Esther was quiet. There was nothing more she could say.

*

Later there was a banquet for the Satrap of Sogdiana, at which Esther was not present, for she was giving a banquet for the Satrap's wife in the Queen's Palace. Xerxes jokingly complained that the Council wanted to cut short his marriage season. Haman, who was within earshot, heard the king's words and saw his opportunity. He was profoundly jealous of Esther because of her closeness to the king, referring to her in private as 'the bewitcher."

"Queen Esther would never wish to hinder the work of the state," he said. "She is so mindful of her duty to the king. I am sure," he added, "that she would never want to come between the king and his responsibilities."

"The queen is never lacking in her duty," said the king stiffly.

"In that case," pursued Haman smoothly, "she will not complain if you spend more time with the Council."

The king gave him a sour look, but did not deign to reply. Haman, however, was satisfied that he had made his point.

In the end, these thrusts did have some effect on the king. He began to spend more time in the administration of the empire, though he was never quite so involved as he had been in the first years of his reign. Now, when difficult matters arose, or when his duties became tiresome, he would delegate his authority to others, and retreat to the queen's palace, or to the stables, to look at prize horses.

Esther, for her part, was well aware that the marriage season had to end sometime. Indeed, she had found it extraordinary that it had lasted so long.

*

Three months after this, Xerxes decided to move to Persepolis in order to present the new queen in the state capital. Esther was very excited about the trip. For the first time in her life she was able to travel and see new places, and despite the discomforts of the journey, for part of the route lay over rugged mountains, she enjoyed each new experience. There were not many towns or villages on the road between Shushan and Persepolis. Officials and servants had been sent out in advance to prepare the royal resting stations on the route, so that when the king's party arrived, the royal beds would be in place and the royal food prepared by the king's cooks. Other unlucky travellers would be relegated to the outhouses for the night, wherever they could find a corner not filled with the king's men. Occasionally they passed through tiny hamlets where the people stared at them with craned necks and wide eyes, too dazzled by the royal panoply to respond to Esther's smiles of greetings. The weather was favourable, and within two weeks they had reached their destination, weary and travel-worn.

As they entered Persepolis, crowds gathered to give the king's entourage a rousing welcome. Suddenly they felt energized again. Esther and Xerxes sat in the elaborately decorated imperial chariot and acknowledged the cheers of the people. The king was smiling happily, hearing the crowd commenting on the queen's beauty. He had chosen well, of that there could be no doubt. She smiled and waved to the onlookers, and her infectious enthusiasm reached the hearts of the people. Xerxes marvelled at the ease with which she fitted into her new role.

The palace of Darius, when they came to it at last, was breathtaking in its magnificence. If the palace of Shushan was fit for a king, this one was surely fit for an emperor. Tall pillars, forty feet high, supported the portico which was flanked by huge lions carved in stone. Wide flights of marble stairs rose to the second and third storeys, where hanging gardens softened the impact of the massive walls. Inside, walls of brilliantly coloured glazed brick stretched for what seemed like miles, while the floors were of tiles laid in intricate patterns. Everywhere there were carvings in metal, ivory and stone, and the furniture was of gold and silver with cushions and hangings of silk in the imperial colours. Esther had never seen such opulence. The palace of Shushan, which she had thought was the epitome of splendour, paled in comparison. Xerxes was very proud of the effort he had made to complete the palace that Darius had begun, and no expense had been spared to make it the showpiece of the Persian empire.

Yet Esther did not feel as comfortable here as at Shushan. The atmosphere was colder, more impersonal. Apart from her own ladies, Bilkah and Kenida, who were always with her, she felt she was among strangers, and although the other ladies at the court were not unfriendly, at the same time their air of bland indifference made her feel an outsider. She was more isolated too, in that the court was run with more formality. She remained for the most part within her own quarters and the gardens that surrounded them. There were no impromptu visits from the king. She rarely saw him apart from formal occasions.

Their stay at Persepolis was taken up with occasions of clourful ceremonies, of which the most splendid was the presentation of the queen. On that day the Adana was crammed with onlookers. Royal musicians with trumpets, flutes and drums, announced the entry of the royal couple. The procession reached the dais, where Xerxes took his place on the golden throne, while Esther sat on a smaller throne at his side. After the proclamation, Xerxes took the queen's crown of state and laid it on her head as she knelt before him. Then, holding her by the hand, he led her forward and presented her to the people amid resounding cheers.

It was a moment of great triumph for Esther. Her belief in her destiny had been vindicated. She felt that this was what she was born for, but years later, when recalling this scene, she knew that she had been mistaken. The hour of destiny still lay in the future.

There followed days and nights of feasting, of formal banquets, of receptions for ambassadors and dignitaries. Esther hosted entertainments for the women, while Xerxes had long discussions of foreign policy with their husbands. Esther was glad that Xerxes was again in total control, and he seemed to have a renewed energy. It was a very busy time, and Esther was not sorry when the summer was over and they all returned to Shushan.

Life at Shushan went tranquilly on. Esther saw more of the king, though not as much as during the marriage season. Scarcely a day passed that he did not summon her to his presence or visit her in her palace. It was during this period that an episode occurred which drew her closer to the king's eldest son, Artaxerxes.

A delegation had arrived from Babylon, and a tournament of athletics had been devised for entertainment. The youths of the court were to pit their strength against each other in various martial arts. In the course of events, Artaxerxes, who was an excellent javelin thrower, was matched against Nemis, a youth who was one of the Scythians, a minority people conquered by Darius. Artaxerxes, at this time a lad of fifteen or sixteen, considered himself to be the champion in this event, and resented having Nemis as his opponent, instead of one of the elite Medes or Persians. He refused to accept him, and when the umpire would not change, on the grounds that all names were drawn by lot and each contestant had to accept the rival assigned to him. Artaxerxes began to create a fuss, threatening to have the umpire replaced. The commotion drew the attention of the king, who sent for his son and demanded to know the reason for the uproar. When Artaxerxes, now very angry, explained what had transpired, the king lost no time in settling the matter.

"If you do not wish to accept the challenge of your opponent, you are at liberty to leave the field."

"But he is a Scythian!" shouted Artaxerxes with contempt. "Surely you do not expect me to take on such an unworthy rival?"

"His parents were Scythians," replied Xerxes coldly. "But he was born into the Persian empire, and he is Persian. Your grandfather, the illustrious Darius made no difference with minorities, and neither do I. Unless you apologize to Nemis, you will take no further part in the this tournament. Now go, and let there be no more of this nonsense!"

Artaxerxes was too proud to give in, and, flashing angry eyes at his father, but not daring to contradict him, he stalked off the field in a fury.

Esther was present at this confrontation, and while she applauded the king for his stand on the rights of minorities, she knew that Artaxerxes was deeply upset. Later that day she went in search of him. She found him eventually seated by the pool in the Garden of the Warriors.

"Artaxerxes, may I sit with you for a little?" she asked.

He turned and looked at her when she spoke, but said nothing, and returned his gaze to the water.

She sat down beside him.

"You are feeling very angry, I know," she began. "Do you want to talk about it?"

"I hate him!" he burst out. "He just loves to humiliate me! He never takes my side."

"He didn't do it to humiliate you," she said softly. "He did what he had to do as a just king. He treated his subjects equally."

"How can you say that Nemis is equal to me?" The outrage in his voice was plain. "I am a Persian, the son of the king. He is nobody, the son of a . . . a soldier of the guard!"

"A soldier who is completely loyal to his king. Persians value loyalty above all virtues, and when you are king, you will value it too. For that alone, he commands respect."

"But he is an incomer! How can he ever be equal to a native-born Persian? It doesn't make sense."

Esther tried another angle.

"Did you ever think of where the Persians came from? They did not always inhabit this land. So Persians are incomers too, from hundreds of years ago. They came and made this their land, just as the Scythians did. In a few decades no one will remember that they were not always part of Persia."

"But surely that is not the same thing," he argued. "The Scythians were a conquered people."

"It doesn't really matter how they came here. The point is that they are now part of the Persian empire, and they deserve to be treated as such."

He was silent for a moment. "I never thought of it like that. But it doesn't change things as they are now. Perhaps after many years they will have earned their place."

"Have you earned yours?" she asked gently.

His head came up sharply.

"What do you mean?" His eyes were cold. She had a vision of him, in a position of authority, years from now, asking the same question of anyone that dared to contradict him.

"Just that you are very privileged to be the son of Xerxes, king of kings. But it is not enough to be born to that position. You have to earn it too."

He raised his eyebrows in disbelief.

She plunged on. "Look, you and I are in the same position. I am queen because your father chose me, but I have to behave like a queen. I must behave with dignity. Because of who I am, I must act in a certain way. Although I have been given the queen's crown, I must also earn it, or else it will be given to someone else. " She paused, and then continued.

" It is the same with you. When you are king, you will have to be a good one, or you will not command the loyalty of your people. You cannot always act in a personal way. I think that is what your father was trying to teach you."

Artaxerxes was silent for a while. Then he said: "Why are you telling me all this?"

She touched his arm lightly. "Because at times we all need a friend to help us see things more clearly."

His face brightened and he smiled at her. "Somehow you made me see things in a different light."

"So, will you apologize to Nemis?"

"Certainly not!" he replied sharply. "No, I... I don't see why I should go that far!" He turned away.

"Tell me one thing," she persisted. "Seeing things the way you do now, if you could go back this afternoon, would you do anything different?"

"I suppose I would," he said slowly.

"Then it should not be difficult for you to tell Nemis, that if you had taken everything into account, you would not have acted as you did. Now that you have had time to think, you realize that you acted impulsively."

"When you put it like that, it sounds simple. But it's not so easy to do!" he said ruefully.

"What do you think of Nemis? Is he a good athlete?"

"He has that reputation."

"All the more reason to apologize, because you will surely meet him at other contests, and if you leave things as they are, you will surely feel uncomfortable. A little discomfort now, and you will feel better. But if you don't, you will be embarrassed every time you meet him— knowing what you know now," she added, hoping to persuade him wholly.

"I suppose you are right, Queen Esther," he said reluctantly. He rose. "I might as well do it now, and get it over with."

He started to go, and then turned back to her.

"I thank you. You are a good friend."

"I will always be your friend, Artaxerxes."

"I will remember that," he said.

Many years later she was to recall that conversation, and realize that he did indeed remember.

*

Later that night, when she was with Xerxes, he said to her:

"You spoke to Artaxerxes earlier. I hope he was more polite to you than he was to me!"

"Yes," she answered, her tone full of surprise. "How did

you know?"

He smiled. "I know everything. Everything you do in this palace is reported to me. You have no idea how confused my spies are that you spend so much time poring over dusty scrolls! No queen has ever been known to do that before. You have set a precedent, Esther." He reached out and touched her cheek. "Do you know how intriguing you are? And kind, too. It was good of you to talk to Artaxerxes. Did you know that he apologized to Nemis? That must have been your doing."

He doesn't know everything, thought Esther darkly. Aloud she said, "Oh, no, I just helped him to see things in a different light. The apology was his doing. That took courage."

"Yes, he's not a bad lad. A bit headstrong at times. But then, we all were at that age." He took her hand and raised it to his lips. "I do appreciate what you did.

I think he loves me, thought Esther, but he has never said so. A little later she learned that he never would. Holding her in his arms he whispered,

"You're so good for me, Esther. I could almost love you."

"Only 'almost'?" she queried with a smile.

"Yes, Esther. Almost." His voice was serious. "A king cannot love as other men. That's why he is surrounded by so many women. So that he will not centre his life on one alone. That way is danger."

"How can it be dangerous to love?" she asked.

"To love is to trust," he replied. A king can trust no one. Just think if men knew that I loved you, they would immediately use you. I have no illusions. A king is only a king as long as he is stronger than his opponents. I know I have people who are loyal and true and I trust them — up to a point. But that's different. With a woman, you tend to let your judgment be swamped by love." He paused, and she wondered if he was remembering Vashti. Then he continued:

"It would be dangerous for you. People would try and influence you, and would use you without you being aware of it. For that reason, we must not be together so much. We have had a longer than usual marriage season. To prolong it would expose both you and me to trouble. From now on you will come to me only when I send for you." He sighed. "This is not my choosing. Do you understand what I am saying?"

"Yes, I understand." He was telling her in an oblique way that he loved her enough to want to protect her. She would have to be satisfied with that. "But don't forget me!" she begged.

He laughed. "How could I forget you! You are the queen." Then his face grew serious again. "Go very carefully in this palace. There are people who would discredit you to gain their own ends. If there was ever any suspicion rumoured about you, I could do nothing for you that would compromise the king. Don't get involved in factions. And even if I seem to neglect you, remember this. I esteem you greatly. For me you will always be the perfect queen. Trust no one." He paused before adding ominously, "not even me." His lips touched hers, and she shivered. But it was a shiver of fear.

*

If, in the weeks that followed, Esther saw less of the king, she found plenty to occupy her. She spent time with the royal children, she wove beautiful fabrics on her loom, and helped the other women making fine pottery. She devised all kinds of entertainments for the women of her household, and often spent time in the library readings the works of the ancient writers. Always, she was treated with great respect. The fact that she had achieved her ambition, that she was in the position she had sought, made her very content, and her happiness was contagious. She made life pleasant for those around her and they all adored her. Even though she knew that eyes might be watching her at all times, she felt it was a small price for her to pay. She was especially aware of the dark figure of Haman always hovering in the background. He was polite to her when he had occasion to speak to her, and she was equally polite to him. But there was something about him that made her distrust him, even if she hadn't known of his enmity to Mordecai. She saw Mordecai from time to time. As Chamberlain he often had business in the Queen's Palace, and it was natural that she should speak to him, albeit very briefly, whenever they met. Sometimes she saw Sarcon in the library, and she would smile at him, and sometimes they exchanged a few words.

One event that brightened her life at this time was a visit from Jacob. He appeared at the palace one day, asking to see the queen. She was with the ladies, Bilkah, Kenida and Amnistra, in the garden salon, and she bade them bring him in.

He entered the room, and made a formal obeisance before the queen, although he could not quite conceal his usual jaunty air. Esther, watching him, almost giggled. She remembered how he used to bow to her in exactly the same fashion when they had play-acted years ago.

"Your Majesty's most humble servant."

Esther acknowledged him graciously.

"Ladies, this is Jacob, goldsmith to the king, " she said, presenting him to the others. "What brings you here, Jacob?"

"Your Majesty, the king commissioned me to make some pieces for your royal person. I am here to show them to you, so that you can choose the ones you want. My boy is outside.

Have I your permission to bring him in?"

She nodded, and he signalled the boy to come in.

A young lad entered, carrying a large casket. Setting it down, he opened it up to reveal an impressive array of gold and silver jewellery. There were gold earrings, some with precious stones, others designed in stylized animal heads, rich with intricate detail. There were necklaces and bracelets set with grey opal, red carnelian, brown jasper and green amazonite, all with rings to match. They were all works of excellent craftsmanship and remarkable beauty.

There were cries of delight from the women as they examined each piece, but Esther was more interested in Jacob. She took advantage of their preoccupation to draw him aside and talk to him.

"It's so good to see you, Jacob. You restore the part of my life that I had to leave behind. You look so fine." She studied him. He had filled out, developed a man's physique, and his dress though modest, was finely made and he carried it well. "You are obviously prospering. It is good to see you like this."

"It is all your doing, Esther — I mean, madam. Since being commissioned by the king, I have more orders than I can cope with. I am now a partner with Barzai, and I've had to hire three apprentices. I spend most of my time designing and overseeing the work."

"I'm so glad, Jacob. What news of our friends?"

They spent some time talking and then Esther called for refreshments. The all sat around, discussing the jewellery, interspersed with much teasing and laughter. Jacob was a born entertainer, and he charmed the ladies with his wit. For his part, he enjoyed the company of four beautiful women who listened to his every word and laughed at his jokes. Amnistra, in particular, took his fancy. She was a dark-haired beauty with green eyes and a ready smile. Not that any of them could compare with Esther, but then he always considered her to be extra special.

An hour passed quickly, and it was time for him to go. Esther picked out the pieces she wanted, and then she asked all her ladies to chose something. When Jacob finally took his leave, he left four happy women in the highest of spirits. Jacob was happy too. He had made a great deal of money and he had a standing invitation to come again.

It was the first of many visits, for she sent for him whenever there were birth day or New Year gifts to be given. Esther especially valued these occasions. Because they were in the privacy of her apartments, she could speak to Jacob freely, and feel again the carefree spirit of her youth. But on one visit, just before he left, Jacob said to Esther:

"Do you know a man called Haman?"

A chill swept over her.

"Yes, of course. He is one of the court officials, a member of the Inner Council. Why do you ask?"

"Be wary of him. He is not your friend."

"I know it. But why do you speak of him? You must have a reason."

Jacob was reluctant to say more, but Esther insisted. "I need to know," she said.

"All right." He smiled ruefully. "I'd forgotten how curious you can be! I wasn't going to tell you this. Anyway, to be brief, I was in a tavern in the city and I overheard him boasting to his friends that he was rising to the top and that soon he would be next to the king. Someone made a lewd joke about the place being reserved for the queen, at which he said he would change that too. He said he meant to be greater in importance than even Xerxes' queen. I'm afraid for you. I don't trust that man and I fear he would stop at nothing to gain his own ends."

"I knew he resented me, and my closeness to the king, but I did not realize how much. Thank you for telling me, Jacob. I will be very careful."

"I will keep my ears and eyes open. If I hear anything, I will let you know."

Later, an incident occurred which revealed how far Haman was prepared to go. One afternoon, Bilkah was nowhere to be seen. Esther herself went to look for her and found her in the little anteroom off her bedroom. When Bilkah saw the queen, she burst into tears. This was so unlike her that Esther became worried.

"What's wrong, Bilkah? You must tell me." Gently she took her in her arms.

Bilkah shook her head and continued to sob. Finally, after much encouragement from Esther, Bilkah told her that one of Haman's men had approached her and ordered her to spy on the queen and report any unusual activity. He threatened that he would have her sent away if she did not comply.

"What am I to do, my lady?" I cannot spy on you, but if I don't who knows what will happen to me!"

"Don't worry, Bilkah, nothing will happen to you. I'll make sure of that. You just report that you see nothing unusual. After all, it's true. I have nothing to hide."

"But he won't be satisfied with that. I don't know what he'll do to me!"

"Listen, Bilkah, if he ever threatens you again, tell him, that I the queen, will speak to the king and have him removed. That should be enough to stop him. I'm amazed that Haman would dare to do this. If I confronted him he would just deny that he knew anything about it. Don't worry, Bilkah, he cannot harm you. Or me. We will make sure that he has nothing to report."

The next time the man approached Bilkah, she told him that she had nothing to report. When he began to threaten her, she did as Esther had advised. After some more threats the man went away. She didn't hear from him again. But Esther and her ladies kept their eyes open all the time. They had to be on constant vigil. Esther knew that she could no longer take any chances especially where Mordecai or Sarcon were concerned.

## CHAPTER 10

A few days after this episode, she was in the library looking for a scroll, when Mordecai entered. He motioned to her to follow him to the far end of the room, where they were out of sight of prying eyes.

"What is it, Mordecai? Is something wrong?"

He answered with a question.

"Are you dining with the king tonight?"

"Yes, but he will be sleeping alone, because of the hunt tomorrow."

He hesitated.

She caught his arm. "What is it? You must tell me."

"There's going to be an attempt on the king's life."

"Oh no!" She stopped herself from crying out loud.

"Don't be alarmed. With your help we will avert this danger."

"My help? What can I do?"

"This morning I took a walk down by the river bank. I sat for a little in the shelter of the cliff, and while I was there I heard two men talking on the river bank above me. I couldn't help overhearing their conversation and what I heard chilled my blood. I recognized the voice of Bigthana, one of the king's bodyguards, and the other was Teresh, another bodyguard. They were plotting to kill the king."

Esther gasped in dismay, but Mordecai went on. "Someone is offering them a large sum of money, two hundred gold coins, but unfortunately they did not mention any name. Their plan is simple. They know the king will be sleeping alone because of the hunt. They are on guard duty at the king's bedroom in the early evening. Just before the guard changes, Bigthana— he is one of them, the other is Teresh— will hide in the king's bedroom. When the new guard arrives, Teresh will say that Bigthana had to leave early to relieve himself. Bigthana will put a drug in the king's drink, and when he falls into a deep sleep, Bigthana will come out of his hiding place and kill him. Then he will make his escape by the window. Teresh will be in the vicinity to create a diversion if needed. It is such a simple plan they could likely get away with it. The thing is, I don't know who is behind them, and I don't know whom to trust. It is obviously someone familiar with the king's movements. We have a traitor in our court, but there is no time to investigate. That's why I came to you. You must tell the king. He will know how best to foil them."

"How terrible! Of course I will tell him! I hope you are not in any danger, Mordecai?"

"No, Esther don't worry about me. They have no idea I was there."

"What good fortune that you were!"

"Fortune, Esther? I think not."

"What do you mean?"

"I mean when evil raises its ugly head, God provides a means to thwart it. You and I are the means, and we must not fail."

"No, indeed," echoed Esther," we must not fail."

"Don't worry. You do your part and all will be well."

That night Esther dined with the king. She did not bring up the subject until the meal was over and the servants had departed. As they sat on the sofas sipping their wine she said,

"My lord king, I have something very important to tell you."

He smiled at her languidly, stretching his legs out in front of him. "What's on you mind, Esther?"

She looked at him, her expression serious. "My lord, tonight there is to be an attempt on your life."

To her surprise he laughed. "Is that all? That's nothing new. Why do you think there are always two guards outside my room."

"It is your guards who plan to do it," she said, looking at him steadily.

At that he sat up. "My guards? What are you talking about?"

"You guards, Bigthana and Teresh. Someone, I don't know who, has offered them two hundred gold coins for your life."

He stared at her, his eyes narrowing. "You seem to know a lot. Where did you hear all this?"

"Mordecai, one of your chamberlains. He came to me, so that I could warn you. He did not know who else to trust. He said you would know what to do."

Now he was all attention. "Did he tell you the plan?"

She related all that Mordecai had told her.

"Hmm. It's so simple it could succeed. Perhaps it is all talk, though."

"But can you take the risk, my lord?"

He smiled, his white teeth glinting. "I never take unnecessary risks. When Bigthana comes out, I will be ready for him. I will pretend to take the drink and fall asleep. The guards will be ready to rush in when they hear a noise. That way, we'll catch him red-handed."

He chuckled gleefully, and Esther realized that he was

actually enjoying the prospect of some excitement.

"However," he went on. "There are always disgruntled or ambitious people who plot against the king, but most of them never come to anything. Perhaps nothing will happen."

"Mordecai seemed to think they were serious."

"Well, we'll see. If Mordecai is right, I will owe him my life."

She left him soon afterwards, relieved that the matter was now in the king's hands.

When the king went to his room there was no sign of Bigthana. He pretended to drink from the goblet, got into bed, slipping a dagger under the cover as a precaution. He left the small lamp burning beside his bed. Then he waited.

After about ten minutes, with ears straining, he heard a slight movement, and from under his eyelids he could just make out a dark form moving towards the bed. He waited until he sensed that his assailant had raised his arm, and then with a swift movement he rolled away, at the same time shouting for the guards. They rushed in, one of them carrying a torch, and there was Bigthana, frozen with surprise, still holding the dagger.

"So, Bigthana, you would kill your king," said Xerxes, getting to his feet "Treachery has its own reward. You will get it, never fear." He motioned to the guards. "Take him away."

So they led him away and in due time he and Teresh were hanged on the gallows. For a few days it was the talk of the palace. Mordecai became known as a hero for saving the king's life, much to the disgust of Haman, who played down Mordecai's part in the affair whenever it was mentioned. The excitement eventually died down, and the whole matter was forgotten, but not before Xerxes ordered an account to be recorded in the chronicles of the Persians.

As it happened, the king had a lot on his mind at this time. There was some unrest in the provinces, not against the king, but between the governors. He was constantly having to settle disputes that arose over the order of precedence. The northern provinces resented the prosperity of those in the south, and accused the central government of making trade agreements that favoured the more fertile lands of the south. Not a day passed, it seemed, but Xerxes had to face angry deputations, and it took all his diplomacy to avert real trouble.

One evening after a particularly trying day, he was taking a hot bath in the royal bath house, a large building with an enormous sunken bath where members of the Inner Council and certain selected men of the king's retinue could come and relax. The floor was tiled with marble slabs heated from beneath, and off the main area were smaller rooms for changing and massage. From one of these rooms Haman emerged, but when he saw the king he turned to go back. Xerxes, seeing him, called out:

"Come, Haman, you may join me in the bath. There is plenty of room for us both."

"My lord king," said Haman, who had been hoping for such an invitation, "I trust I am not disturbing you."

Xerxes, a feeling of goodwill now oozing through his tired body, closed his eyes, and immediately forgot about Haman. About ten minutes later he opened his eyes to find Haman watching him.

"What is it, Haman? Have you something on your mind?"

"Since you ask, Sire, there is something I would like to talk to you about."

Xerxes groaned. "I can never get away from problems, not even in my bath!"

"Oh, there's no problem, Sire. At least," he continued, "there's no problem now. There was a deputation from Ajax, one of the minor kings-"

"I know who he is!" interrupted Xerxes testily. "Get to the point, man!"

"Yes, well, Sire, he wanted to know why he had received notice of the Confederate Council at Shushan next month. He heard it from some passing ambassador. Anyway, I ordered a meal for them in the dining hall and while they were eating, I made inquiries and found that none of the minor kings had been informed. Accordingly, I arranged for special messengers to leave tomorrow and then I told the deputation that we had been waiting for reports to come in, hence the delay. Now that we had the reports, special messengers would be sent out tomorrow with detailed notes of the agenda. They went away mollified. I trust the king approves of my actions?"

Xerxes, who had listened to all this in silence, chuckled. "As devious as ever, Haman! Just what I would have done myself." Abruptly he stopped smiling. "Find out who is responsible for this lapse. Have them suitably reprimanded. It must not happen again."

"It wouldn't surprise me," put in Haman, "if Mordecai were at fault here. He—"

"Well, it would surprise me!" interrupted the king. "He follows orders meticulously as a rule. He probably did not receive the order. But enough of business! What pleasures does the court offer tonight?" he asked, rising from the bath, and taking the towel the servant had rushed forward to hand him.

"There's a troupe of minstrels newly arrived from Ispahan," replied Haman, following him out of the bath." They are to perform in the great hall."

"Too boring to listen to them all evening. Perhaps I shall look in on the queen and her ladies. They know how to entertain."

Haman made another effort. "The king's guard is having a wrestling competition in the gymnasium. That should be interesting."

"A competition, eh?" The king could never resist trials of strength. "We mustn't miss that!" He clapped Haman on the shoulder. "Come and dine with me, and we'll pay a visit to the gymnasium afterwards."

This was the start of many evenings that Haman and the king spent together. Haman played on Xerxes' weakness for self-indulgence, and he went to great lengths to provide a variety of diversions that the king could not resist. They became inseparable companions. Xerxes sent less and less for Esther to entertain him, and even when he did send for her, he would end up so drunk that he would order the invitation cancelled. On one occasion, when Esther came to the king's quarter he was not there. She went out on the balcony to wait.

In the meantime, Haman had delayed Xerxes, ostensibly because of a special report that had just come in by courier. After he had dealt with the matter, Xerxes rose to go.

"The queen awaits me in my chamber," he told Haman.

"I'm sure she won't mind waiting a little longer while you taste this wine that I have just received. Let me pour some for you."

"Very well," said the king. "A little wine will relax me after all this business."

Haman filled the goblets, and while they drank, he pro-ceeded to engage the attention of the king relating to gossip about one of the commanders of the army. He knew how to tell an amusing anecdote, and he soon had the king roaring with laughter, while at the same time he kept refilling the goblet. When at last the king rose he was less than sober.

"It's time I was off, he said. "Time you finished here too. Come on, walk me down to the courtyard."

When he entered the chamber where Esther was waiting, she saw at once that he had been drinking. He was irritable and abrupt, knowing that he had kept her waiting, but, as the king he would not dream of apologizing. She made an effort to soothe him, and when that didn't work, she got her lute and began to sing. Xerxes stretched out on the couch, and in a short time he had fallen into a drunken sleep. Calling for his menservants, she ordered them to carry the king to his bed, and then she went back to her own suite. Although Xerxes had often kept her waiting, this was the first time that he had come to her drunk, but she did not consider that significant in itself. Not until it happened a second time.

Later that week the king summoned her, but when she arrived there was no sign of him. An hour had passed. She strolled out onto the balcony. The stars shone brightly out of a calm sky. Xerxes used to call me his star, she thought, as she surveyed the heavens. Could it be that his love for her was waning? She walked along the terrace and as she did so, she caught sight of Xerxes and Haman emerging from the administration offices, the king's arm round Haman's shoulder, exchanging joking comments, obviously close companions. Even as she watched, she heard Haman's voice as it drifted to her on the still air.

". . . the wife of general Verentes. She gives great parties. Especially when the general's away!"

There was a loud guffaw and they both broke into raucous laughter. She saw Xerxes clap Haman on the shoulder, and together they strode across the courtyard, in the direction of the barracks. He had forgotten all about her!

It confirmed her fears. Haman was undermining the king, pandering to his weakness, while at the same time ingratiating himself more and more into the king's favour. It was becoming common knowledge in the palace that Haman was close to the king and people began to accord him special deference. Esther had no doubt in her mind that Haman had deliberately kept the king late the other evening. And now he was taking him to Isandra! How she would gloat that the king was spending his time with her and not with the queen!

She feared Haman more than ever. He was in a position where the king was coming to depend on him, and that gave him an exceptional influence above anyone else in the palace. It bore out what Mordecai had told her. Haman was becoming known for offering to relieve the king of any duty he found tiring, and often these were the duties that kept him in touch with his subjects. Haman was assuming more and more power at the king's expense, and if the king was aware of what was happening he was either too lazy or too complacent to care.

Xerxes was only too glad to be relieved of his commitments. Esther felt powerless to help him. She could never prove to the king the subversive nature of Haman's motives. The king was happy with the situation, and would only fly into one of his rages if anyone tried to interfere. She felt very sad for him, especially since she had dismissed the rumours, whispered about the palace, of drunken orgies, of nights of revelry with Haman, and his cronies. She had thought them untrue, because when he was with her, he treated her, as he always had, with respect and affection.

She sighed deeply and turned to go inside. At that moment, Sarcon emerged from the shadow of the pillar and she was face to face with him. He said nothing, just looked at her, his eyes reflecting the pain in her own. Their gaze held for a long minute. Then she walked past him. There was nothing she could say. She knew what he was thinking. 'I would not have treated you like that.' But I am queen, she wanted to tell him. I got what I wanted and I will not complain. She had gone only a few paces when she heard his voice.

"Queen Esther, would you allow me to escort you back to your palace?"

She turned and looked at him. There was no mistaking the sympathy in his eyes. She didn't want his sympathy. About to refuse, she realized belatedly that she had dismissed her ladies. It would not be appropriate for her to be walking alone about the palace at night.

"Thank you Sarcon." She could not trust her voice to say more without betraying the sobs that were welling up in her throat. She could feel his love reaching out to her, and it was all she could do to stop throwing herself into his arms. She turned and walked ahead, and he began to follow her leaving a distance of two paces between them. She did not hurry in order that she could savour the fact that she was sharing a few minutes of his time. She dared not speak to him. Everywhere there were unseen eyes and ears. Yet it was balm to her to know that even if Xerxes had spurned her company tonight, at least in someone else's eyes she was highly esteemed.

All too soon they reached the door of the palace. He gave a quick bow and left without looking at her.

What a friend you are, Sarcon, she thought. You would do nothing to compromise me in front of the guards. But she felt his love wrapped round her, as surely as if he had taken her in his arms.

It was not an easy time for her. She was worried too, about Mordecai. They met infrequently, either in the gardens, or in the library, taking care not to be seen, Kenida and Amnistra acting as look-outs. When she questioned him, Mordecai told her that the possibility of marrying Zinna was becoming more remote. He had to be so vigilant, always on the alert for Haman, that it was impossible for him to think of bringing a wife to the palace. His time was wholly taken up in performing his duties with such zeal so that Haman would have no cause for complaint. If there was an omission, on the part of an underling, Mordecai would correct it himself, so as not to draw the attention of Haman. He had to be vigilant not only for himself but for all those in the household over whom he had oversight. He worked from early morning until late at night, only occasionally snatching a few hours away from the palace. It became increasingly difficult for him to meet Esther, and finally their visits petered out altogether.

With more time to herself, now that Xerxes was preoccupied with Haman, she busied herself with the royal children. Knowing that they knew little of the history of the empire, she decided to write it down for them in a simple form. Having obtained permission from the king to enlist the help of the keeper of the archives, she sought him out. To her surprise, and pleasure she discovered that Sarcon had been elevated to that office.

"The king made me Keeper of the Scrolls," he told her. "I think it was on Mordecai's recommendation." The emphasis he laid on Mordecai's name told her that it was a deliberate move to keep in contact with her. Now he was smiling at her openly. "I will be happy to assist your majesty in any way I can."

Again the double meaning. She felt her heart lift. Here was a source of strength and support whenever she needed it.

It was fortunate that I didn't know when I asked the king

for permission, she thought. Now we will be able to work together quite openly.

She spent many hours in the library working on her scrolls. Sarcon was not always present, and even when he was they exchanged only a few words so as not to draw attention. Yet she looked forward to these times, living her life on a secret level, when even a glance from Sarcon would buoy her up for hours. She completed her scroll and began to read the stories to the little princesses. Before long they had started to follow along as she read, and quite soon they would recognize some words.

Shortly after the lessons began she met with opposition from an unexpected quarter. One day, on reaching the schoolroom she found the princesses were not there. Instead she was met by Areba, the mother of one of the princesses, along with two other mothers. Although they had all been mere concubines, they had special status as royal mothers. Areba was a powerful woman, statuesque, still attractive in a full-blown way. Rumour had it that Xerxes had captured her in some campaign and taken her back to Shushan. Now she wasted no time.

"No more teaching the princesses to read. We don't want their heads to be filled with that nonsense!"

Esther smiled, confident that she could win them over.

"Surely it can do no harm, and to think how it will enrich their lives. They will be accomplished and in great demand when they come to marry."

Areba laughed without amusement. "You think so? That shows how green you are! Men don't want learned wives. Let me tell you, it was not because you could read that Xerxes chose you as queen!" Her eyes narrowed. "Oh you're very beautiful, no question about that. But there must have been some way you beguiled him into choosing you. There's something about you we can't fathom. What are you hiding behind that inscrutable face? What's under that calm you present to the world? You're too perfect to be true!"

Esther blanched as a dart of fear licked her heart. What was she talking about? Did she know of her relationship to Mordecai? Or perhaps she knew about Sarcon? No, she couldn't know anything. It was merely a shot in the dark, she thought, pushing the fear down. She looked at the other two women. They gazed back at her, unblinking. Her eyes came back to Areba's face.

"About the princesses, I'm sure the king will be happy to have his daughters learn to read."

Areba's face darkened. "We'll see about that! Don't think that you can come here and change our ways. We decide what's best for them, not you!"

"Let the king decide what's best for them," said Esther complacently.

"He will!" returned Areba. She swept out, followed by the other women, who tossed malevolent glances as they passed.

Esther was not overly concerned. Areba's insinuations were insubstantial. Was that how most people thought of her, she wondered? A model of perfection? Certainly she did not trust anyone enough to let down her guard, except her own women. I suppose it's true, she admitted to herself. I am leading a double life. There are few people with whom I'm completely myself. Even with Xerxes she had to be on her guard in case he found out where she came from. Not that he would mind, she knew, but his advisers would take quite another view, and if it came to choice, she had no illusions. His empire would always come first. As to the matter of the princesses she was sure Xerxes would take her side.

In the evening the king summoned her to dine with him. He greeted her warmly, and over dinner he talked to her about his horses and the chariot races his team had won. He was in good spirits. When he had dismissed the servants he led her to the couch in the alcove overlooking the terrace, where he had sat the first night she had spent with him. He handed her a goblet of wine, and taking his own goblet he walked over to the parapet. Without looking at her he remarked:

"I hear you are teaching the princesses to read."

"Oh, you heard about that?" she asked, setting down her wine. She stood up and took a step towards him, but he had turned to her, and something in his expression made her stop.

"My dear Esther, everything you do, every flower you pick, every song you sing, is reported to me. I thought you knew that."

"Yes, but . . . it just seems so unimportant," she faltered, not quite knowing what was coming next.

"Everything in the palace is important. For all sorts of reasons." He turned away again. "That's why you must stop the lessons."

"But Sire . . . " She moved close to him. "I didn't think there was any harm in it. After all you have never objected to my reading."

"It's different with you. You are the queen." He gave a rueful smile. "And one learned woman at the court is enough!" A serious look crossed his face. "No, even princesses must learn to keep their place. With the marriages I have in mind for them, reading would be superfluous. Indeed, it would be a decided disadvantage from the point of view of the bride-groom." He drained his glass. "So, no reading."

"But . . . "

He moved over to the wine table to refill his goblet.

"No, Esther. A royal princess with learning could be dangerous. She could create factions, stir up trouble, want power for herself. I overlooked your learning because it would never pose a threat to me. You came from nowhere and have no connections. I made you, and you know I could unmake you with the snap of the fingers. You would never be a threat to me, would you?"

"No, no, of course not." her eyes were downcast, her voice low.

"Then," he said, his voice smooth as silk, "I expect you to follow my wishes in this matter. To the full."

"Yes, Sire. Of course." She bowed her head.

His hand was under her chin, tilting her face towards him. He looked into her eyes, as his lips brushed hers. "Go and get your lute," he said lightly. "I'd like you to sing for me."

She did as she was bidden, thinking that the mothers had won after all. They knew Xerxes better than she did. Her singing that night was lacklustre, but afterwards Xerxes comforted her with kisses.

The disappointment she suffered lasted only for a few days. She accepted that there were some things that could not be changed. Sarcon's presence was a great consolation to her at this time. She came to rely on him, grateful for the information he gave her about Mordecai, and about other goings-on at the palace. She remembered Xerxes' warning not to trust any one, and she wondered if she should trust Sarcon quite so much.

Yet she was sure that he loved her. She could read the signs, although he never spoke the words that might betray it. Sometimes when he looked at her, she glimpsed his feelings, and wondered if her own eyes mirrored them. She loved him too, but her destiny did not lie with him. She belonged here, in the palace, whatever difficulties she had to face. Somewhere in the deep recesses of her heart there was a special place, locked tight, that was especially for him. But nothing must ever jeopardize her position as queen. That was the most important thing for her. It always had been.

She reckoned without the force of circumstances that were already gathering momentum, which would place her in the position where she would have to risk her crown or face certain death.

# CHAPTER 11

H aman's star continued to rise. Sarcon, who heard it from Mordecai, brought the news to Esther. Xerxes had made Haman Prime Minister.

It all happened, he told her, at a meeting of the Inner Council. Xerxes put forward a plan whereby some revenues intended for the satrapies could be diverted into the royal treasury. He meant to use the money to build a new arena for chariot-racing. The Inner Council refused to sanction the expenditure, contending that the arena in current use was perfectly adequate, and they were adamant that they should not deprive the satrapies of their revenues. Xerxes was determined to have his way, and Haman, seeing his opportunity to win favour, devised a plan which would please the king. He suggested that they should invite the satrapies to contribute a pre-determined sum of money for the building of the arena, where teams of charioteers from the satrapies could compete annually for a grand trophy. In this way, the satrapies would feel that they were getting a return for their money.

The members of the Inner Council debated the new plan, and finally consented, provided that the satrapies gave their approval. Xerxes was so delighted with the outcome that he announced that he was making Haman Prime Minister, since he had shown such initiative and wisdom.

"The king has made a bad move," said Sarcon. "He will

live to regret it. I think we are in for troublous times in Shushan, with a man like that at the head of government."

It was not long before he was proved right. Stories began to emerge of bribery and corruption. Haman was subverting the justice of the king, and lining his pockets at the same time. Xerxes was quite happy to leave Haman in charge while he spent more and more time watching the races and seeing to the building of the new arena. People began to realize Haman's great power, and would bow low whenever he appeared. Some of the courtiers even went down on their knees to make sure that Haman noticed them. Gradually it became an expected part of the protocol of the palace, but not everyone observed it. Mordecai alone of all the officials in the palace refused to bow down when Haman appeared. The first time it happened, Haman pretended not to notice, but inwardly he seethed with rage. When it happened again and again, Haman, who now regarded obeisance as his due, decided to broach the matter with the king.

"Your majesty. there is a small matter I would like to discuss with you. Your loyal subjects hold you in so much honour and esteem that when even I appear, as the representative of the royal person, they bow down before me. However, some are not sure that it is the proper thing to do. Would it be possible to have an order in council to the effect that it is mandatory, so that all will know what is required?"

The king stared at Haman in surprise, and gave a short laugh.

"You're very zealous for my honour, Haman. To the point of being obsessed with it. Do you really think the matter is so important?"

Haman bowed low so that the king would not see his irritation.

"My lord king, people like to know where they stand, and when the little things are attended to, it is my experience that the big things take care of themselves. It is merely a point of protocol, sire."

"Oh of course," said the king dryly. "Protocol! Very well, if it will please you, it certainly can't do any harm. But there's no need for an order in council. Just issue an order yourself. Now can we talk of something else?" Xerxes was thoroughly bored with the whole subject.

"By all means, sire." Haman bowed again, this time to hide his satisfaction. This would fix Mordecai! He would not dare to disobey now!

So the order went out from Haman's office, that all should bow to him, as the king's Prime Minister. It became mandatory that all the officials of the palace should observe it. One of the officials, Varensis by name, laughed at Mordecai.

"You'll have to bow to Haman now, just like the rest of us."

"No," he told them, " I believe that I should bow only to the king, and kneel before God."

"But Ahura Mazda, the good spirit, does not require us to kneel before him," said another.

"Look," said Mordecai, "I am a Jew. I belong to the minority of captive people. I believe the God I worship is the only true God. Only before him will I kneel, and I will bow before no one but the king."

"You're mad Mordecai." insisted Verensis. "Don't you know that you are putting yourself in danger? Haman will not stand for it He'll have your head."

"So be it," said Mordecai calmly. "My God is more important to me than Haman. Let him do what he will."

"But Haman is the king's favourite" said Varensis. "See

all the honours he has heaped on him. They will say you insult the king."

"Never." Mordecai was emphatic. "I honour the king. I am completely loyal to him."

"Well, if you won't listen . . ." Varensis shrugged his shoulders. The others shook their heads. They respected and liked Mordecai, and did not want to see him punished.

Not long afterwards, Agog, Haman's son, came to his father in the office.

"Father, I found something interesting. It's about Mordecai, the one who refuses to bow to you. He's not Persian. He's a Jew one of the minority peoples. The Jews keep their customs and worship their own god. They remain separate and refuse to be assimilated. That's why Mordecai won't kneel before you."

"So that's it." A slow smile spread across his face. "I knew there was something different about him. A Jew. A curse on all Jews! We Amalekites have an old score to settle with them. This may be our chance."

"But father," said Agog, looking puzzled, "what are you talking about? What's this about Amalekites? Are we not Persian born?"

"Yes, yes, of course," said Haman, hastily. "You need not concern yourself with that. The important thing is Mordecai. It happened again today, you know. Yes," he nodded, as Agog looked surprised. "Even after the order was read, he still refused to bow. But this time he has gone too far." He thought for a moment. "How many of these people are there in the country?"

"I don't know exactly. Thousands, probably. They remain different because they worship this god of theirs."

"Hmm." Haman pondered. "It would be really smart to get

rid of them all at once. That's it!" he shouted, slapping his hand on the table. "I'll get at Mordecai through his people. Yes, now I can make plans."

"What plans, father?"

"Never mind. Send for the magicians. Go! Go!"

When the magicians arrived, Haman ordered them to cast lots to find the most auspicious day to put his plan into action. They decided, after much consultation, that the thirteenth day of the twelfth month was the most suitable.

His next step was to enlist the help of the king. He waited for a suitable moment, when Xerxes was in a relaxed mood, before he brought up the subject.

"My lord king," he began," I have a matter that I wish to bring before you. There is a certain race of people scattered all over the empire, and found in every province. They observe customs that are different, customs which go against the laws of the empire. It is not in your best interests to tolerate them. If it please your majesty, issue a decree that they are to be put to death. If you do, I guarantee that I will be able to put three hundred and seventy-five tons of silver into the royal treasury, for any purpose which your majesty shall devise."

Xerxes was busy poring over the plans for the new arena. Reluctantly he gave his attention to what Haman was saying.

"Who are these people?"

"They are captive from the west, from Babylon and Judah."

Xerxes frowned, and fiddled with his ring. "You know it has always been our policy, and the policy of my father, Darius, and my grandfather, Cyrus, that the minority peoples should be treated equally within the empire, and that they should be free to pursue their own traditions and to worship in their own way. I see no need to change that policy. It has been a unifying influence in the country."

"Yes, sire, but these people, the Jews, refuse to integrate. There cannot be unity as long as they feel they can ignore the laws of Persia whenever they conflict with their ideas. You don't know how subversive these people are. They encourage people to defy our laws. Surely refusing to obey the law is treason, punishable by death."

Xerxes stroked his chin. This was just the kind of problem that he hated. But obedience to the law was of paramount importance. He was very sensitive on that point. Otherwise the empire would not hold together. It was one of his biggest fears that he would fail to hold the empire that had been so hard won by his ancestors. Suddenly he thought of his beloved queen Vashti. Even she had not been spared when she had refused to obey the king. If these people did not obey the law, that was worse than disobeying the king, and they ought to be punished. Haman was right, but still... He shook his head and sighed.

Haman saw that he was wavering and added a little more encouragement.

"I wouldn't have mentioned it, sire, except that I feel it should be dealt with at once, before it gets out of hand. As a lesson to others. If we let it go, who knows how far it will spread."

Xerxes had had enough. He wanted to get back to his plans.

"Oh very well," he said. "You deal with it. Here is my ring." He removed the heavy seal ring from his finger. "That will give you all the authority you need to do whatever is necessary. As for the money, it's yours to use any way you want. Now, don't bother me any more." He turned back to the plans on the table.

"As you wish, my lord king." Haman bowed and left, scarcely able to contain his glee. He could hardly wait to put his plan into action.

He called for the secretaries and told them to prepare a proclamation.

"Take down what I say, and make sure every governor and satrap in the empire gets a copy. Translate it into every language and system of writing used in the empire. Then he dictated the following:

> This proclamation is issued in the name of King Xerxes, under his authority and sealed with his seal.
>
> To all satraps, governors and officials in the Persian Empire:
>
> Be it known that on the thirteenth day of the twelfth month, all peoples belonging to the captive peoples of Judah, namely all who call themselves Jews, young and old, are to be eliminated by whatever means necessary. There are to be no exceptions. Furthermore, all their possessions are to be confiscated. Preparations to carry out this order are to be commenced without delay.
>
> This proclamation is made in every province of the land. Let the king's will be done.

When Haman finished dictating, he saw that all the secretaries were looking at him, dismay evident on their faces.

"Well, what are you staring at?" he demanded harshly. "See to it that you get this done as quickly as possible. And not a word of this to anyone or I shall have your heads."

The secretaries bent their heads and set to work. They had no doubt that Haman meant every word he said.

Haman was full of impatience for the next few days. He kept the scribes working constantly until all the proclamations were ready. He used the king's ring to set the seal on each one. When they were all ready he took a copy to show the king.

"This will rid the empire of your enemies once and for all!" he said.

"Let's drink to that," cried the king, cynically. He and Haman spent the rest of the evening drinking, while the couriers set off across the land, carrying their deathly message.

The proclamation was read out in the city square at Shushan the next day. The citizens, many of them Jews, were stunned.

"This is mass murder!" they protested. "Massacre!" The whole city was thrown into confusion, for even those who were not Jews suddenly felt insecure. Once that kind of killing started, who knew where it would end up?

As it happened Mordecai was at home in his own house when he heard the news. He could hardly believe his ears. Such a thing was unheard of, that decent law-abiding citizens should have to face death for no apparent reason. He went to the city square, where a huge crowd of people had gathered. He heard a man addressing the people, and moving forward, he recognized Barzai, the goldsmith.

"Let us march to the palace, and demand to see the king!" he urged. There were shouts of agreement. Mordecai at once perceived the danger, and strode quickly to the front.

"Fellow Jews!" he shouted. "Let us give thought to what action we should take. If we march on the palace, they will say we are rebelling against the king's authority, and they will feel justified in killing us all without delay. We have time on our side. There are still some months before this order will be carried out. Let us use this time to ask God for deliverance. Let every one of you go to your house, and pray to the God of our fathers, Abraham and Isaac, to save us all, fast and pray that he will send an advocate who will plead our cause before the king. Let us all behave with caution, and give our enemies no cause to annihilate us, while we search for a way of escape."

He finished speaking, and while there were some who still wanted immediate action, most of the people recognized the wisdom of Mordecai's words, and agreed to follow his advice. The sight of the women weeping tore at Mordecai's heart. He went home and dressed in sackcloth, and covered his face with ashes. He walked through the city to the palace, and sat down outside the palace gates, for no one dressed in mourning clothes was allowed to enter.

*

Esther was sitting in the garden with some of her ladies when Bilkah came rushing up.

"Madam, I must talk with you." She seemed upset, and Esther drew her to one side.

"What's the matter, Bilkah?"

"It's Mordecai! He sits outside the palace gate dressed in sackcloth and ashes! They won't let him in" Bilkah was nearly in tears.

"What! Who told you this?" She thought it strange that Mordecai had not thought to let her know what was wrong. Perhaps something had happened to Zinna.

"It was Meshullam." Meshullam was one of the keepers of the Harem. "He was at the gate when it happened. The guards wouldn't let him in!"

"I must find out what is wrong," said Esther desperately.

"Send Hathach to me." Bilkah, glad of something practical to do, went off in search of him.

Esther paced up and down the garden. What on earth had got into Mordecai? He knew better than to appear at the palace gates in mourning dress. It couldn't be a death of someone close, other wise he would not be sitting outside the palace. When Hathach appeared she ordered him to go and find out from Mordecai what was wrong.

Hathach found Mordecai sitting in the square outside the palace gate.

"The queen has sent me to inquire the meaning of all this," he said, noting the sackcloth and the face streaked with ash.

Mordecai groaned. "It is bad news, terrible news. We have survived so much as a people, so much suffering, so much oppression. We all thought it was behind us, a thing of the past. It was bad enough for our people to be carried off by Assyrians to Babylon, and then when Cyrus and Darius both brought our people here. We thought that nothing worse could befall us, we thought we were safe here. Where else could they send us? But now they want to wipe us out altogether!"

Hathach listened in silence as Mordecai poured his heart out, not understanding what he was talking about. When Mordecai stopped he said:

"Queen Esther is concerned about you. She asks how she may help."

"Doesn't she know what has happened? About the proc-lamation?" Seeing the mystified look on Hathach's face, Mordecai showed him a copy of the proclamation that he had managed to procure.

"Look at it! The destruction of the Jews! Take it to the queen. Show her what King Xerxes has done!"

He handed Hathach the paper, then a thought struck him.

"Wait! It has just come to me. Queen Esther may be able to save us. Yes, she must speak to the king, plead our cause. Beg him to have mercy on our people. Go, tell her what I said!"

Hathach went back to Esther with the proclamation. She read it with growing dismay. It left her speechless. Why had Xerxes done this? She could think of nothing that would explain his actions. When Hathach relayed to her Mordecai's message, she was even more astounded.

"How can I, a mere woman, influence the king and his advisers? Mordecai of all people should realize that I have no power. I can't believe he is serious."

Hathach was very curious. "Your majesty, when Mordecai spoke he mentioned 'your people'. Are you one of them?"

"What? Oh, he was talking about his own people. Perhaps he got mixed up."

"Yes, of course," said Hathach diplomatically.

Privately he suspected there was more to it than that. "What shall I tell Mordecai?"

"Tell him what he asks is impossible. I can't go and see the king uninvited, and it might be long enough before the king sends for me. Tell him he will have to think of another way."

"Very good, madam." Hathach bowed and went away.

Esther, however, was deeply troubled. It was a terrible thing that was going to happen to her people, but there was nothing she could do to help. No one knew she was a Jew and Mordecai himself had told her not to divulge it to any one. How could she come out now and say she was one of them? There must be some other way, if only she could think of it. She took the proclamation and studied it again.

'Sealed and enacted by Xerxes.'

There was no way around that. Once it was law it was

immutable. Even the king himself had no power to change it. She thought of all her friends in the city, Jacob, the Shulmans, Zinna, and all the Jews scattered throughout the empire. It was unthinkable that they all should die. "They are all doomed!" she breathed. "Doomed!" She put her head down on her hands and wept.

All that day she could think of nothing else. She let it be known that she was not feeling well and was not to be disturbed. She lay on her bed and wept intermittently. She was going to lose all her family and friends. Mordecai himself could not escape. She would be the only one left. She tried to think of ways by which they might escape the death sentence, but always she came up against the immutable law of the Medes and the Persians that could not be repealed.

After dark, Bilkah came to her and whispered, "Madam, Sarcon is in the library and wishes to speak to you."

Sarcon, thought Esther. Perhaps he will be willing to help. She made her way to the library and found Sarcon seated at a table piled high with scrolls. He was alone. He rose as she entered, and beckoned to her to follow him.

"Is it not dangerous?" she whispered. "We will be seen."

"No, I have arranged everything. The king's spies are elsewhere. Trust me."

She felt she had no option but to comply. He led her through a door into the corridor. Making sure the way was clear, he took her through a maze of back rooms and passages that she didn't know existed. She had no idea where she was when finally he stopped at a door and drew her inside. A lamp burning on a table lit up the room. It was some kind of storeroom, filled with merchandise of all kinds.

"This opens onto the outer wall," he whispered. "Don't worry, you are quite safe here. I've made sure of that. Wait here. I'll send Mordecai to you. He wants to speak to you."

He left her then and she sat down on a box, trying hard to calm her fears. After a few minutes the door opened and a hooded figure entered. She had a moment of panic until she recognized him. Without a word she rushed to him and he held her close.

"What is happening, cousin? Are you all right?"

"Yes, I'm all right for the time being."

They sat down, Esther still clinging to his hand.

"Esther, my dear, I had to talk to you. This is a very grave situation. You don't seem to understand that the Jews will all be wiped out."

"I do! I do!" she protested.

"Then you must help us."

"I? What can I do? You know I can't interfere in the affairs of state. I'm only a woman, after all," she added, a trace of bitterness in her voice.

Mordecai smiled wryly. "That never stopped you before!" Then his face became serious. "Don't think you will escape, Esther. When Haman finds out you are a Jew, he will kill you too."

"Haman?" She looked astonished. "What has he got to do with this?"

"He has everything to do with it! Who do you think thought up this plan? Not Xerxes. It's not his style. He may have his faults, but killing innocent people is not one of them. No, Haman is getting rid of our people because of me. He has always hated me, and especially since I refused to bow down to him. He is an Amalekite, you know, and they have always hated the Jews. He wanted to get me, and he saw a way to do it through our people. So you see, you will not escape either."

"But he doesn't know that I am a Jew!" she protested.

Mordecai regarded her steadily. "How long before he finds out?"

She was silent. She knew very well that Haman would like her out of the way. He always resented her closeness to the king, and already he had come between them. It would only need a whisper to orchestrate her downfall. She suddenly remembered Hathach's question. He had only to voice his doubts to someone and then they wouldpoint the finger at her

"What do you want me to do?"

"You must go to the king and plead for our lives."

At his words, Esther jumped up in consternation.

"The king hasn't sent for me for more than a month. Who knows when he will summon me again!"

"Then you must go to him, said Mordecai quietly. "There is no other way."

Her face drained of colour.

"You must be out of your mind! It is certain death for me if I go to the king without being summoned. And even if the king holds out the golden sceptre to me and bids me to approach him, there is no way of knowing how he will react. He once warned me not to trust him. At the very least, I might be banished from the palace. I cannot risk my position. This has been the goal of my life, and now you ask me to risk it all?"

Mordecai moved away from her and breathed deeply, struggling to remain calm. Then he turned to face her and spread his hands. "What has happened to you, Esther?" he asked softly. "Have you forgotten who you are?"

She couldn't meet his eyes. "No, no, of course not!"

The grim look returned to his face, and he pressed her relentlessly.

"Don't imagine that you will escape just because you are in the palace! If you keep quiet at a time like this, God will find another way to save his people, but you will die, because you withheld your help." He paused. "Who knows, maybe it was for such a time as this you were made queen!"

Esther's eyes seemed to grow larger. Mordecai's last words had silenced her. Was it true? Had she been made queen because she was part of God's plan to save her people? It was an astounding thought. All this time she had taken it for granted that to be queen was the sole purpose of her life. She had never thought beyond it. Now she had to face a far greater challenge. To be an instrument of history, responsible for the fate of thousands of people. She was shaken to the core of her being. Finally she faced the hopelessness of her situation. She was doomed if she acted, doomed if she did nothing. Then she rallied her resources. If I am to go down, she told herself, I might as well go down trying to help my people.

"All right," she told Mordecai. "I'll do it. But I am not strong enough to do it on my own. I will need all the support I can get. Get all the Jews in Shushan to hold a fast and pray for me. Don't eat or drink anything for three days and nights. My ladies and I will do the same. After that I will go to the king, even though it is against the court protocol. If I must die as a consequence, then I must die."

Mordecai put his hands on her shoulders.

"Bless you, Esther! You have always been strong. You have more strength than you know. We'll do exactly as you say. We will pray for you without ceasing. Now I must go."

He hugged her close for a minute. "Don't be afraid. God is on our side. We would not have survived till now had it been otherwise."

When Sarcon returned she was still standing where Mordecai had left her. Tears were streaming down her cheeks and her body was trembling all over. She looked up as she entered, and seeing the despair in her face, he was beside her in an instant, his arms gathering her to him in a close embrace. He held her, caressing her hair softly, murmuring words of love in her ear.

"I've never stopped loving you, Esther. You are the reason I stayed here in the palace. As long as you need me, I'll be here. At first, I thought your talk of destiny was just the fancy of a young girl, but as I watched you take your place beside the king, I realized that you were indeed meant to be queen." He paused. "Though even in that I was mistaken."

She lifted her head to look at him. "Mistaken?"

"I mean that this your real destiny, this hour. When you are asked to risk your life on behalf of your people. Yes," he said in answer to her unspoken question. "Mordecai has told me everything. It is a desperate situation. He would not ask you to do this if there was any other way." He looked into her eyes. "You must be strong, Esther. I know you are strong. You have shown it in the past months, when life with the king has not been easy."

He must watch me very closely, she thought.

As if he read her mind he went on: "I made it my business to know every detail of your life at the palace. Don't worry, I did it for your protection. And Lady Bilkah keeps me informed. We both love you and would do anything for you. You are surrounded by people who love you. So never think that you are alone." He held her closer. "I wanted to take you away from all this. Instead it has been my destiny to stay and serve you."

"I know," she whispered. The comfort of his arms around her, his body close to hers, was indescribable. She wanted this moment to last forever. If only she could remain here in his arms, sheltered, protected, never having to face the fiery trials ahead. Time passed, measured in heartbeats, eternal and fleeting. A whole lifetime of love with Sarcon condensed into a few moments. She lifted her face to him and they stared into each other's eyes. Gently, very gently, he laid his lips on hers, a kiss with infinite tenderness, full of the significance of what might have been. It was too much for her. With a soft moan she clung to him, her arms around his neck, and kissed him with all the pent-up emotion and passion of years. For a few moments they were lost in each other, overcome with the excitement of expressing their feelings at last. Then he was drawing back, loosening himself from her grasp, unclasping her hands from his neck.

"Come, we must get back. Our time has run out."

With a great effort she stifled a sob and stood mutely by while he snuffed out the lamp. Taking her hand, he led her noiselessly from the storeroom, through the passageways, back to the little room off the library where Bilkah was waiting anxiously.

"Oh, madam, I was afraid something had gone wrong!"

"It's all right, Bilkah." Esther found to her surprise that she felt quite composed. They waited while Sarcon searched through the library. In a few minutes he was back.

"There's no one there," he told them. "Take this scroll—it's the one you came to fetch. The guards at the entrance have just come on duty. They can have no idea how long you have been here. Go now!" His voice was urgent.

Quickly they made their way to the entrance. The guards eyed them but made no comment. They were used to seeing the queen coming and going from the library.

As soon as they were safely back in the queen's apartments, Esther sat down on the couch, and motioning Bilkah to sit down beside her, she told her everything. "You must help me, Bilkah," she finished.

Bilkah, visibly overcome, assured Esther that she and the other Jewish women would help her in any way they could. They decided too, that they should keep their activities secret. No one must know that Esther was Jewish until she told the king herself.

Only when she had dismissed Bilkah did Esther allow herself to think of the scene with Sarcon. At first she felt ashamed that she should have given way to passion, but the more she thought about it she realized that she needed at that point to feel the closeness of another human being, to be more than her solitary self, to be identified wholly with someone else. Sarcon, because of his great love for her had recognized her need, and in so doing had given her the necessary strength. She would never forget these moments, just as she knew with certainty that they would never be repeated. She fell asleep, her mind at peace, ready to face her ordeal.

For three days and nights Esther and her women fasted and prayed. During that time she searched her soul. It had been a long time since she had taken her God into account. Surrounded by the worshippers of Ahura Mazda, she had forsaken the uniqueness of her faith. Now she decided to go back to it and find strength there as her people had done for generations. She got out a scroll of the psalms of David, and found comfort as she read the words aloud.

What time my heart is overwhelmed,
Lead me to the rock that is higher than I.
I am in trouble, God. Listen to my prayer.
I am afraid of my enemies. I am gripped with fear.

Mordecai's words burned into her being -- "It was for such a time as this that you were made queen." She had always thought it was her destiny to become queen, but she had never gone beyond that. To her it had all seemed an end in itself.

Now she had to face the fact that her destiny required more of her. There was a price to pay. The queen's crown which she had striven to acquire, and which for four years she had considered to belong to her, had never been reality hers to possess. It was a blow to her pride and self-esteem. She felt very vulnerable. She thought of the way she had found favour with the king, and been accepted with the people, not just because she was worthy of it, but because God had willed it. It would have happened anyway without all her strivings. All she had to do was to be herself. She understood for the first time in her life that her sense of herself, with all her strengths and weaknesses, was the important thing. Because of who I am, she mused, with all that makes me unique, I will be able to do all that is asked of me. As long as I am true to myself and what I believe. For the first time she felt at one with herself and with her destiny. Destiny is not something you achieve, it is something you live up to, she told herself. Then she read how David rose above his fears:

I will trust in God, and not be afraid.
He will save me and confound my enemies.

In this way, she thought her way through from despair to calm and peace.

She slept soundly that night, and in the morning she called for her maids to dress her in her royal robes. They brought out the blue and white dress of heavy silk, and the blue robe trimmed with peacock feathers. Bilkah dressed her hair, piling it high on her head to make her look as regal as possible. Then she took the gold crown studded with blue and white precious stones, and with shaking hands placed it on her head. The tension among her ladies was almost tangible, but Esther, in contrast, manifested a calm serenity. She thought of how, as a young girl, she used to practise assuming an air of complete calm, when inside she was churning up with excitement. She smiled at herself. She would need every ounce of outward calm when she faced the king.

She looked at herself critically in her mirror. Her face was pale, despite the rose powder Minna had patted on her cheeks. Bilkah had surpassed herself in dressing her hair. It was set in layers of curls so that the crown seemed to grow out of them. She had never looked more impressive.

It was time to go. She had chosen the time of day carefully. Xerxes would still be in the Hall of Petitions, but the deputations would be finished, and most of the officials of the court would already have dispersed to other duties. With only a few of his close advisers around him, he would be taking stock of the morning's business. She gathered her women around her for a last prayer, and with them chanted a verse:

Our trust is in the name of the Lord
he will give us the victory
Blessed be His name for ever and ever.

Some of them were weeping as she left the room, followed by Bilkah and Kenida. They were not sure if they would ever see her again.

Esther made her way slowly through the corridors and halls of the palace. She spoke to no one, although she was aware of the stares and whispers as she passed. At last she came to the courtyard of the Hall of Petitions. She told her ladies to leave her. Standing alone, she recalled her first visit to the king, all those years ago. I thought that was the test, she remembered, but this is the real test. Taking a deep breath, she walked forward and stood in the doorway, directly facing the king.

# CHAPTER 12

When Xerxes looked up from the scroll he was studying and saw Esther in the doorway he could hardly believe his eyes. He was astonished that she should be there at all, and her appearance was so striking, so imposing, dressed as she was in full royal regalia, that he could only gaze at her in awe. His advisers, equally impressed, looked on in silence. What a sight, he thought to himself, what a beauty! Was there ever a queen like Esther? Then he became aware of her unusual pallor, and even as he looked at her, she trembled and swayed and he thought she was going to faint. It dawned on him belatedly that she was terrified. Quickly he picked up his sceptre and held it out towards her. Her eyes never left his as she moved towards him. My beautiful Esther, he thought, I have neglected you. I'd almost forgotten how beautiful you are. I must make it up to you.

She touched the tip of the sceptre and knelt before him. Taking her hand he raised her up. He looked into her huge dark eyes and smiled.

"My dear Queen Esther," he said. his voice gentle, "what can I do for you? You shall have whatever you want . . . even up to half of my kingdom!"

For a few moments she hesitated, gathering her strength.

"If it please your majesty," she said, "I would like you and Haman to be my guests tonight at a banquet I have prepared for you."

He understood at once that she had something to ask him, but she did not want to make her request publicly here in front of his advisers.

"I shall be delighted to come to your banquet," he answered. "I shall make your request known to Haman, and I'm sure he will be equally delighted. I thank you for your kind invitation."

"Thank you, my lord king," she said, bowing low, and as she straightened up Xerxes saw the relief in her eyes. It must be something really important, he said to himself, for her to risk coming here like this. He smiled at her reassuringly.

"Until tonight, then," he said.


Esther returned to her ladies, trembling with relief. Quickly she told them all that had transpired.

"A banquet?" said Bilkah. "You didn't tell us you were planning a banquet!"

"I only thought of it at the last minute. I realized as soon as I walked into the room that I couldn't speak freely to the king, not with all his advisers listening. I was going to put myself at a disadvantage, having to confess my origins in front of the court officials. The king would be at a disadvantage too, because he would have to uphold the law. No, I felt the only way was to appeal to the king in private, and it would have to be on my ground, where I have some kind of control. It was then I thought of the banquet."

"That was a brilliant idea," said Kenida, and they all agreed. "But why did you invite Haman too?"

"To please the king, because he is his favourite. And also

to make sure the king would come. If I did not invite Haman he might make some excuse to keep the king from coming, as he has done before."

"You think of everything," Kenida said with admiration.

"We have to be wise as serpents," said Esther, "and use every means we can. There is too much at stake. We must not be simple-minded when we are dealing with the likes of Haman. We have to sharpen our wits so that he will not succeed in his evil designs. Now, we must get to work and plan everything for tonight so that my banquet will be prefect in every detail."

When Xerxes and Haman arrived at the Queen's Palace, Esther knew a moment of fear, but she walked forward calmly and did obeisance before the king. She received Haman with a graciousness she did not feel. He was her enemy, and she would expose him as such, only it had to be exactly the right moment.

She led them to the dining hall, where tables were laid with all kinds of delicacies. A troupe of musicians played soft music at the far end. Silk tapestries embroidered in vivid pinks and greens lined the walls, and everywhere there were masses of flowers whose scent pervaded the air with fragrant sweetness. Hundreds of candles bathed the room with soft light. Thick carpets covered the tile floor, and the couches and chairs were piled with silk cushions in a myriad of colours. Esther, and her servants had combed the palace, looking for vases and artifacts that would add to the opulence, and the result was an ambiance of luxury and beauty. She had made every effort to create an effect which would appeal to the senses. Esther herself was no less of an adornment to the room, in a gown of purple silk, its low neckline encrusted with tiny amethysts. She wore a gold necklace and earrings made for her by Jacob in an unusual openwork design, and her hair was held in place by a gold clasp studded with more amethysts. With her stunning appearance and charm of manner she set out to keep her guests entertained.

Xerxes was enchanted with her, it was plain to see, as he laughed and chatted in his most relaxed manner. Haman, for his part, was filled with a sense of his own importance at being present at this exclusive royal dinner. He imagined that the queen had realized he was worth cultivating, as the person with the ear of the king, and he surpassed himself with courtliness and gallantry. Esther appeared to be receptive to his flattery, and gave not the slightest hint of her deep distrust and fear.

After dinner they sat on the cushioned sofas while the wine servants filled their goblets.

"Now, Queen Esther," the king said, sipping his wine, "tell me what is on your mind. Whatever you want, I will give it to you, up to half my empire."

Haman gave the king a wary glance.

It was the first he had heard of a request. His eyes narrowed. Just what was the queen planning to ask for. He looked at her suspiciously, and she, noticing the expression on his face, felt instinctively that this was not the right moment, when Haman was on his guard. She must not arouse his suspicions in any way. Turning to the king with her most charming smile she said:

"If your majesty is kind enough to grant me my request, I would like you and Haman to be my guests tomorrow night at another banquet. At that time I will tell you what I want."

She looked at them both engagingly, and they accepted with pleasure.

Haman was relieved. The queen's request was obviously

nothing of any importance. Probably just a woman's ploy to get them to come again. Why should I mind, he thought, as long as she invites me too. It will be good for my image, when everyone hears that I'm being asked a second time. And, give the queen her due, she really knows how to entertain.

Another thought entered his head which he quickly suppressed. He would never risk his position by making any untoward overtures to the queen, but he couldn't help being aware that she was a very desirable woman.

Haman escorted the king back to the palace and then set off to his own house, full of good humour. As he was leaving the Administration building, he passed Mordecai, who was sitting near the door, talking to an official. The official rose quickly when he saw Haman and got down on his knees as Haman approached, but Mordecai did not move. Haman was furious although he gave no indication that he had noticed Mordecai, smiling instead at the official.

He went on his way, his good humour turned to ashes. He felt that his evening had been ruined, but then he remembered the fate that was in store for Mordecai and his good humour surfaced again. By the time he reached home he was in such high spirits that he decided to have an impromptu party. He called his wife and family and some of his closest friends to join him. When everybody was served with wine he told them that he was celebrating his good fortune. He boasted to them of his riches, his family of fine sons, his position as Prime Minister, second only to the king himself.

"As if all this was not enough, the queen put on a banquet just for the king and me. And to show me that it was not just a one-time event, she invited me back tomorrow night to another banquet. What do you think of that?"

Haman beamed round his friends. They were all suitably

impressed with his achievements, and they congratulated him on his success. He received their congratulations with satisfaction. As far as he was concerned he had reached the top. He was second to the king in power. Even the queen recognized that. He could now contemplate her with equanimity. He had nothing to fear from her. He had placed himself between her and the king, and he meant to stay there. Then his face clouded.

"None of this means anything," he told his friends, "as long as I see that Jew Mordecai, sitting at the entrance to the palace, and not paying me any respect!"

His friends commiserated with him, and put forward various suggestions as to how he should deal with Mordecai.

"You are powerful enough now," they said. "You don't have to put up with him. You can ask the king to get rid of him. Better still, why don't you have a gallows made, so that there will be no delay. If you ask the king in the morning, he will be hanged by noon, and you can go to the banquet happy."

Haman brightened up at this idea. "Yes, it would be such a relief to have him out of the way. I can easily make up some story that will annoy the king and he will be only too glad to leave the details of his punishment to me."

His wife looked at him in awe. "You are so brilliant, my husband. It is only right that you should want to rid yourself of someone who refuses to show you the respect you deserve."

So it was decided that he would order the gallows the next day, and he went to bed a happy man.

*

In the king's palace, it was a different story. Dining with Esther had invoked in the king all kinds of pleasant memories. He lay awake remembering the happy times they had had together, the evenings of fun and laughter they had shared in the company of the ladies. When did it change? he asked himself. In truth he had to admit that he had exchanged it for drinking orgies with Haman and his cronies. The thought that he had deprived himself of all the pleasures of Esther's companionship, the warmth of her personality, and the uncomplicated friendship of those who were not motivated by self-interest, made him feel uncomfortable. Sleep eluded him, hour after hour, and at last he could stand it no longer. He called for his servant and ordered him to light the lamps. Then he sent for the Keeper of the Records, and ordered him to bring the official records of the empire.

Sarcon, (for he was the Keeper of the Records) was roused from his bed and hurried to do the king's bidding. The king asked him to read to him from the scrolls that covered the period since Esther became queen. When he came to the conspiracy plot of Bigthana and Teresh, the bodyguards that Mordecai had exposed, the king stopped him.

"How have we honoured and rewarded Mordecai for this?"

"Nothing had been done for him," replied Sarcon. Then he added, "It is part of Mordecai's duties to see rewards of that nature. He would not order a reward for himself."

"He is an unusual man," commented the king. "Most men would have taken advantage of a situation like that to fill their pockets."

"Mordecai is an honourable man, sire," Sarcon dared to say. "He is completely loyal to the service of the king. He probably thought it was no more than his duty."

"All the more reason for us to reward him. He really deserves a very special reward. It is a grave oversight on our part that he got no reward for saving my life."

He looked out the window. Daylight was already streaking the sky.

"Are any of my officials in the palace?" he asked. One of the servants went to find out.

At that moment, Haman entered the courtyard. He had risen early in order to see to the building of the gallows, and having given the workmen instructions, he was now at the palace to see the king before his morning auditions. He knew exactly what he would say to the king in order to convince him that Mordecai should be put to death. The servant spied him and returned to the king to report that Haman was at hand.

"Show him in," said the king.

Haman entered and bowed low, giving his usual morning greeting to the king, who wasted no time on preliminaries.

"Haman, there is someone I wish to honour in a very special way, but I am not sure of the best way to go about it. How do you think a person should be honoured for exceptional service to the king?"

Who could that be? Haman asked himself. Surely it can be none other than myself! There is none else of such importance in the kingdom. He considered how he would most like to be rewarded, then he answered:

"Have the royal robes brought out for this man, the robes you yourself have worn, for we Persians consider this to be the highest honour. Have a royal headpiece put on your own horse. Then have one of your highest noblemen dress the man in these robes and lead him, mounted on the horse, through the main streets of the city. Also, the nobleman shall announce to all as they go that this is the way the king rewards a man whom he wishes to honour."

"You think that would suffice?" asked the king. "Very well, see that it is done. Now hurry, get the robes and the horse ready. You yourself will do the honours. Lead him through the streets and so forth. Do everything just as you suggested. And I want it done today. We have wasted too much time already. It should have been done long ago. Go now and fetch him. You will probably find him at the entrance to the palace."

The colour drained from Haman's face. He realized with a shock that the king was not talking about him.

"But sire," he managed to ask, "who is the man to be honoured?"

"Oh, Mordecai, of course. Did I not say so?"

"Mordecai? Surely you are not going to honour him?" Haman's tone betrayed his rising desperation.

The king's eyes glittered. "Do you dare to question me?"

Haman hastened to make amends. "No, no, sire. I mean, for what reason do you honour him?"

"Because I owe him my life. And he is a loyal servant."

Haman blinked. He was having difficulty breathing. He opened his mouth and shut it again. There was no argument he could offer to shake the confidence of the king. In a daze he took his leave and went to carry out the king's orders. He felt as though his world had turned upside down. This was not the way it was supposed to be. He had envisioned himself rushing off to arrest Mordecai, and instead he had to honour him. And to add to his chagrin he was obliged to do all the honours himself. Why, oh, why had he not kept his mouth shut? But how could he have imagined that the king was talking about Mordecai? It was almost more than he could bear, yet he did not dare disobey the king's orders.

No one was more surprised than Mordecai when Haman, along with his assistants, came to give him the news that he was to be honoured by receiving the acclamation of the king and the people. Indeed, it would have been difficult to discover who was the more reluctant, Haman or Mordecai. On the one hand was Mordecai, under the sentence of death, being held up to honour by the man who was the cause of his condemnation. On the other hand, Haman found himself having to acclaim the man who had publicly refused to show him respect, whose death he had planned, and for whom he was having a gallows built.

Mordecai, still shocked at the turn of events, allowed himself to be led off to the king's wardrobe, and dressed in the king's robes, for it would have been a grave insult to refuse the king's reward. Then he was escorted to the courtyard where the king's white charger waited, complete with royal trappings. Mordecai got on the horse, and Haman, trying to hide his distaste, led him out through the main entrance gate. They were followed by a troop of the king's guard. Every so often Haman had to call out the announcement:

"See how the king regards the man he wishes to honour!"

Hearing the noise, people came running from all corners to see the procession. When they saw it was Mordecai who was being honoured, they clapped and cheered, and the cheering burned into Haman's soul. It was all he could do to keep going, but to save his dignity he acted as though the proceedings had his complete approval. Over the bridge they went, and down through the main thoroughfare until they came to the city square. There a large crowd gathered to listen to Haman's announcement. The Jews, all Mordecai's friends, wondered what was happening. Here was Mordecai, whom they had last seen in sackcloth and ashes, receiving the highest honours the king could give. It was quite incredible. Mordecai, for his part, when he saw his friends, smiled and waved to them. They rushed forward and showered him with congratulations, crowding round so that the procession had to stop.

Haman's face grew redder each time he had to make the announcement, and he had to grit his teeth to force himself to go on. Finally when the procession had filed round the city square, they started on their way back, only to find the way lined by even more people. Mordecai looked so handsome, dressed in the blue and white royal robes, with his black curly hair and beard, his white teeth flashing as he acknowledged the cheers of the onlookers, that they cheered even louder, and joined in the procession, making it a parade of triumph. Slowly they made their way back.

They were half way along the Processional Way, when a woman ran forward out of the crowd and stood before Haman and Mordecai. It was Alcytes, the prophetess. Such was the magnetism of her presence that the procession drew to a halt, and everyone waited with bated breath to hear what she had to say. Pointing her finger at Haman, she proclaimed in ringing tones:

> There will be war with Amalek from generation to generation until his name is blotted from remembrance of men! This is the word of the Lord.

In the moment of silence that followed, while everyone puzzled over her words, she turned and disappeared into the crowd. Haman stood, rooted to the spot, his face a deathly pallor. Of all the people there, only he and Mordecai realized the significance of the prophecy. In spite of himself Haman found his eyes drawn to Mordecai, who returned his gaze steadily. There was war between them, of that there was no doubt. Would the outcome be as Alcytes had said? From the expression on Haman's face it was evident that he feared the worst.

The restless champing of the horses brought Haman back

to the present. Throwing a venomous look at Mordecai, he motioned for the procession to continue.

At the palace the news had got around, and Bilkah rushed off to tell Esther.

"Madam, you'll never guess what has happened! Mordecai has been honoured by the king!"

"Honoured? What do you mean?"

Bilkah described the triumphant procession, and the circumstances that led to it. Esther was amazed at this development and could not contain her delight.

"Come, Bilkah, let's go out on the terrace, so that we will watch them return. This is wonderful news. It shows that the tide is turning."

"What do you mean, madam?"

"There is more to this than coincidence, Bilkah. I see it as a sign that Haman's star is waning, and Mordecai's is on the rise. This is a great encouragement for me. Tonight when I speak to the king, I will feel more confident that he will listen to my plea. Yes, it will make a great difference." She breathed a silent prayer of thankfulness. For the first time she began to hope firmly that God would deliver his people.

By the time the procession reached the palace gates, the crowd had swelled to hundreds. Esther watched from the terrace, as Mordecai acknowledged the people one more time, and then went through the palace entrance. Once in the courtyard, he got down from the horse, which was led away by the groom.

Haman kept his eyes averted. It was odious for him to have to look at this man, who had caused him so much frustration. He waited impatiently while Mordecai took off the fine robes. Then he carried them to the king's quarters and handed them to the king's eunuch. At last he could escape from the charade, and he hurried off to his own house. He could still hear the cheers of the crowd ringing in his ears, and see the gleeful looks on the faces of those who knew of his enmity to Mordecai. He put his hands over his face to hide his humiliation.

When he entered his house, his wife and friends gathered round him. They all had heard what happened, but they were eager to hear every detail from Haman himself, and to hear his explanation of the extraordinary turn of events. If he expected sympathy from them he was disappointed. Far from comforting him, they only added to his misery.

"It looks like you are losing your power, Haman," said his wife. "That Jew Mordecai will get the better of you yet, you mark my words!"

When she heard of Alcytes' prophecy she threw her shawl over her face and ran from the room.

"You certainly can't move against him just now," remarked his son. "But you are still Prime Minister. There will be other opportunities. Meantime you must act as if nothing happened."

Haman shook his head. All he could think of was his own humiliation and Mordecai's triumph. "I should have been the one honoured by the king! I should have kept quiet when the king asked my advice. If I had only known he meant to honour Mordecai, I would have suggested that he receive a gift of silver, or something like that. But to see that man wearing the king's robe! It doesn't bear thinking about!"

While they were talking, a servant came in to announce that the palace chamberlains had arrived to escort Haman to the queen's banquet.

Haman jumped up in consternation.

"The queen's banquet! I forgot all about it! I must bathe

and dress! I'll be late ... Oh, what a terrible day this has been! Tell the chamberlains to await me in the courtyard." He rushed off to get ready.

A servant led the two chamberlain to the courtyard behind the house and left there. They looked around, admiring the elaborate marble walkways, the flower-filled bowers, the rows of bronze statues. Then they noticed the gallows, half hidden behind a wing of the house. They went closer to investigate. It was obviously newly built, waiting to be transported to its destined location. One of the chamberlains, Harbonah by name, voiced the thought in the minds of them both.

"I wonder what poor wretch this is meant for?" He wandered about round the courtyard until he came across a servant who was loading casks on to a cart.

"Tell me, who's the one under the death sentence?" He nodded in the direction of the gallows.

"The Lord Haman has built it for Mordecai. He's our master's enemy. He was supposed to be hanged today at noon, but our master was away all day on the king's business. Probably the hanging will take place tomorrow."

Harbonah could hardly hide his surprise. He hurried back to the other eunuch and passed on the information.

"But I don't understand." said the other. "Why would Haman want to hang a man whom the king honoured? It doesn't make sense."

"Obviously the king doesn't know what's going on. Haman is mad because Mordecai won't bow down before him."

"Why won't he bow down? It's not wise to make an enemy of Haman."

"Mordecai is a Jew and it is against his religion to bow down before anyone but before his own god and the king."

"Well," shrugged Harbonah, "you heard the king's proclamation against the Jews. They are all going to be killed sooner or later."

"Imagine honouring a man one day and hanging him on the gallows the next!"

They were still discussing it when Haman emerged from the house, dressed in his finest robes. They hurried to his side to escort him to the Queen's palace. Harbonah eyed him warily. He looks a cold-blooded brute, he thought. I'd better show him as much respect as I can or I'll end up with my head in a noose!

*

Esther prepared carefully for the evening. She knew the time had come to confront Haman in the king's presence. As Minna brushed her hair she turned the matter over in her mind, wondering what would be the best way to tell the king. So much depended on how Xerxes reacted. Would he believe her, or would he take Haman's part? Haman had been the king's favourite for so long. With his cunning he had relieved Xerxes of so many onerous tasks, and had wormed his way into the king's good graces by pandering to his wishes, indulging his weaknesses, and always saying what the king wished to hear. She suspected that Xerxes was too shrewd to be taken in by Haman's machinations, but it suited him to go along with them. She had to believe that he would act independently, if he saw the need. If there was any blame to be laid, she thought, he would soon shift it to Haman.

Esther sighed. Xerxes had changed so much over the years. When she married him, he was always so dutiful in matters concerning the empire. He had been conscientious then, ever anxious to live up to the achievements of Darius, his father, and Cyrus, his illustrious grandfather. What had happened to the king who had reformed the administration of government so that the whole realm enjoyed peace and prosperity and was the envy of other countries? Somewhere along the line he had given up caring and allowed Haman to take charge. He must have known what kind of man he was, but in his self-indulgence he had ceased to care.

Despite all his protestations about carrying on the work of his ancestors, he had abandoned the principles on which they had built the empire, especially the principle of allowing freedom of worship to all his subjects. That was evident in his treatment of the Jews. Esther knew that Xerxes himself had no personal animosity to her people. He had just ceased to be vigilant on their behalf. Who knew what minority Haman would focus on next? It was high time that Haman was exposed, and she was the one who had to do it. The king's Inner Council could not do it because Haman was too good at covering his tracks, and it would be impossible to accuse him when he always carried out the king's wishes. No, she would have to be the one, and since she was under sentence of death anyway, she had nothing to lose. She smiled to herself.

*Look at you, Esther, the little orphan girl, going to save your country and your people! The crown has really gone to your head!* The she thought soberly of the people who were depending on her as their last chance of survival. *I truly am an instrument of destiny, but it is not the destiny I imagined when I came to the palace.* Suddenly she was no longer afraid or worried about the outcome of this evening. It was auspicious that the king had thought to honour Mordecai today of all days. Surely he would be open to her request. Bolstering her courage with these thoughts she went off to her robing room to dress for what was to be the most important evening of her life.

She stood in the reception hall, waiting for the arrival of her guests, resplendent this time in a dress of midnight blue, simply cut, except for the pleats that fanned out from below her knees as she walked. Minna had brushed her hair until it glistened and swept it up on top of her head, fastening it with gem-studded clasps. She was even more beautiful than she had been nearly five years before, when she first met the king. Her face had acquired a ripeness of beauty, and her poise and dignity had been enhanced by her years as queen. There was a strength there, a presence that affected everyone around her.

When Xerxes entered the palace, and saw Esther coming forward to greet him, he was struck again by the sheer force of her beauty. A remarkable woman, he thought, and she curtsied before him. He took her hand and kissed it, and she smiled at him as if she had nothing on her mind but to entertain him. Xerxes felt his spirits rising. It was amazing that Esther always had this effect on him.

Realizing that Haman had not yet arrived, she drew the king aside out on to the terrace, ostensibly to show him a new fountain that she had installed in the garden. What was keeping Haman, she wondered? He should have arrived before the king. What if he had decided to stay away? What should she do? It was imperative that he was present when she accused him.

Esther talked to the king, keeping her eye on the doorway. After a few minutes her servant appeared, and signalled to her that Haman had arrived. She led the king indoors to the dining hall where they found Haman waiting. She took a deep breath to relieve the tension, thankful not only that Haman had come but also that an incident had been averted. Had the king known that Haman was late, he might have taken it as a breach of protocol, and there might have been a few unpleasant moments. As it was, the king was quite unaware of anything amiss, as Esther graciously greeted Haman and led her guests to the tables.

According to custom, Esther had arranged three small tables with one at right angles to the other two, and close enough that they could easily carry on a conversation. The tables were of wrought- iron overlaid with gold, and each had a matching chair and a little footstool. Esther seated herself between Haman and Xerxes and signalled to the servants to bring in the food.

The banquet was, if anything, more sumptuous than the night before. Esther knew all the king's favorite foods and had sent into the city to find special delicacies. While they ate, the musicians played soft music, and towards the end of the meal, a troupe of dancing girls appeared to put on a display of traditional dances. Xerxes applauded heartily and Haman was no less appreciative. He was beginning to recover from his earlier humiliations.

When the meal was over, they moved over to the sofas set by the long windows, and a wine servant poured wine into gold goblets. Xerxes sat back and sipped his wine in a relaxed frame of mind.

"Now, Esther," he said, "you have kept me in suspense long enough. Tell me what you want, and I will give it to you, even up to half my kingdom, as I promised."

Esther cleared her throat.

"If it pleases your majesty," she began, "to grant my humble request, my wish is that I may live, and that my people may live."

Out of the corner of her eye she saw Haman's head jerk up

and he leaned forward in his seat. She looked at Xerxes, seeing the mystified look on his face, and went on.

"My people and I have been sold for slaughter. If it were nothing more serious than being sold into slavery I would have kept quiet and not bothered you about it, but we are about to be destroyed -- exterminated!"

"Your people being wiped out! What on earth are you talking about?"

"It is true, my lord, there is a plan to destroy us." Esther's quiet voice convinced the king that she was serious. "My people are the exiles from Judah, taken into captivity to Babylon, and later brought to Shushan under king Cyrus and king Darius. I was born here, as were my parents, but we never forgot our heritage. And now we are to be wiped out, because we continue to worship our God."

"Why was I not told of this?" Xerxes threw a sharp glance at Haman. "I want to know who is responsible!"

He had hardly got the words out when Esther stood up and pointed at Haman.

"Our enemy, our persecutor, is this evil man, Haman!"

There was a moment of ominous silence as the king, comprehension dawning on him, stared at Haman, who was stunned into speechlessness and made no attempt to deny her charge. Then Xerxes rose up, his face thunderous.

"You! You have done this against the queen and her people!"

Flinging his goblet aside, he turned and strode out into the garden to get control of his thoughts. I didn't know she was one of them, he told himself, otherwise I would never have let Haman make that decree. He felt himself to be at fault in some measure, no matter how he tried to excuse himself, and his anger at Haman intensified.

Meanwhile, inside, Haman sat immobilized, quailing at the force of the king's anger against him. He had not foreseen this. How could he have known that the queen was one of them? His wife's words came back to him. She had said he could not prevail against the Jews. Horror seized him. The king would not forgive him for this. He was finished. What would happen to him? Looking up he saw that the queen was still sitting on the couch. In his confusion and terror the thought flashed into his mind that she might help him, that she would have pity on him. He got up and threw himself at her feet.

"I beg of you, Queen Esther, believe me! I would not have done this thing if I had known you were one of them. I am devastated! It is all a terrible mistake! Please help me!"

Esther's eyes opened wide. "I help you! You, who have condemned me to death!"

"No, no! Never you!" In his agitation, he reached up and caught her by the shoulders, intent on saving his skin.

"You must speak to the king for me! Tell him I did not know! Don't you see?" His voice was almost a scream now, as he pressed the queen. She tried to pull away from him, leaning back as far as she could against the cushions of the sofa. Haman continued to hold on to her, crying for mercy, quite unaware in his distress, that his body now lay on top of hers.

At that moment Xerxes came back into the room and found Haman sprawled over the queen, his robe all but hiding her from sight. All he could see were her white face and terrified eyes. The king's wrath exploded.

"What! Are you now going to violate the queen before my very eyes? In the royal palace?"

Haman drew back, his mouth open in astonishment. He

was struck with horror at the depths of his own misfortunes. He could not utter a word. Waves of despair washed over him. How had things gone so wrong? He knew it was useless to protest. No one would believe him now.

The king's bodyguards had rushed in on hearing the commotion, followed closely by the queen's chamberlains. They all stood transfixed, staring at the scene as Haman slowly disengaged himself from the queen and prostrated himself on the floor before the king, waiting for Xerxes to pronounce the inevitable sentence.

"Let this . . . this betrayer be put to death!" declared the king, his voice hoarse with anger.

"If it please your majesty . . ." This was Harbonah, who never let an opportunity pass without seizing it.

"Well, what is it?" growled the king.

"Your majesty, this man has built a huge gallows at his house. He meant to hang Mordecai, who saved your majesty's life."

"A gallows? For Mordecai?" The king was incredulous. He looked at Haman with revulsion. "Let him be hanged on his own gallows. Tomorrow, publicly, in the palace square. At noon."

Even as the king was speaking, the chamberlains covered Haman's head with a cloth and the guards led him away, a doomed man, followed by the rest of the company.

Xerxes sat down beside Esther who all this time had been sobbing quietly. "My dear Esther," he said, feeling her tremble, "it's all over. He won't harm you again."

"But the decree, my lord," she whispered. "What of the decree?" She looked at him with pleading eyes.

Xerxes frowned. "Hmm. It's true the decree cannot be revoked. But don't worry, my love, we will think of something. There has to be a way to save your people."

Under his calming words she recovered a little. "Thank you, my lord king. I thank you with all my heart."

He continued to hold her, his lips touching her hair, until he was satisfied that she had stopped trembling. Then he called for her ladies, who came and took her to her room.

Xerxes returned to his apartments deep in thought. 'I trusted Haman and he abused that trust. I allowed him too much power. It was his job to protect me from unwise actions. I should have listened to the Inner Council. I should have been more vigilant. And to think that I might have lost Esther! She is so brave, to fight for her people at the risk of her own life. But I could still lose her. It would be intolerable if I had to find another queen. There must be a way to save her and her people.'

He went to bed, still wrestling with the problem.

# CHAPTER 13

The day dawned cold and bleak, in keeping with the mood of all in the queen's palace. Esther's sleep had been intermittent. She kept on waking up, the scenes of the night before rushing into her mind. It bothered her that she had remained silent when Xerxes accused Haman of rape. She knew it was the farthest thing from his mind at that point—he was more intent on saving his own skin. Yet, it really didn't make any difference. Even if he was not guilty of rape, his heinous crime of planning genocide merited his death. Besides, even if she had told Xerxes the truth, he would not have believed her then. His anger against Haman had been kindled earlier, when he learned of the intent of the edict. No, she consoled herself, the only thing that mattered was that her people were safe from Haman. As for the edict, the king had said that he would find a way to save her people.

When she was dressed, Esther called her ladies together and told them in detail all that had transpired.

"We are not safe yet," she said, "but the king has promised to find a way to deliver our people."

There were expressions of great joy and relief, and the ladies praised Esther for her great courage in confronting their enemy.

"God gave me the strength when I needed it," she replied, "and I could not have done it without your support. My thanks to you all."

At that moment Harbonah appeared to say that the Prince Artaxerxes wished an audience with the queen. Esther hurried to the reception hall to greet him.

"Queen Esther," he began, taking her hand in his and kissing it," I have just heard what has happened. I am sorry for the distress you have suffered."

"Thank you Prince Artaxerxes." She smiled at him. He was very tall, at eighteen, already a man.

"We should be thankful for you! You have rid the palace of an evil influence."

Her eyes widened. "What do you mean?"

"Oh, he was a clever man. He ingratiated himself with everyone, and when he obtained a position of power he began to use it for his own ends. Look what he did to my father, undermining his authority while pretending to preserve it. Alienating him from me, his son, and from you, the queen. "Oh yes," he added, as he saw Esther give a start, "don't think that the people around you didn't notice! We watched it happening, but we were powerless to do anything, as long as he had the king in the palm of his hand. I had a long talk with my father this morning. He now suspects that Haman planned to eventually take over the throne with the help of his followers."

Esther was astonished. "Would he really have gone that far? I had no idea. I thought he acted out of enmity for the Jews."

"No doubt he wanted to get rid of them first because he knew they were absolutely loyal to the king. You know, it's strange," he went on with a half smile, "it took a woman to deliver our country from the usurper. When men are helpless you can be sure a woman of courage will come forward to save the day."

Esther smiled. "Now you are teasing me and my sex!"

"Not at all!" he assured her. "I'm perfectly serious. One only has to look back on history. Men can win victories with armies, but when it comes to battles involving the security and well-being of the country, women have ways of succeeding when all else fails. It has happened in the past, and no doubt will always be so. Thank God for brave women, I say, and thank God for you, Queen Esther."

"Oh, I'm not brave," she protested. "I was terrified. It was God who gave the strength to accuse Haman."

"Well, we thank Ahura Mazda, the Wise Spirit, that you were able to do it."

"Thank Jehovah. He is the true God."

"Probably he is the same God. The one Creator must be also the one Almighty God. Just that we use a different name."

"You are a wise young man, Prince Artaxerxes. You will make a fine king one day."

"I hope not for a long time." He flashed her a wide grin. "I have many things I want to do before I am burdened with any responsibilities of the empire. And now I must go. The hanging is to be at noon, and my father has said that he expects me to be there. Will you be present?"

"Oh no, I think not," responded Esther quickly, a shudder of horror running through her. "I don't want to look on Haman's face again."

"Well, no one could blame you for that."

"Before you go, let me thank you for coming to see me. You have made me see things differently. Not just from my own point of view."

"It was a pleasure to see you, madam. It always is."

With that, he gave a brief bow and left.

Esther was thoughtful. So it was possible that Haman had had designs on the throne! Then everything had worked out for good. The whole empire was well rid of him. She felt better as she made her way to her ladies.

*

Towards noon, there came a break in the clouds, and as Xerxes crossed the Palace square, the sun glinted on the gold insignia emblazoned on his tunic and the gold thread in his purple cloak. Across his broad chest lay the heavy gold chain of the Emperor of Persia, which he always wore on important occasions. It was less than the full regalia of a state affair, but nevertheless impressive in its symbolism. He was flanked on either side by two of his imperial guards and behind him there followed the seven members of the Inner Council. In the square, in front of the balcony, the soldiers were completing the erection of the huge gallows that had been transported from Haman's courtyard. Xerxes barely glanced at them as he passed, but went quickly up the wide steps so that his entourage had to hurry to keep up with him.

At the top of the stairs, Sabona, the Master of Ceremonies came forward to greet the king, who acknowledged him with a peremptory glance. Xerxes looked around.

"Where's the queen?" he asked.

Sabona was quick to reply. "Your majesty, the queen sent word that she would not attend."

The king's mouth tightened to a straight line. Turning round he beckoned to one of the chamberlains, who hurried up.

"Tell the queen I wish her to be present. In full royal attire."

The chamberlain bowed and left immediately. Xerxes moved to the front of the balcony and surveyed the scene for a few minutes. The soldiers had finished and were standing in formation on either side of the gallows. Behind them the drummers and trumpeters were readying their instruments. The king turned to Sabona.

"I shall be in the office. Let me know when the queen arrives."

He entered the main hall and crossed over to a small office at the side. As he went he motioned to Memucan and Carshena who followed him inside and closed the door. All the other officials were left to cool their heels, standing about aimlessly in the hall, waiting for the hanging to get under way. None of them dared to leave in case they missed the action. There was an air of tension over everyone. A public hanging was rare enough, but the hanging of the Prime Minister was, to say the least, a once-in-a-lifetime spectacle. There were few who contemplated Haman's demise with any degree of sorrow, yet all were conscious of the solemnity that the occasion demanded. The officials were at a loss as to how to pass the time, and either shifted from one foot to the other, mumbling meaningless remarks to anyone within hearing, or else paced, stony-faced and silent between the pillars. In the palace square a crowd, unusually quiet, had gathered.

Meanwhile those in the queen's palace were feeling the strain of suspense. When the chamberlain delivered the king's message, Esther and her ladies were sitting in the gallery above the inner courtyard, intent on embroidering a bedspread; work which Esther hoped would engross them and keep their minds off events taking place in the palace square. But their strained faces betrayed the tension they felt, however hard they tried to hide it.

On hearing the king's message, Esther rose immediately and went to her room, calling for her maids to attend her. She had hoped to avoid this, but she knew she could not disobey the royal command. A vision of Vashti sprang to her mind. She, Esther, would not make the same mistake, no matter what it cost her in feelings of revulsion and horror. She did not know how she would react when she saw Haman actually being put to death. One part of her rejoiced that the enemy of her people should be removed, but another side of her cringed at the idea that when she witnessed his death, she would know that she had been the chief instrument in bringing it about. The part she had played in keeping silent still troubled her, no matter how she rationalized it, and dimmed the elation she felt at the possibility of reprieve for her people. Yet, Artaxerxes was convinced that Haman meant more harm to the king and the empire. She resolved to keep that thought in mind as she witnessed the hanging.

Her maids helped her with the elaborate dress of state, of heavy blue silk. It had long sleeves hanging out at the cuffs to show the white silk undersleeves that clung to her wrists. There was a broad band of white silk at her throat, over which she placed a gold neckpiece, studded with sapphires and pearls. The openwork gold crown lined with blue patterned silk lay on top of her dark hair and round her shoulders was a heavy dark blue cloak fastened with filigree clasps in the shape of winged lions. At last she was ready.

My life seems to be a succession of ordeals, she thought. Yet, I don't seem to show it. Looking at herself in the burnished bronze mirror, she marvelled at her queenly appearance, as if the turmoil inside her did not exist. Little did I know, she mused, when I dreamed of being queen, what demands it would make on me, the depths of resources it would require. If I had known, I would never have pursued the dream.

Then she remembered Mordecai's words: "It was for such a time as this that you came into the kingdom." They would sustain her through the ceremony. It was all part of her destiny, and the destiny of her people.

Now, surrounded by her ladies, she made her way to the balcony overlooking the palace square. As she reached the main hall, Xerxes emerged from the office and waited until she had reached him. His face was stern as she curtseyed to him, but as he took her hand and led her out to the balcony, she detected something in his eyes, a look that she could not quite interpret. She caught a glimpse of Mordecai, distinguished-looking in a dark blue tunic and cloak. His face was solemn, but he flicked her a glance of recognition, the tension round his mouth easing for a moment.

Xerxes led her forward to the front of the balcony, while the advisers stayed a few paces behind. He looked sideways at her, noting the pallor of her face, and he realized how much of an ordeal it was for her to be there.

"It is necessary for the queen to be present, when all are ordered to attend," he whispered, as if to mitigate the severity of his command.

"I understand, Sire." Her voice was so low he barely caught the words, but she shot him a glance to show that she appreciated his concern.

"When this is over, I want to confer with you. There is still the business of the edict to attend to."

She nodded, but he didn't notice, for he was already giving the signal to the Master of Ceremonies.

The trumpets blared, the drums rolled, and from across the square came a small parade of soldiers, followed by Haman, clad in black, guards at his side, his hands tied behind him. Slowly he mounted the steps to the platform of the gallows, his head held high, a defiant look on his face, denying the shame of the situation. He came to a stop facing the company on the balcony. The drums ceased to roll and in the ensuing silence the herald stepped forward to read the proclamation.

By order of King Xerxes, Emperor of Persia.

Be it known to the citizens of Shushan and all the empire. This man Haman, one-time Prime Minister of this state, is pronounced guilty of plotting against the king and queen and guilty of plotting to massacre certain of the king's loyal subjects. According to the laws of the Persians, the penalty for plotting against the king, and pursuing treasonable acts, is death. This man Haman is therefore sentenced to death by hanging. Let the order of the king be carried out now in the presence of his subjects.

There was another roll of drums and Haman stepped forward, raising his head deliberately so that he stared directly up to the king, his eyes glittering with hatred. Xerxes returned the stare, unblinking. Then Haman's gaze moved to Esther. The naked malice in his eyes made her start involuntarily. A vivid memory flashed across her mind as she remembered the first time she had seen him, at the hanging in the market square, so many years ago. No wonder she had been so terrified. So justice had come full circle. She closed her eyes, almost overcome. Xerxes reached out and took her hand in his, squeezing it gently in reassurance. Strengthened by this, she managed to keep her face void of expression. The moment passed.

Then the drums rolled again. Esther stared straight ahead, but her eyes were unseeing. She did not see the noose placed over Haman's head. The executioner in a loud voice gave the prisoner leave to speak a last word, but Haman looked on disdainfully and remained silent. He had witnessed enough hangings to know that words made little difference in the end.

The platform was moved away. When the fateful moment came, the crowd remained in a hushed silence. No one stirred. Abruptly an officer shouted an order to the soldiers who turned and marched off in formation. Still the crowd were silent, all eyes fixed on the body now hanging limply from the gallows. A trumpet blared, and the people, as if loosed from a spell, shouted with one voice:

"Death to the traitor! Long live King Xerxes! Long live Queen Esther!"

It was over. Xerxes turned to Esther, his face grim.

"So may all the enemies of the king perish!"

She shivered at his tone, feeling weak as he led her inside. In the hall he spoke to her again.

"Meet me in the Blue Pavilion in one hour. We will discuss what is to be done."

He left her then, with a small bow, and her ladies rushed forward to escort her back to the queen's palace.

Esther took off her royal robes and jewels and dressed in a simple linen gown. She sipped the hot honey drink that Minna bought her, while her maids fussed round her, massaging her feet, brushing her hair, doing whatever they could to make her feel better, all aware of the strain she had been under, and what it had cost her to make that appearance in public. Bilkah came and held her hand.

"My lady, it was necessary that he should perish, to save many from death.

257

Esther nodded. "Yes, Bilkah. Of course. It had to be."

She began to feel somewhat revived, and when the time came to go to the king, her colour was almost back to normal.

Leaving the ladies in the ante-room, she entered the pavilion. There was no sign of the king. She found Mordecai seated on a couch by the window. Seeing her, he rose and came forward to meet her, drawing her into a warm embrace.

"Esther, my dear Esther, how can we ever thank you for what you have done? My brave girl!" He held her tight.

"Oh, Mordecai! I only did what I had to do. You were all there with me. I could feel your support, and God strengthened me. Now you won't ever have to cope with Haman again."

"No," he agreed. "But his evil deeds live on. The sentence of death still hangs over us."

"Don't worry. The king has promised to help us. A way will be found."

"You're right." He smiled at her. "Let's just enjoy the day and celebrate." He hugged her to him again. "Do you remember when you were a little girl, how you would find excuses to have a party, sometimes for the most unlikely reasons?"

She laughed, nodding in recollection. "Remember the day the pedlar came and I made you buy gifts for everyone and then we had a party so that everyone could have their gifts at once?"

They were standing there, still with their arms around each other, laughing and looking into each other's eyes, when they became aware of the figure in the doorway. Xerxes was watching them, his expression like stone.

Oh no! thought Esther in dismay. She saw in a flash how it must appear to the king, Mordecai now cast in the same role as Haman, compromising the queen, but this time with her acquiescence, a willing participant, deceiving the king.

"Leave us." The king addressed Esther, his tone as icy as the look he threw her.

She had to act fast, even if it meant ignoring the command.

"Sire," she said in her most pleasant voice, as if there was no reason for dismay, "may I present to you my guardian?"

"Your guardian," he repeated flatly. He looked from Esther to Mordecai.

"You . . . are her guardian?"

"Yes, your majesty." Mordecai bowed. "I brought Esther up from the time she was a small child. She is like a daughter to me."

Another small pause. Then surprisingly, the king laughed and shook his head. He clapped Mordecai on the shoulder.

"Well, at last I get to meet you! For years I have listened to Esther talk about you, and she promised that I would meet you one day." He turned to Esther. "Why did you not tell me that he was right here in the palace? That he was my loyal chamberlain Mordecai? You know how much I esteem him."

"If it please your majesty," said Mordecai, "I asked her not to divulge our relationship. I thought it might jeopardize her position as queen." And as the king still looked puzzled he added, "because we are Jews."

"I see." The king pondered this for a moment and then went on. "It seems no matter what laws we make, discrimination continues to exist. Human nature being what it is. But we have to overcome these prejudices. Even I have been remiss in this matter, by allowing Haman to issue the decree. Come, let's sit down and discuss what is to be done. That is why I asked you both to come here." He smiled at them. "I didn't realize that it was going to be a family affair!"

They sat down, the king on one couch, Esther and Mordecai opposite on another.

"You know, of course, that the decree has the authority of my seal, and therefore cannot be revoked. Esther, my dear you look pale. Let me send for some wine." He was silent, waiting while the wine servant filled the goblets.

Esther sipped her wine and began to feel better. Gathering her courage, she addressed the king.

"You must do something," she pleaded. "I don't care for myself, but don't allow my people to suffer. You know they serve you loyally."

"Don't worry. Esther." The king leaned forward and spoke earnestly. "You have pleaded the cause of your people well. You must realize that I feel responsible for giving Haman the power to issue the edict in the first place. I gave him a free rein, because I thought he was looking out for my interests. Had it not been for you, I would have a horrible massacre of innocent people on my conscience. I thought about it long into the night, and I think I have found a solution. I will order a letter to be sent to all the satrapies in the empire to the effect that the proclamation as issued was an injustice against the Jews, and I will advise the Satraps and governors to refrain from putting it into action. Also that the Jews are free to organize themselves into units for defence of their people by force of arms if necessary on the day appointed." He looked at Mordecai. "What do you think? Would that be enough to protect your people?"

Mordecai set his goblet on the table. "Such a letter would have to be carefully worded, to give as much protection as possible to the Jews, and to ensure that it would take precedence over the decree."

The king nodded. "Granted. You will write the letter in

my name and I will give the royal seal to stamp it."

"In that case," said Mordecai, slowly, "it might just work. It will not have the force of the edict, but it might be enough to prevent a massacre. It is the best we can hope for under the circumstances. And if there are those who will prefer to follow the edict, as I am sure there will be, then our people will be prepared to defend themselves. It is a great improvement on the present situation. It will then be a matter of waiting to see what happens."

Xerxes turned to Esther.

"Does that allay your fears, Esther? At least to some extent? If your people are armed and ready to fight in self-defence and if it is known that the king himself is favourably disposed towards them, it will act as a deterrent."

"Oh yes, sire." She knelt down at his feet and kissed his hand, her voice trembling with emotion. "I thank you. On behalf of my people I thank you with all my heart!"

The king clasped her hands in his, and rising, drew her to her feet.

"You know, Esther, it grieves me that you had to suffer so much pain. I am going to make it up to you. Today I am going to order all of Haman's property, which of course is now confiscated, to be transferred to you, to do with it whatever you want. And Mordecai," he turned to him, "I am going to make you Prime Minister in Haman's place,"

Esther gasped, and then went to embrace Mordecai. "I am very happy for you. You deserve to be Prime Minister, and you will be the best. You deserve it."

"You both deserve my thanks," said Xerxes. "You are both completely loyal to me, and Persians value loyalty above all virtues."

It was time for them to take their leave of the king, but

before they could do so the king said, "There's still one thing that puzzles me. When I made inquiries, I discovered that Haman himself was not of Persian lineage. I would have thought that he of all men would have sympathy with the minorities."

"There is an explanation, my lord king," said Mordecai. "It goes back to our history. He belonged to the people called the Amalekites, who for centuries have been the traditional enemies of the Israelites. Haman was probably reviving the old feud and avenging his people for the many defeats we have inflicted on them in the past when they attacked us without provocation."

"I see," said Xerxes, thoughtfully stroking his beard. "We would do well to forget the enmities of the past. I learned that during the Greek campaign. We gain nothing by inflicting the animosities of the past on the present generation. Well, we must get on with the work that is to hand. Now Mordecai, we will call a meeting of the Inner Council this afternoon, at which we will confer on you the insignia of the Prime Minister. Then I think it would be a good idea if you were to show yourself in public wearing your badge of office. Perhaps a procession would be in order. That's the quickest way to let the people know that you and your people are favoured by the king. And Esther, I would like you to dine with me tonight. Come to my suite at seven."

Expressing their thanks again, they took their leave.

"Come with me and have something to eat," said Esther, once they were in the corridor. So Mordecai went with Esther to the queen's palace and as they ate they talked over all that had transpired with the king.

"I was most pleasantly surprised by his attitude," said Mordecai. "He seems to have got some of his old decisiveness back. I think he was shocked by the realization that what happened was due to his own negligence. And I doubt if I will be afforded as much freedom as Haman had as prime Minister."

"At least he knows you won't abuse his trust."

Mordecai shook his head. "It is easy for power to go to one's head. No one is immune from that temptation, given the right circumstances."

"With me to keep an eye on you, you'll have nothing to fear," laughed Esther. "I'll make sure you don't get too big for your badge of office." She patted his hand. "Do you know what is the best thing about this whole business?"

He raised an eyebrow inquiringly.

"That I can now talk to you freely, without fear of being discovered. Oh, I know that you'll be very busy and at the king's beck and call, but I'll see you from time to time."

"You'll be at the king's beck and call too, from what I gather. Without Haman to come between you, he will probably spend more time with you now. He really seems concerned for you. I hope it lasts. Somehow I can't imagine Xerxes as a reformed character for long. But he has tried to make amends for the wrong done to our people, and if only for that he will have our eternal gratitude. We must have a party to celebrate with our friends here."

"What do you think will happen?" asked Esther.

"God has remembered us thus far," replied Mordecai. "When the time comes, He will deliver his people. So, don't worry. And now I must go and prepare for the Inner Council."

Esther sat on after he left. How life can change from one day to the next, she mused. Yesterday was full of fear and foreboding, and today is full of hope. And I am back in favour with the king.

For the first time in many long days she could look forward to the future, however short a future it might be.

# CHAPTER 14

The next day Mordecai carefully composed the letter to be sent to the one hundred and twenty seven provinces of the empire. The translators were called to translate the letter into all the different languages of the realm, so that it cold be read in every town and village, just as the edict had been. The scribes worked all through the night to make copies, and when they were ready couriers carried them with all speed to every governor of every province. From there, riders fanned out to bring the letters to every town and village. When the Jews of all the regions heard the letter read, their initial reaction was one of great jubilation and thanksgiving to God that he had provided the means for their deliverance. They realized, however, that the danger was still there, and all they could do was prepare to defend themselves and await the fateful day to see what happened.

Following his investiture with the khelaat as Prime Minister, Mordecai had his inaugural parade. He dressed in fine new robes in the blue and white colours of the royal court. He wore a dark blue cloak of linen, fastened at the shoulders with gold clasps, the gold badge of office pinned to his breast. Esther was there to see him off.

"How handsome you are, Cousin Mordecai!" She could now address him freely as her kinsman without fear of the consequences. "How well these fine clothes become you," she said. "As if you were born to them."

"Well, as cousin to the queen, perhaps I was!" he replied, smiling, carefully adjusting the sleeve so that it hung perfectly.

"What about Zinna?" asked Esther. "Will you marry her now?"

Mordecai's face grew serious. "We are not out of the woods yet, Esther. None of us can breathe freely until the thirteenth day of Adar is passed. This is only a respite. I'm going on this parade as the king suggested, to encourage our people not to lose heart. And when our enemies see that our king favours me, perhaps they will not dare to take up arms against us. It is all a gamble, in a way. While they still fear the king to a certain extent, they know that Xerxes has been careless in recent years. It would not be surprising if some unscrupulous people would use the edict to usurp the king's authority. They might say he is not obeying his own edict, and so justify an uprising against him. In a way he took a risk on our behalf."

Esther looked stricken. "It is a worse situation than I thought. Will it never end?" she asked despondently.

Mordecai put his hand under her chin and lifted her head.

"We must hope for the best, Esther. And you can be sure I will do everything I can to see that the worst does not happen. We must support the king in every way. Now," he said, taking up his rod of office, "I must be off. I have declared today a holiday in Shushan and there will be celebrations all over the city tonight. Zinna is preparing a feast and inviting all our friends. Why don't you arrange a party for the ladies?"

"Yes, of course, I will. All our friends will be so happy when they see you wearing the official robes and badge of office. Give my love to Zinna. She must be proud of you."

"Yes, Zinna has been very patient all these years. If we get through this safely, I will find a house close to the palace and we will be married." As he spoke, two chamberlains appeared at the door, ready to escort him to the waiting procession.

Esther watched from the balcony as Mordecai mounted one of the fine horses from the king's stable. The members of the Inner Council also on horseback, lined up behind him. Two horsemen of the Imperial Guard led the way, with two more taking up the rear. The small cavalcade moved off down the Processional Way to begin the tour of the city. It was the second parade of honour for Mordecai in so many days, but now he was coming as one who was second only to the king, a man of honour in his own right. It was a great encouragement to the Jews, and they crowded into the streets in festive mood, to cheer Mordecai. Although they realized that there was still a day of reckoning ahead, they were thankful for even a short time of reprieve. It meant a great deal to them to see one who was a Jew being held in such esteem and favour by the king.

With Haman gone, a new atmosphere prevailed throughout the palace. All his spies and henchmen, on whom he had relied to create fear and suspicion, disappeared on the day of the execution. It was rumoured that they had escaped into the city, and had attached themselves to Haman's sons before they could be rounded up and punished for their crimes of brutality. Everyone was so relieved they were gone, that they did not give them another thought. The Inner Council decided to take no further action, a decision they would come to regret. Meanwhile life at the palace took on an air of relaxation. People went about their business without feeling that they were being watched every moment. Even the eyes and ears of the king, the Sabat, did not inspire the dread that Haman's spies had.

Esther found her life was much easier. The burden she had

carried since she first heard about the decree had been lifted. Xerxes, now that Haman was out of the way, seemed to want her company more than ever. One day he even came in search of her himself.

"You are always surrounded by these damned women," he complained. "Come" he said, not waiting for her reply, "I want you with me. Alone." He took her off to his own palace, to the garden on the roof where he ordered wine and sweetmeats to be brought. They sat, reclining on the silk cushions of the sofa, shaded from the sun by the gently swaying palm trees.

"Esther, I'm going to make some changes. I'm tired of always having to send for you when I want to see you. You are always secluded in that palace of yours. I would like you to feel free to come here whenever you like. There is no need for you to be treated like just one of the other women. It has occurred to me that sometimes we let our traditions rule us excessively. Look at the difficulty you had in approaching me to tell me about Haman. Because of our custom, you had to take your life in your hands. Well, there is a way around custom," he smiled, "just as there was a way around the decree. So, from now on, you are free to rove as you wish, as long as you don't interrupt affairs of state." He spread his hands. "I'd like to be able to talk to you, without having to send a page in search of you. What do you say?"

"I'll do whatever you wish, Sire," replied Esther, wondering greatly at his change in attitude. The affair of Haman must really have shaken him. "It has always been my pleasure to do your will."

He beamed at her. "Good, that's settled. Now there is one more matter. Haman's sons and all the family have fled into the city. Today I arranged for the ownership of all his property to be transferred to you. It's yours, to do with as you like."

Esther could not hide her astonishment. "Mine, Sire? But I have everything I want. What will I do with all that property?"

Xerxes grinned, showing white teeth. "No doubt you'll think of something. You usually do!"

She smiled back at him. "Thank you, my lord. You are most kind." She would give it to Mordecai. It was the perfect house for him and Zinna.

As soon as she could, she went to see it. She was amazed at the opulence of it. It was situated at the perimeter of the palace compound, surrounded by tall trees. Pillared columns supported the verandah, and in the courtyard, willow trees shaded the large pool in the centre. Inside, she found the rooms richly decorated with elaborate tapestries and furnishings. Couches of acacia wood were decorated with gold designs and covered with purple cushions. It was splendour fit for a king. Esther ordered everything to be removed and stored. She wanted no reminders of Haman when Mordecai took over the house.

On the surface, Esther's life returned to normal, but every day brought her nearer to the fateful reckoning. There were still three months to get through before they would know their fate. She did not see much of Mordecai, for he was constantly busy with the affairs of state, and much of her own time was taken up by the king. He continued to pay her a great deal of attention, when he was not engaged in his chariot-racing or hunting. He still delegated much of his authority to Mordecai, but he was much more diligent in calling meetings of the council, and he kept his hand on the helm of state in such a way that he knew exactly what was going on. Sometimes Esther would arrange a dinner party for the king and Mordecai, and afterwards they would sit and sip their wine, discussing the events of the day. The king enjoyed Mordecai's company, for he liked learning, and was well-read. Esther was happy then, even although under the tranquil existence there was an undercurrent of fear.

A few weeks later, Sarcon came to her as she sat alone reading in the garden, while her ladies were playing a game of skittles a little distance away.

"Your majesty, Queen Esther," he began, "may I speak with you."

"Sarcon! Yes, of course." She had only spoken to him once since the affair of Haman, when he had expressed his sympathy for the plight of her people. "I have not seen you for some time."

'My lady, that's what I want to talk to you about. I feel that I am not of further use to you here, and I have decided to go back to Idumea. Please let me finish," he said, as Esther made as to interrupt him. "My father is growing older and he wants me to take over some of his responsibilities. It was always understood that I would go back some day, and I have already stayed longer than I expected."

"Of course, Sarcon. You must go back. Your family needs you, and we have no right to keep you." She paused. "I'm going to miss you. We will all be sorry to see you go, but you have your own life to live. I will never forget what you have done for me. There were many times when I thought you were the only friend I had in the palace. Certainly you were the only one I could trust."

"You have more friends than you know, Queen Esther. Now that Mordecai is Prime Minister, and you are back in favour with the king, you no longer need my help."

"I hope you will have a happy life, Sarcon. You will find

269

a wife among your own people and live the life you have always wanted."

He smiled ruefully. "I thought I wanted you, my lady. But now when I see how you have helped your people, and the influence you have had on the palace, making it a much freer place, I know that you were meant to be here. It was your destiny, just as you said."

Esther laughed. "Little did I know then what that destiny entailed. I just wanted to be queen. How long is it since we first met, Sarcon? If things had been different . . . but I was not free to do what I wanted."

"I understand that now, although for years I thought that I could change your mind. We were caught up in something bigger than ourselves."

"And it is not finished yet." She bit her lip. "Who knows what will happen on the appointed day!"

"That's another reason I must go. As I travel home, I will visit the Satraps on the way. They will receive me for my father's sake, and I will make sure they know everything so that they will act in your interests. When they know how much the king favours you and your people, they will not go against you."

"Thank you, Sarcon. I will forever be in your debt." She was silent for a few moments, then she went on: "I want to give you something, Sarcon. A keepsake, that will remind you of me."

He looked into her eyes. "I need no keepsake to remind me of you, Queen Esther!"

She smiled. "Yes, Sarcon. One day you will. I want your life to be so filled with loved ones that there will be only a very small place for me, just large enough to hold my keepsake. I will send it to you before you leave."

He bowed, but said nothing, not trusting himself to speak. She wanted to embrace him then, but she did not dare risk it. There were limits, after all, to the liberties she could take. Instead she put her hands on his shoulders, and, stretching up, she kissed him first on one cheek and then on the other.

"Goodbye, Sarcon."

"Goodbye, Queen Esther."

There was nothing more to be said. She watched him go with tears in her eyes, knowing that she would never see him again.

That night she searched out a pair of gold engraved wrist bands that she had ordered from Jacob as a gift for Xerxes. She sent them to Sarcon's apartment. Jacob would just have to make another pair for Xerxes.

*

The days that passed slowly for Esther passed all too quickly for Mordecai. His duties as Prime Minister took up most of his time, and the rest he spent making contact with the Jews spread out in every province, ensuring that they had weapons with which to defend themselves. Every day Jews arrived at the palace, pressing him to sell them arms in exchange for gold and silver. The story of what Queen Esther had done was told in every household, and it seemed as if every Jewish woman had relinquished her rings, necklaces and earrings in order to finance the defence of her people. Mordecai, with the king's help, was able to supply the needs of all who came.

It was some time, therefore before Esther got a chance to tell him about Haman's estate. At first Mordecai refused it outright.

271

"I want nothing that belonged to that man," he said adamantly.

"It doesn't belong to Haman. It belongs to me. I removed all the furnishings, and it is now an empty shell. I would like you and Zinna to have it. Why don't you take it?"

"I told you. I must have the permission of the king before I can marry. Besides, I have no time to think about it just now. There is no point in making plans until . . . "

"The king will not refuse you now. In fact, I think he would be happy to see you settle finally in the palace." She paused and glanced at him sideways. "Zinna might like to see it. Would you mind if I showed it to her?"

"What?" Mordecai's mind was obviously on something else. He looked up from the paper he was studying. Suddenly he smiled. "I know that look. You have set your mind on this, and you won't stop until I give in. All right, I might as well save myself some trouble. Show it to Zinna and if she likes it, well, it will be up to her. But only on the condition that it remain your property. You may want to have it for yourself some day. Perhaps for your children . . . "

"It doesn't look like I'm ever going to have a child, Mordecai. It didn't happen all those years."

"Well, who knows? Now that you are in the king's favour again?"

"If I live long enough."

"Yes." Mordecai's face was serious again. "There is no point in planning anything until the thirteenth day of Adar has come and gone."

"I think you said that already," said Esther. "It's obviously time for me to go. Just think about what I told you."

She left him to his work.

On the twelfth day of Adar, the eve of the fateful day,

Esther decided to go to bed early, and her ladies followed her example. Before long, the queen's palace was silent, with only the guards at their posts and the two chamberlains on duty.

Just before midnight there was a commotion at one of the side doors. Someone was knocking insistently. Cautiously the chamberlains went to the grill to look out. A young man, well dressed but obviously not a nobleman, was standing impatiently on the steps. When he saw them he called out.

"I must see the queen immediately. It is most urgent. A matter of life and death!"

"The queen has retired," they told him. "Whatever your business, it must wait for the morning."

The chamberlain made to close the grill again, but he set up more noise.

"The queen will see me if she knows I am here. There is great danger, and your heads will roll if you don't let me in."

That gave the chamberlain pause and they conferred with each other. In all their years of service such a thing had never happened. Since when did the queen have any involvement in life and death situations? It was very perplexing, but so many unusual things had taken place recently, and it was true the queen was close to the king and the Prime Minister. To be on the safe side, they decided to tell the queen.

"Here," said the man, urgently, "take this." He slipped a ring off his finger and handed it to them through the grill. "Take this quickly to the queen. I will wait here for your return."

The chamberlain took the ring, noted it was made of real gold, and hurried off to the queen's suite.

When Bilkah woke up Esther and showed her the ring, she recognized it at once. It belonged to Jacob. Quickly she donned a robe and ordered the chamberlains to bring him at once to her private room.

"Jacob," she said, as soon as he was shown in, "you have some news?"

"I ask your pardon for waking you up, Queen Esther. Yes, I have news. It's not good. I thought you should know at once. There is a conspiracy afoot. Haman's sons have organized a small army in the city. They plan to carry out the edict and they have incited men to join them. Not only that but if they get enough on their side, they plan to march on the palace, and kill all the Jews. Then in the confusion, they will kill the king and seize power and so avenge their father's death."

Esther covered her face with her hands. "It is what I have dreaded all along. Are you sure about this? How did you find out?"

"I have a friend who keeps a tavern. He knows of my friendship with you. At great risk to himself, he came and told me. There have been secret meetings. Men came to his tavern three weeks ago and hired a room. There's been a lot of coming and going. He heard snatches of conversation which made him suspicious. Then tonight a group of men arrived and asked not to be disturbed. My friend hid in a secret storeroom and listened as they discussed their plans."

Jacob's voice became urgent. "There is not a moment to lose. They plan to make their move at first light. As soon as the edict takes effect. They have already marked all the Jewish homes in the city and they will go and kill everyone."

"This is terrible. We must go to the king at once. It's a good thing I have access to him. The guards are used to me. They will let me in, even at this late hour. Come with me and you will tell him what you have told me."

They found the king's chamberlain in the king's quarters,

and sent him with a message to the king. In no time at all they were shown in to his chamber. He was seated at a table piled high with scrolls, and had obviously been reading. He smiled a welcome to Esther, but his expression changed quickly when he saw Jacob behind her. He rose at once.

"Esther, there is something wrong?" He looked from her to Jacob.

"You remember Jacob, the goldsmith?" she asked. "He has something to tell you."

"Ah, yes. What brings you to the palace at this hour?"

Jacob recounted to the king all that he told Esther. When he had finished, Xerxes looked grim.

"Haman's sons. We expected something of this sort. They will stop at nothing to avenge their father. My spies have been aware of a conspiracy, but they knew no details of the plot. I will order Haman's sons arrested, and be assured of this, they will be punished. They are as treasonable as their father and they deserve the same fate." He turned to Esther. "Send for some wine and remain here until I return. Jacob, you will come with me and tell your story to the captain of my secret guard. He will appreciate your information." He quickly left the room, followed by Jacob.

It was an hour or more before Xerxes returned. Esther looked at him anxiously and he came to her, putting his arms round her.

"Don't worry," he told her. "Everything is being done. My secret guards have just received a report that corroborates all that Jacob has told us. He has given us some valuable information. They will all be caught in the very act of conspiracy. I have ordered that they should be hanged publicly in the city and their bodies displayed as a warning to others." He raised an eyebrow as he noticed Esther shudder.

"Would you prefer to leave them alive to continue to act against your people?" he asked, sardonically.

"No, no, of course not."

"Then there is no more to be said. Incidentally, the order was put out in the name of the king and queen. I thought it best to include you, to leave no doubt as to your status and power in the realm. No one in Shushan is likely now to take up arms against you or your people. Does that satisfy you?"

"I am most grateful to you, my lord, as are my people."

She looked up at him, feeling his ruthlessness, and yet at the same time realizing that there were times when it was necessary.

"Good." He smiled at her, a calculating look in his eye." "I like my subjects to be grateful. Now there is still an hour or two before dawn. Come to bed."

Esther woke up to find Xerxes had risen and was standing out on the terrace, fully dressed. It was bright daylight. She donned a robe, and joined him.

"I tried not to wake you. It's going to be a long day. Why don't you go back to bed and sleep on for a while? You didn't get much sleep last night."

She shook her head. "I can't rest any more. Did you here of any more of Haman's sons?"

"A report was brought to me a little while ago. That's what woke me. They have all been apprehended. You have no more cause to worry. There has been no uprising in the city so far, and we do not expect there will be."

"Thank God," breathed Esther. "And the rest of the country? How soon will we know what has happened?"

"I have arranged for fire signals to be lit at dusk in every corner of the land. Every town and village is to light a bonfire as a signal that all has gone well. The outermost provinces will light their bonfires first. Only when they see a fire on the horizon will the neighbouring provinces light their bonfires. So if the chain of signals continues until it reaches us at Shusan, the we will know for certain that all is well. No town will light its signal if there has been a massacre of the Jews."

"Then, when will we know here?"

"Towards midnight. By that time we should be able to see fires on the horizon."

"And if we don't?" She hardly dare pose the question.

"And if we don't," he smiled, pulling her on to his knee, "we will not assume the worst. For one reason or another, rain, accident, who knows, somewhere along the line a signal may fail, but then our couriers will race back and let us know. Don't worry, we won't fail. Xerxes is still a name to be reckoned with." He buried his face in her silky hair. "You please me, Esther. You please me mightily." As if with reluctance he pulled away from her. "I must go. It is going to be a busy day. Dine with me tonight and we'll watch for the fires together."

When Esther returned to her own palace, she found Jacob waiting.

"Jacob!" she greeted him. "I'm so glad you're here. I was going to send a message to you. You are all right?"

"I'm fine. I spent the night here at the palace. The king suggested that it might be dangerous for me to go back to the city. I think he was afraid I might interfere with the plans of his secret police. But you have heard that they got Haman's sons?"

"Yes, the king told me. There has been no uprising in the city. We have so much to thank you for, Jacob. Had it not been for you, we might not be alive today."

"Well," he gave a lop-sided grin, "my skin was at stake

too, you know!"

"Still, we owe you a lot. The king will reward you."

"He already has." He drew himself up in a gesture of importance. "As from today, you are talking to the king's Chief Goldsmith."

"I'm so happy for you, Jacob. You deserve it. Does that mean that you will work at the palace?"

He shook his head. "No, but it means I can buy my own workshop in town. There's a large house I have wanted to buy for a long time. I can set up my workshop at the rear where there is a large garden. And Esther, sorry, Queen Esther, you are the first to know that I am going to be married. We drew up the marriage contract some months ago, but because of the decree there was no betrothal. Now we can start to make plans."

"Congratulations, Jacob. I hope you will have a long and happy marriage. Who is she? Do I know her?"

"She is Deborah, the daughter of Eli Benachin, the merchant."

"Well, Jacob, I am glad things have worked out so well. Do you remember the plans we used to make when we were young? What confidence we had then!"

"Had it not been for you, I wouldn't be here."

"Had it not been for you, I might not have been here either!"

They laughed, and as it seemed there was nothing further to be said, he took his leave. Esther was more aware than ever of the changes that were driving them further apart. Their relationship was changing She recognized that Jacob would have a life in which from now on she would play only a small part. She was confined by her life in the palace. She would see him only if he came to show her designs, or deliver pieces that she ordered. She would have no more claim on his time or his allegiance than on any other craftsmen. She would keep her memories, as he would, but life would never be the same.

The long day dragged on. News came from the city that the conspirators had confessed and it was revealed that a major coup had been averted. A tribunal, set up at short notice, pronounced the sentence and they were all put to death. Mordecai sent word to Esther throughout the day to keep her advised of all events. The city and the outskirts remained calm. There was still no word from the provinces.

At dusk Xerxes sent his chamberlains to conduct Esther to the dining hall. She could eat little, but Xerxes seemed in high spirits. After the meal they sat on the terrace, watching the night grow ever darker. The torches lit around the palace, and the lights of the city were all that could be seen. Esther could not conceal her anxiety, and to divert her, the king asked her to sing for him.

"Please, sire, excuse me. I have not felt like singing for some time. I'm afraid my singing would not entertain you."

"Nevertheless, I would like you hear you. I'm sure your skill has not left you. Besides, here is your lute. You must not neglect it."

She had no choice but to comply. At first her heart was heavy and she could only sing softly, but gradually the music that her fingers made over the strings began to have an uplifting effect. She sang the words of the song that she had sung to Xerxes the night of their first meeting.

Lord, hear my prayer.
Because you are righteous, listen to my plea;
Because you are faithful, give me an answer;

My enemies have hunted me down,
They have completely defeated me.
I am ready to give up
My heart is desolate.
For thy name's sake bring my soul out of trouble.

But I remember the days gone by,
I think about all you have done for me.
I bring to mind all your deeds.
And when I remember your love,
I know you will deliver me from my enemies.

Because you are righteous,
Because you are faithful,
I will triumph because of your goodness.

Even as she sang the words she began to feel calm and confident. When she had finished, Xerxes motioned to her to sit beside him. He held her in his arms, and they sat in silence as the daylight faded and darkness fell. At last he said, "It is time. We will go up to the observation tower. We cannot see from here because of the lights of the palace."

They walked down the long flight of stairs that led to the courtyard. Just as they were crossing the square, a voice rang out. Looking up, they caught sight of a woman on the terrace above them.

"It's that damned soothsayer, again," said Xerxes. "I wonder what's on her mind now?"

Just then her voice was heard again, loud and clear.

The name of Xerxes, the mighty king, is known throughout the world, but the name of Esther the queen will be known from generation to generation! Generations yet to come will bless her name!

Esther caught her breath. She glanced quickly at Xerxes to see how the words had affected him. "What does she mean?" she asked.

"She means," said Xerxes dryly, "that your name will be remembered when mine is forgotten."

"Does it anger you that she said that?" Esther could not help asking.

"Of course not," replied Xerxes with a laugh. "I don't believe it for a moment. When did that old hag ever make a true prediction?"

But she had, thought Esther. She had.

They entered the doorway of the tower and slowly climbed the five flights of stairs, pausing at each level to look out over the countryside. Still they could see nothing. At last they came out on the platform high above the palace. A lone figure stood beside one of the pillars. It was Mordecai.

"Your majesty," he bowed to Xerxes and then bowed to Esther. "I was looking for the signal. There is nothing yet. With your permission, Sire, I will go down."

"Don't go, " said the king. "Stay and watch with us."

The three of them stood silently side by side, looking out into the darkness. To the west, a few isolated lights were visible, probably the fires of the shepherds, and in the city, the glow of torches petered out to a few pinpoints of light down by the river, where the merchant ships lay at anchor. The hills in the distance remained black shadows, the beacons still unlit. Esther shivered in the cold night air, and Xerxes called for a servant to bring a fur wrap. The time stretched on and on. The tension becoming almost unbearable.

Suddenly Xerxes gripped her arm.

"Look, there, to the north! On the horizon!"

With excitement rising she turned her head. Yes, there it was, a tiny pinprick of light in the far distance. Even as she watched, another light appeared, and immediately there was another. They gazed in silence as fire after fire broke the darkness, until the chain of lights drew nearer and was answered by a fire on the hill above the city.

Esther was filled with elation. She hugged the king and Mordecai in turn.

"There, Esther, your people are safe now." Xerxes was smiling broadly, not hiding his own satisfaction. "Thanks be to the Good Spirit Ahura Mazda, there is peace in the land."

"Thanks be to Jehovah," said Esther. " and thank you, my lord king. Without your intervention we would all be destroyed by now." There were tears of relief running down her cheeks.

"Yes, your majesty," echoed Mordecai. "We thank you for defending the rights of the people. It is because of your justice that our people have survived."

"When I had the help of a brave queen, and a wise counsellor, it was an easy task. And I have learned too, that it is not enough to establish just laws. One has to be constantly vigilant to maintain them from the forces that would ever seek to undermine them. So my thanks are due to you both also. Now let us go down and celebrate together."

They went down to the great hall of the palace, where the celebration had already started. Musicians and dancers were entertaining the assembled company, which was made up of many of the princes and nobles and all the palace staff from the highest to the lowest, for the king had ordered that all should be present. The king led Esther up to the royal seats on the dais, Mordecai following behind. The people cheered, and it was noticeable that the loudest cheers were for the queen. When the cheering died down, the king made a short speech, outlining all the events that had taken place that day, and giving details of the triumph of the king's supporters over the conspirators, and the victorious outcome for the minority peoples.

"We all owe a great debt of gratitude," he went on, "to our beautiful Queen Esther, who, with great bravery and courage, first accused the perpetrator of these evil designs, and so brought to our notice the terrible injustice that was about to be carried out. Luckily, with the help of the Good Spirit, we were able to avert what would have been a disaster for the whole empire.

"We must always preserve our great land for our people, who are one people, no matter what their origins, and we must never let anyone, no matter who, undermine the rights of the minorities to worship their gods in their own way. All must honour the law, and the law must not discriminate. May the laws of the Medes and the Persians last for ever!"

There was loud applause for his words, but he held up his hand for quiet.

"It is also thanks to the wise direction of our Prime Minister that this matter was brought to a successful conclusion. At this time he wishes to make an announcement."

He motioned for Mordecai to come forward and address the people.

"With the permission of our mighty emperor, King Xerxes," he began, "I have ordered that this day will be proclaimed a holiday every year, for all time. It will be an annual celebration for our people, to remember for posterity the way the minority people, the Jews, were delivered by God, through the courage of the queen."

The applause that greeted this statement drowned out the rest of his speech, and he sat down, unable to continue.

The king leaned over to Esther.

"I'm beginning to think that the soothsayer was right after all," he teased. "See how popular you are! I certainly made a good choice when I chose you as queen."

Esther's eyes danced. "I would not presume to disagree with you, Sire!" Then her face became serious. We have a wonderful cause for celebration."

"Then let's celebrate," cried the king. "Fill your goblets," he shouted so that all could hear. And then, raising his golden goblet, he declared in ringing tones"

"To Esther, the most beautiful, most courageous queen Persia has ever known!" Then when all had toasted her, he turned to her and raised his goblet again.

"To Esther, my star!" he said softly.

# EPILOGUE

On a mild sunny afternoon in late spring, the dowager queen walked with her ladies in the fields down by the river. They were gathering the lilies that grew there in profusion, in preparation for the spring festival in the temple. It was a ritual which Queen Esther had started in her first year at the palace many years ago.

The beautiful spring day, with its warm breezes, the fresh greenness of the land, the carpet of blue flowers, the cloudless sky, all combined to lighten their mood, and they laughed and joked among themselves as they filled their baskets. On the river they could see the boats of the fishermen, and now and again snatches of shouted conversations reached them from across the water. As she surveyed the scene, Queen Esther felt almost young again, remembering the fun and laughter that had always accompanied these outings. Nowadays, the laughter was more subdued, the fun more sedate, but she was content. She had had plenty of excitement, of uncertainty and intrigue, enough to fill a lifetime.

Looking around, she saw that some of her ladies were beginning to tire, and she called the servants to bring up the wicker chairs so that they could all rest for a while. Bilkah and Kenaida, those two had been with her from the beginning, came up with the others and seated themselves around her in a semi-circle, all chatting happily, glad to be free of the confines of the palace for a while. It was a pleasant change for all of them.

Suddenly Kenaida, who was always on the alert, noticed a troop of horsemen riding by the river, coming in their direction. As she pointed, they all turned to look, trying to discern the identity of the riders, but a screen of trees kept them hidden. Then, as they emerged into the open, the royal pennant could plainly be seen flying from the standard of the advance rider.

"It's the king! The king is coming!" The ladies began to flutter about in consternation, and began to withdraw. The dowager queen, however, motioned them to stay where they were.

"Calm yourselves," she told them. There is nothing to be afraid of. The king has seen us. He will decide whether he will approach."

At the same time excitement tremored through her. It was years since she had spoken with Artaxerxes, but if he had meant ill to her it would have happened long ago. She did not think that she had anything to fear from him.

They stood and waited in silence as the troop of riders drew near, noting that there were only three men with the king. He did not often go about with such a small entourage. Evidently he did not intend to travel far.

Could it be that he has come specially to see me, she wondered? Well, she would soon know.

The riders came to a halt about ten yards away. The king greeted the dowager queen and her ladies.

"Good day, Queen Esther. They told me I would find you here."

He dismounted and came towards her. She immediately sank in a low obeisance before him.

"My lord king, you honour us with your presence."

He smiled and stretched out his hand to lift her up.

"Come, walk with me a little. I have some news for you."

They moved away from the others, out of earshot, and then he turned and scanned her face.

"The years do not leave their mark on you, Queen Esther. You are still a beautiful woman. You must tell me the secret of your youthfulness."

She tried not to show her surprise. The Artaxerxes she knew of old, although she had never known him really well, had not had much time for flattering women. He was tall, taller than his father, and she had to look up to him. She saw that he had not aged noticeably. But then, Artaxerxes had never looked particularly young. She forced herself to smile.

"There is no secret, sire, except contentment. I am always thankful to God for the life he has given me here at the palace."

"And you deserve it. You have been a good and dutiful queen to our people. We all appreciate the wisdom and dignity you brought to the throne."

These were the words of formal courtesy; nevertheless, shunted as she had been into the backwater of court life and all but forgotten, she took pleasure in them all the same.

"If I have done anything, it is by God's grace."

The king's expression softened. "I know how much your God means to you, and it is about that subject I wish to speak. I have just returned from Babylon," he put in, as if such an event were not common knowledge in the palace. "My cupbearer there is a man called Nehemiah, a Jew like yourself. One day, noticing his sad appearance, I asked him the reason, and he told me that the city of Jerusalem was in a bad way, that the walls were in ruins, and that the morale of the people was very low. He mentioned your name, saying that though his people had been inspired by your brave stand on their behalf so many years ago, they had grown weary of the struggle and forgotten their commitment to God. When I questioned him further, he told me of his desire to return and rebuild the city walls. He requested a leave of absence and letters of safe conduct through the provinces, which I was very willing to grant, and also supplies for the rebuilding. I decided to make him governor of Judah, so that he could carry out his plans without interference, and so that he could send me regular reports on the state of affairs in the city."

All the time he had been speaking, the king had been looking into the distance. Now he turned to meet her eyes, and added, "I thought you would like to know about the rebuilding of Jerusalem, and what is going on with your people."

Queen Esther felt the tears pricking her eyes as her emotions threatened to overwhelm her. With an effort she sought to control her swelling heart, in case she should disgrace herself before the king.

"Thank you, my lord king, for telling me this, and thank you for helping my people. God will reward you for your kindness."

"It was the least I could do, considering what you did for your people, and what your people have done for us. You were kind to me when you were queen and I was still a youth. However," and here he smiled wryly, "I also learned that your people are loyal subjects, and even more loyal when they are free to worship their God in their own way. It will be good for the province of Judah to have Nehemiah as governor. He is an excellent man with many talents. Your ancestral homeland is in good hands."

Then he took her hand in his.

"I must be off. Take care of yourself, my good mother

queen. You are still an inspiration to us all."

With a nod he strode back to his horse, and mounting quickly, was away along the river bank, while his attendants spurred their horses and struggled to catch up with him.

She stared after them, unable to move, unable to speak. The whole episode was so extraordinary she wondered if she had dreamed it all. Her ladies ran up to her, full of questions, but she waved them off, wanting to savour the moment, to recall every word and gesture so that she would not forget them.

How wonderful that Artaxerxes had helped her people, and how wonderful that he had come to tell her himself, knowing that it would uplift her spirits. She had misjudged Artaxerxes. He was so different from his father. Not warlike, certainly, but much more self-disciplined, concentrating his energies on consolidating his empire. She wondered, not for the first time, if he had been involved in his father's sudden death. There had been much speculation at the time, but no evidence had ever come out to link him in any way to a plot to remove his father from the scene. He was considered to be a reserved man, inscrutable, not given to warm personal contact, which made it all the more amazing that he had come himself to give her the news.

Her thoughts turned to his father, Xerxes, dead now these twenty years. He was a great man, she mused, although weak where women were concerned. I loved him, and I think he loved me too, in his own way. We had many happy times together. The trouble was, he always loved novelty, and when I could no longer provide that he looked elsewhere. But things changed after he brought that Babylonian woman to the palace. Even though she didn't last long, it was never the same between us after that, and I knew then that I would never have a child. Still, he was always kind to me, treating me with respect, and giving me my place as queen on formal occasions. But there were only a few short years, and then he himself was gone.

She picked up a flower and sniffed it absentmindedly. She had often wondered, in the years that followed, if anything permanent had been achieved. Her people were still exiles, still at the mercy of others, and the plans to rebuild Jersualem had never materialized. Now, today for the first time, she understood the true importance of the part she had played in the history of her people. Now she could contemplate the past with equanimity. All the pain, anguish, loneliness and heart-ache had been worth it, because it was all part of God's plan. Her memories would no longer be coloured by personal disappointment. She had fulfilled her destiny, and although it had not turned out as she had thought in her youth, in reality it was a far more lasting destiny, linked forever with the destiny of her people.

She turned and called her ladies, and collecting their baskets, they made their way in the gathering dusk up the slope towards the palace.

.